# ADVANCE PRAISE FOR *ANOMALY*

"*Anomaly* grabs the reader and refuses to let go. From the introduction to misunderstood anomaly, Thalli, to the boy she loves, one is never completely sure what is fact and what is a horrifying virtual reality. This is sure to be a favorite of teens everywhere."

"A razor-edged look at the resilience of Christian faith, *Anomaly* is taut, high-stakes dystopia that grips on the first page and twists all the way through."

"*Anomaly* is a fabulous read! Krista McGee is a fresh and gifted voice in YA apocalyptic fiction. Excellent characters and an intriguing plot provide readers with great entertainment—as well as a call to go 'outside' themselves. I can't wait for book two!"

"A beautiful story that has me wondering if I would have the strength to be an Anomaly. Fans of James Dashner's Maze Runner will love Krista McGee's *Anomaly*."

# ACCLAIM FOR KRISTA MCGEE

"McGee's debut novel is an absolute gem. Anyone who enjoys reality television and a well-told story shouldn't hesitate to read this great book."

—*Romantic Times* TOP PICK! Review of *First Date*

"[A] touching, fun, edifying, campy, quick and downright delicious teen read."

—USAToday.com regarding *First Date*

"Good things come to those who wait—and pray."

—*Kirkus Reviews* regarding *Starring Me*

"... an abundance of real-life problems ... should keep this story relevant for many teens ..."

—*Publisher's Weekly* review for *Right Where I Belong*

# ANOMALY

# OTHER NOVELS BY KRISTA MCGEE

*First Date*
*Starring Me*
*Right Where I Belong*

# ANOMALY

WITHDRAWN

## KRISTA MCGEE

### THOMAS NELSON
*Since 1798*

NASHVILLE  DALLAS  MEXICO CITY  RIO DE JANEIRO

Published in Nashville, Tennessee, by Thomas Nelson. Thomas Nelson is a registered trademark of Thomas Nelson, Inc.

Published in association with literary agent Jenni Burke of D.C. Jacobson & Associates, an Author Management Company, www.DCJacobson.com.

Thomas Nelson, Inc., titles may be purchased in bulk for educational, business, fund-raising, or sales promotional use. For information, please e-mail SpecialMarkets@ThomasNelson.com.

Publisher's Note: This novel is a work of fiction. Names, characters, places, and incidents are either products of the author's imagination or used fictitiously. All characters are fictional, and any similarity to people living or dead is purely coincidental.

**Library of Congress Cataloging-in-Publication Data**

McGee, Krista, 1975–
  Anomaly / Krista McGee.
    pages cm
  Summary: Living in a post-apocalyptic State that has supposedly eliminated emotions, Thalli is slated for annihilation by the Scientists when her carefully-kept secret that she is an anomaly becomes known, but when she becomes their test subject, instead, she learns that she may actually be part of a Creator's greater design.
  ISBN 978-1-4016-8872-1 (pbk.)
  [1. Emotions—Fiction. 2. Curiosity—Fiction. 3. Science fiction.] I. Title.
  PZ7.M4784628Ano 2013
  [Fic]—dc23                                              2013002060

*Printed in the United States of America*

13 14 15 16 17 18 RRD 6 5 4 3 2 1

To my son, Thomas

"I thank my God every time I remember you."
Philippians 1:3

# PROLOGUE

Fifteen minutes and twenty-three seconds.

That's how long I have to live.

The wall screen that displayed the numbers in blood-red letters now projects the image of a garden. The trees are full of pink and white blossoms, the green grass swaying a little in the wind. I hear the birds as they call to each other. I smell the moist soil.

But the countdown still plays in my mind.

Fourteen minutes and fifty-two seconds.

It isn't really soil I smell. It isn't really the garden breeze I feel on my face. That is simply the Scientists' "humane" means of filling my bloodstream with poison, of annihilating a member of the State who has proven to be "detrimental to harmonious living."

The wall screen is beginning to fade. The colors aren't as bright. The blossoms are beginning to merge together. They look more like clouds now. I don't know if the image is changing or if it is the effect of the poison. I could try to hold my breath, to deny the entrance of this toxic gas into my body. But I would only pass out, and my lungs would suck in the poison-laced oxygen as I lie here unconscious.

No. I will die the way I finally learned to live. Fully aware. At peace. With a heart so full of love that even as it slows, it is still full.

Because I know something the Scientists refuse to acknowledge.

Death is only the beginning.

# CHAPTER ONE

I suppose I've always known something was wrong with me. I've never quite been normal. Never really felt like I fit. Don't get me wrong. I've tried. In fact, I spent most of my life trying.

Like everyone in Pod C, I was given a particular set of skills, a job I would eventually take over from the generation before us.

I am the Musician of Pod C.

My purpose is to stimulate my pod mates' minds through the instruments I play. I enable the others to do their jobs even better.

And that is important because being productive is important. Working hard is important. I have always been able to do that. But being the same is also important.

This is where I have failed.

I started realizing this in my ninth year, the year my pod mate Asta was taken away. We were outside in the recreation field and our Monitor had us running the oval track. We ran nine times—one time for each year of life. This was part of our daily routine.

Sometimes, I would like to say no. To just sit down, not to run. Sometimes I want to ask why we have to do this. And why we always do everything in the same order, day after day. Why couldn't we run ten laps? Or eight? Or skip laps altogether and do something else? But I knew better than to ask those questions, to ask any questions. We are only allowed to ask for clarification. Asking why is something only I would consider.

I am an anomaly.

So was Asta. But I didn't know it until that day. She always did what she was told, and nothing in her big black eyes made her appear to be having thoughts to the contrary. She was training to be our pod Historian, so she was always documenting what we were doing and what we were discovering. Her fingers could fly over her learning pad faster than any I'd ever seen. But that day, when we were running, she stopped. Right in the center of the track. I was so shocked that I ran right into her back, knocking her to the ground.

"I apologize." I reached for her hand, but when she looked up at me, I saw a yellowish substance coming from her nose. I had never seen anything like it. Her eyes were red and she was laboring to breathe—all of this was quite unusual. I pulled my hand back and called for the Monitor to come over and help Asta.

But the Monitor didn't help her. She looked down into Asta's face and her eyes grew large. She pressed the panel on her wrist pad. "Please send a team to Pod C. We need a removal."

The Monitor motioned for me to finish my laps. No one else had stopped to see what happened. The rest of my pod mates simply ran closer to the edge of the track, eyes forward, completing the circuit.

I stood and tried to run, but I did not want to run. I wanted to stay here, to help Asta. She looked . . . I do not know how to describe it. But whatever it was made my heart feel heavy.

Berk ran up beside me. "You will never beat me." His grin shook me from my thoughts. I was determined to beat Berk. He always thought he was faster, but I knew I could outrun him. So I picked up my pace. Berk did the same.

We were on our fifth lap when I saw a floating white platform with four Medical Specialists land beside Asta on the grass inside the track. "Where will they take her?"

"I don't know." Berk slowed a little. He was watching the medics lift Asta onto the platform, then wrap her in some sort of covering. "Maybe take her to the Scientists. They will help her."

Berk was going to be a Scientist. One of *the* Scientists who govern the State. That made him different—but in a good way. The Monitors never corrected him, and he was allowed to study any subject that interested him during the time the rest of us worked on improving knowledge in our specialty areas.

I didn't say anything else, but the image of Asta being taken away—removed—stayed with me. And somehow I didn't think she was going to be helped. The look on the Monitor's face was not the look she gets when one of us falls and scrapes a knee on the track. It was the look she gets when we do something we shouldn't. But Asta hadn't done anything wrong. She just had something wrong inside her.

Like me.

A few days later I asked the Monitor if Asta would be coming back. I had worked on how I would phrase that question for days. It could not sound like a "why." It had to sound like I simply wanted information, clarification. I had to sound like my pod mate Rhen. Logical. Not emotional.

"Excuse me." I tried to ask with an air of indifference. "Will Asta be returning to Pod C?"

The Monitor did not even look up from her communications pad. "No."

And that was all. I had to bite my lip to keep from asking why. I imagined all kinds of reasons. None of them made sense, and none of them, I knew, could ever be voiced.

In the quiet of our cube, I asked Rhen, "What do you think happened to Asta?"

But Rhen just looked at me like she did not understand the question. "She was removed."

And that's all she needed to know.

When I still couldn't stop thinking about it, I asked Berk. We were back on the track several days after Asta's removal. "If she went to the Scientists, why don't they fix her and send her back?"

Berk slowed his pace a little before answering. "Maybe they will keep her with them."

"But she's our Historian." I could argue with Berk. He actually enjoyed it, liked questions. "They already have one of their own."

"Whatever they are doing, it is right." This is what we have always been taught. And, of course, it is correct.

"But I want to see her."

"When I leave to live in the Scientists' compound, I will tell her that."

That made me feel better. And worse. Better because I knew Berk would do what he said. Worse because I knew that when he did, I would lose another pod mate. I would lose Berk.

I did not want to think about that.

"I will win this time." I pushed all thoughts of Asta from my mind and ran as hard as I could to the line marking the end of our circuit.

I won.

:: :: ::

Berk left when we were twelve. It was very different from when Asta left. Lute, our Culinary Specialist, created a pastry that was huge and delicious. We are rarely given pastries—the Scientists say that we function best with vegetables and pro-teins. We are allowed fruit once a day, but pastries are only for special events: like Berk leaving us to begin his training with The Ten. One day he would be one of the leaders of our State, with a variety of specialties and more knowledge than any of us could imagine.

I always knew he would have to go. But I did not want him to. Berk was the only one who understood me. He was the only one who would argue with me. He let me ask questions and did not think I was peculiar for having them.

"Will you ever come back to visit?" Berk and I sat in the

gathering chamber. Everyone else had returned to their cubes. But the Monitors allowed Berk to stay. And because they allowed Berk to do anything he wanted, they allowed me to remain behind as well.

Berk shrugged. "If I can."

I knew then he would be just like Asta—gone forever. Suddenly, my throat felt tight.

The lights flickered off.

Berk groaned. "Power outage."

It happened often. Berk was sure he could help solve that problem. The solar panels, he said, were overtaxed. They needed to either add more panels or find a way to use less energy. When he got to the Scientists' compound, he would make solving that problem his priority.

Berk tapped his communications pad and the small square made enough light for me to see his face. He leaned close to me. "I have an idea."

I could smell the soap on his skin. His teeth glowed blue from the light his pad cast on his face. Berk took an eating utensil from his pocket, scooted off the sofa, and pulled me down with him. "No cameras." He reached under the sofa, utensil in hand, and started scratching on the ground.

"What are you doing?" I looked toward the door, making sure no Monitors were here to see this.

"You will see." His head was on the ground, his arm as far under the sofa as it could go. His other hand held his communications pad. I leaned down too, but his head was in my way and I couldn't see what he was doing.

Finally, he pulled his hand out and smiled a big grin. I would miss that grin. "Look."

I bent down and, in the blue glow of the communications pad, saw that he had scratched our names into the chamber's hard floor.

My eyes burned. I didn't know what was happening, but it felt awful. Like my heart would explode and leak out, one drop at a time.

"Is it that bad?" Berk's face was in the shadows.

A tear slid down my face and Berk wiped it away with his thumb. "I will always be here." He pointed to our names, a secret testimony to our secret bond. Me, an abnormality, and he, a leader.

The lights were back on—which meant the cameras were too. I stood and turned my back to the wall where the cameras were hidden. "Good-bye, Berk."

I went back to my cube and buried my head under my covers, trying to push down the emotions threatening to spill out, like the tears that dampened my pillow and the substance, so like Asta's, that dripped from my nose. My heart felt like it was being ripped out. Berk was my best friend in the whole State. And he was gone. Forever.

In the years since, I learned that when I am missing Berk or Asta, I can play my tears through my instruments. And the Monitors think I am just improving. They don't know the truth. I play laughter and frustration. I play feelings I cannot define. But the music defines them for me. I don't feel out of place when I am playing. I feel just right. I wish I could play all the time.

But we have other responsibilities. Like right now. I am supposed to be in my cube, reading my lesson on the learning pad. I am in my cube. And I have my learning pad. But I am using it to write music instead. Sometimes notes come into my mind and

I need to get them out, on the screen, so I can play them later. The Monitors see me doing this. I know they will come in and tell me to stop, to complete my lesson. I know this and yet here I am, fingers flying over my pad, getting as many notes on my program as I can before—

"Thalli." The Monitor arrives. She is the sixth Monitor we have had this year, although I know she has been here before. More than once. But the Monitors rotate every two months. The Scientists don't want us becoming dependent on them. The Monitors are older than we are, from the generation before us, Pod B, and their lives will end before ours.

Productivity is key, as is peace.

The Scientists determined long ago that generations who live and die together will be more productive and more peaceful than those who live integrated with other generations. So we live only with our generation, seeing other generations only occasionally and only for short periods of time.

"History." The Monitor taps on my screen and my lesson pops up. "You have free time next hour."

I wait until I hear the Monitor's sharp heels fading into the distance, then I finally look at my screen. I don't know why I wait. Rhen wouldn't wait. She would do exactly as she was told right when she was told to do it. Rhen wouldn't work on music when she was supposed to be studying history either.

But I am not Rhen.

History is my least favorite subject. There is nothing new. At least with the other subjects, new layers are added each year. But as I scroll through the lesson, it's exactly the same material we've had since we learned how to read.

"In the era before ours, the world was chaotic. People did

terrible things." I look up from the pad. I would like to know about those terrible things. But if I even asked, I'd be taken away for sure. No one asks questions like that. Questions like that do not promote peace.

I look back down and pretend to read while my thoughts run away, back to my music. If I am being completely honest, I know I am flawed. But no one else has to know. I need to force myself not to give in to those flaws. Which means I need to force myself to study history.

Ah yes. Terrible things. The final terror was what the Scientists called a Nuclear War. Something that destroyed everything aboveground. Billions of people died in one moment.

I try to imagine billions of people. I see them as notes crammed on a pad of music, so many notes that the screen is black with just little dots of white peeking through whole and half notes, shining through the crevices of the treble clef.

I must concentrate.

The only survivors were The Ten, the Scientists who now rule the State. Before this war, they had been creating the underground State for almost a decade because the government of what they called their country wanted to have something in place to protect their rulers. The rulers never had time to make it underground, though. But The Ten were here. They had known this was coming—not the Nuclear War exactly, but something terrible. They watched people become slaves to emotion and be driven by conflict. The end result of emotion and conflict is devastation.

So they decided to begin again with a State that required peace, that did not allow for any conflicts so there would never be any wars. Emotions were limited for the same reason. Before the State began, children were born in a way the history lesson called "primitive."

"Primitive." I mouth the word, barely above a whisper. It sounds awful. What does it mean?

Children were designed by The Ten, designed to be healthy and intelligent and know their places in the State. When their incubation period ended, they were placed in pods with other children whose incubation periods ended. Mine is the third generation of children, with each generation having just enough citizens to maintain productivity and fill the vacancies left by those who were no longer productive.

Ours will never be a world of billions.

I look back at my learning pad. I can answer all the questions at the end without having to read the information again. But the learning pad watches my eyes, making sure I read everything, not letting me complete the evaluation until I have looked at every word.

Finally, I finish. I return to my music when a sound erupts in the cube next to mine. Rhen's cube.

I have heard that sound before. A long time ago.

It was the sound Asta made before she was taken away.

Rhen steps into my cube. Her nose drips a yellowish substance.

Before I can stop her, she presses the emergency button that summons the Monitors to our wing.

# CHAPTER TWO

I t was my fault." I step in front of Rhen, blocking the Monitors from seeing her face, her nose.

"No." Rhen's hand is on my shoulder. She wants to report herself. It is logical—she realizes she is flawed so she must leave.

But something greater than logic makes me stop her. I don't know what it is, I only know that I have lost two friends already. I cannot lose another. I cannot stand the thought of waking up every day and not seeing Rhen in our cube.

"I hit the button." I look at the Monitors. The one who had come to me earlier stands beside a new one. They look almost identical. All Monitors do. Dark hair, dark eyes, tall and thin, hair pulled away from their heads. They are designed with heightened senses of sight and hearing. Nothing escapes their notice.

"I didn't hear you move from your seat." The first Monitor looks at me, her dark eyebrows lifted.

I don't say anything. Rhen looks at me, and I see the question in her eyes. I close my own in response. We will not discuss this with the Monitors.

"You are seventeen, Thalli." The Monitor folds her arms. "You must stop playing tricks. That is not acceptable anymore. Do you think the Scientists play tricks?"

Of course the Scientists do not play tricks. They work hard and they work together and they help this world to function in perfect order and harmony. I lower my head to acknowledge that I understand that fact and am ashamed for having been frivolous with my time.

Rhen breathes in deeply through her nose, the substance making a liquid sound as it goes up. I do the same, trying to make a similar sound. The Monitor's look of surprise turns to one of annoyance. "Rhen, please do not allow Thalli to encourage you to behave in ways that are unseemly for one your age."

"Of course." Rhen's voice sounds different, deeper. The Monitors step forward. They are going to examine Rhen. I have to do something.

"Attention, please." The wall screen lights up. I want to shout in relief. But I do not, of course. I do glance at Rhen and smile just a little.

The Announcer's face fills the screen. His face is flawless. Announcers are plastered on our walls at least twice a day, and so they must be pleasant to look at. They all look slightly different. I like this one the best. He has hair that is a mix between Rhen's blond and my brown. His eyes are a bright green.

Berk's face pops into my head and I realize that is his coloring too. He has been gone from our pod for five years, and yet I still think of him. Does he look like this man now, or has his face changed?

I need to stop thinking about Berk because the Announcer is discussing something important.

"The moon will be visible tonight through the southeastern panel. Pod C, this is your night to go to the viewing."

I sneak another smile at Rhen. I love these nights. We are told that before the earth was destroyed, people could see the moon every night, no matter where they lived. But here, in the State, we must take turns. I do not enjoy taking turns. I would like to go to the panel and see the moon every night. It makes me think of music—soft violins and the trill of flutes.

The window is very high and very thick. There are dozens throughout the State. Sunlight floods through them during the day. The clear panels soak in the energy from the sun, converting it into the power that allows our pods to function.

Berk hasn't solved the problem of the solar panels yet because we still experience power outages. Perhaps he has some other, more important work to do in the Scientists' compound.

We can only go to one window for the viewing, the one closest to us. I wonder what the moon looks like from the other windows. I wonder what the State looks like from the other panels. I wish we were allowed to travel beyond the perimeters of our pods. No one else seems to mind that we must stay in our building or our recreation area, that the farthest we are allowed to travel is the ten-minute walk to the window once a week.

The Monitors will be focused on preparing for our viewing. They will not have time to interrogate Rhen when the announcement is over. I release a breath I didn't know I was holding. Rhen is safe. For now.

The Announcer's face is replaced by the image of an ocean. We do not have any oceans down here. We just have huge tanks of water that are pumped down from the oceans and taken through many years of cleansing processes so we can drink it. But The Ten want us to know what the earth was like before the war, what it could possibly be when it once again becomes habitable.

I love the ocean scene. The vents release the smell of salt water and the speakers pipe in the music of birds and waves. I close my eyes and pretend I am really there, that the sun is on my face without the barrier of a window panel miles above my head.

The Monitors leave and I grab Rhen's hand. Pressing a button on my learning pad, I pull up the music I had been writing. I play the notes through the speaker, loudly, then I speak quietly to Rhen so the Monitors won't hear me.

"Do not press that button again."

Rhen closes her eyes. I know what she is doing—her mind is being flooded with all the reasons why she must turn herself in.

"It is nothing. Very minor."

"But Asta . . ."

"Asta was worse." I wave my hands, wanting to make those thoughts fly away like a piece of lint off her smock. "She couldn't even get up, could barely breathe."

"But it started like this." Rhen shakes her head, her blond ponytail swaying. "I am sure of it."

"How can you know that?" I sit on my sleeping platform, certain that even she can't deny the logic of my argument. "We were young. Our brains were not fully developed. You know we cannot trust those memories."

The music stops suddenly. That was as far as I got before I was interrupted by the Monitor.

"It is beautiful." Rhen points to the screen. "Will you finish it today?"

"Yes." The Monitors can hear us now, so our conversation returns to what is safe. But Rhen is not pushing the button. She will not turn herself in. Not today, anyway. I smile to myself in victory. "I will play it for everyone tonight on the way to the viewing."

Rhen nods and returns to her cube. She uses her free time to clean her already spotless area. I do not understand what drives her to do that. The Scientists must have left that particular gene out when they were weaving together my DNA.

I pick up my pad and finish my music. I pour in my longing for the beach scene. The notes become my wishes, my dreams, the thoughts I can never speak out loud, not even to Rhen.

Because I know my malformation goes far beyond a sickness of the body. My mind is sick, my heart is sick. But I will never tell. Because, if I am perfectly honest, I like my sickness.

# CHAPTER THREE

Tonight isn't an ordinary viewing. The Scientists are coming. That rarely happens. The Scientists usually remain in their compound, creating life and developing technology that will make our State even better. They are also busy training the next generations. Because the Scientists, though brilliant, are still mortal.

They are the oldest people in the State. They were all in their twenties and thirties when the Nuclear War occurred. That was forty years ago. And they weren't designed by other Scientists. They were created in the primitive way, which means they could get sick and die.

I wonder about death. What is it, exactly? In the past, I

have read, people died of "natural causes." That means that they could be walking along, talking, working, and just drop dead. Or sometimes, I read, they would get a sickness that would last for months—sometimes years—and they would slowly die, right in front of everyone. Some even got so sick they couldn't care for themselves and needed others to care for them, like the Monitors do for the newborns.

This is why the Scientists annihilate those who are sick. No one should have to watch others die, they say. It could create conflict and unnecessary emotions. The Scientists' technologies have eradicated most illnesses, but even minds as brilliant as theirs cannot prevent occasional mistakes.

Mistakes like Asta.

The reality that she may have been annihilated did not occur to me until my fourteenth year, when we studied the human body in our science module and learned about the life cycle. I had not thought about it before that. We were all alive. We were all fine. I did not know what Asta had would be called a sickness because I did not know what sickness was. I still hoped that she was alive, though. That Berk was right and the Scientists had brought her back with them, helped her, and given her a position there. Surely they wouldn't annihilate someone because of something so minor.

Rhen cannot be taken away like Asta. We need her logic. She will help us as we move on from our lessons to our occupations. How could our pod survive without her? Certainly, there are other logically gifted pod members. But there's only one Rhen.

"Thalli." Rhen taps my shoulder. My mind has been wandering. Again. From the way she says it, I am sure this isn't the first time she has called me. "Please bring your violin, and let's go."

I do as I'm told, grabbing my learning pad as well. I want to play my new song, but I haven't memorized it yet. I will attach it to the "pad holder" Berk made for me before he left. It attaches to the underside of the violin by a double-sided magnet that hardly weighs anything. A lightweight but sturdy wire loops out and forks into three thick fingers at the end. I slip a case on my learning pad and slip the case into the fingers. A perfect fit. And because Berk is brilliant, my learning pad is sturdy and the added weight is insignificant.

I lift my bow and move forward, trailing behind Rhen, my fingers itching to play this new piece. I have named it "Moonlight in C." Not the most creative name, I know. But the Scientists do not like creativity in words. They appreciate technological creativity, scientific creativity, creative solutions to difficult problems. But words, like music, are tools. That is all. Excessive use of words is seen as wasteful. But if I could name it something else, I would call it "Musings of Moonlight."

We leave our pod, lining up in pairs. Rhen and I are together. Behind us stand Moly and Senic. Ahead are Lute and Nic. There are twenty-eight in our pod. We silently, slowly, orderly walk through the hallways, our shoes tapping a rhythm in unison as we walk. I want to add in more percussion to the sound. Cymbals. A bass drum. Then a trumpet playing loud and clear over the rhythm section.

Rhen pokes her elbow into my side. I am dancing when I should be walking. The Monitors would not be pleased if they saw that.

I give Rhen a thank-you smile and keep walking, pushing the orchestrations out of my head.

We reach the end of our pod. The Monitors open the large double doors.

"Please return to your pods immediately." The wall screen beside the front doors blinks on. The Announcer is slicking back his hair. The camera is off-center. "No pods may go outside tonight. The moon viewing is canceled for Pod C. I repeat, no one leaves your pod tonight. Monitors, all exits will be locked in five minutes. Make sure every pod member is accounted for at that time."

We are all in shock. This never happens. Plans are made and followed through. Plans are never canceled. Rhen looks at me, her blue eyes wide.

The Monitors motion for us to return to our cubes.

I look at Rhen. "What do you think is going on?"

"I don't need to know." Rhen shrugs her thin shoulders.

Rhen can exasperate me at times. "Aren't you even a little curious?"

"No." Rhen lowers her voice. "And neither should you be."

"Something unexpected must be going on out there." My mind begins to race with all the possibilities.

"Thalli." The Monitor steps beside me. "You are aware that talking in line is against policy, correct?"

"I am aware."

"And yet you chose to talk anyway."

"I did." I do not like that rule. I was talking quietly, not disturbing anyone. I was peaceful about it. Why should it be a problem? But I lower my head, acknowledging that I have disobeyed. Again. There is nothing to be benefited from attempting to deny that fact.

"You will spend tonight in isolation." Her fingers grip my

arm and guide me to the isolation chamber. She takes the violin from my hands and programs my learning pad to the behavior-modification module.

I hate the behavior-modification module. And the isolation chamber . . . normally I hate that too. I have spent more time in it than almost any of my pod mates. But tonight is different. Tonight I have an idea.

The isolation chamber is in the far corner of the pod, behind the kitchen. The Monitor locks me in and then walks away. She will not come to check on me. This is part of the punishment. I must sit on the sleeping platform and complete my lesson and then sit in silence until morning.

"The power will be out for the remainder of the evening."

Lights flicker out as soon as the Announcer finishes. The power is never out for the night. Plans for the moon viewing are never canceled. Something is happening outside. Something exciting.

I find that, more than anything, I want to know what that is. I need to know.

A plan begins to form. A plan so outrageous I should refuse its entrance into my brain. But I cannot.

I will find a way to sneak outside and find out what is happening, why the viewing had to be canceled, why the Announcer was so harried. The power is out, so the cameras will not see me and the doors will be easy to unlock. I know this pod. I have lived here for seventeen years. I am sure I can get out and return without being caught.

The thought alone is enough to get me sent to something far worse than the isolation chamber. But the possibility is so exciting, my curiosity is so overwhelming, I find that I don't care. My desire to know what is going on outweighs any other desires.

Further confirmation that I am an anomaly.

But I don't think about that. I plan. Tonight I will get outside the pod.

I will escape.

# CHAPTER FOUR

ell no one what you see." One of the Scientists leans over the body of another Scientist. He hands complicated-looking pieces of machinery to a younger Scientist who is bent over the body.

I have been outside the pod for ten minutes. When the Culinary Specialist brought dinner to the isolation chamber, I followed her to the door, made sure the latch didn't catch when she shut it. I rushed through the behavior-modification module, then I slipped out.

It was so exciting. The hallways were dark—even the panels above that look outside had been switched to the opaque setting—providing further confirmation that something was going on outside, something they didn't want us to see. I peeked around the corners. No Monitors. They were all asleep. They would never even think that one of us would consider leaving during the night. Escape was ridiculous. Insane. I only knew the word because I read about it in a history lesson. It was what the ancient government leaders were not able to do and so they perished aboveground.

I walked through the kitchen to the back. I knew this way from my rotations in cooking duty. There was a chute that led to a trash bin outside. I remember thinking, *I could fit into that chute.*

And I do.

The slide out was dirty and slick. The thought struck me, halfway down, that I could not enter the way I exited. That I would smell like potato and banana peels. But the thrill of escape was greater than any fear I had. Surely I could crawl back in up the chute. Like a trombone sliding back up the scale.

And then I was out.

I landed on the hard ground and looked around. Lights filled the space to the east of my pod, between the greenhouse and our pod's back wall. I heard voices. People were speaking quickly, some at the same time as others. That never happened. The voices did not sound peaceful.

And then I saw the Scientist on the ground. One of The Ten.

"Tell no one what you see."

Who is that younger Scientist? Something about the way he nods his head is so familiar.

Then he turns to the older Scientist, and my heart beats faster. Berk.

His profile has changed. The fat in his cheeks is gone, replaced by a squarer jaw. His lips are full and his hair, still a light brown, is a little longer and curls at the ends. The Scientists must be more lenient with their hair rules than the Monitors are.

"His heart . . ." Berk's voice has changed too. It is so deep. Deeper than the voices of the boys in my pod. The sound of it does something strange to my stomach.

"Try this." That is one of The Ten too.

I recognize him and the one on the ground from my history books. I have seen videos of them talking, but those were obviously ancient. This man has white hair and his face looks like my pillow after a difficult night's sleep. The one on the ground looks just as bad. I had no idea age did those things to the skin, to the hair. The Monitors are right to keep this from us.

Berk takes a syringe from the older Scientist. That man's hands are shaking. Another effect of age? Berk's strong fingers tap the glass, then point the needle directly into the prone man's chest.

I cover my mouth to keep from crying out. What is he doing? Nothing.

"Dr. Grenz, I think he is gone." Berk has a sad look in his eyes. I know that look. It is what I felt when Asta was taken away, when Berk left our pod.

The Scientist Berk called Dr. Grenz straightens himself. The effort is obviously difficult. "You are right. I did not expect . . ."

"What should I do?" Berk's voice sounds strained.

"This was supposed to be an educational experience for you." Dr. Grenz seems to be looking into the distance, at something only he can see. "For the pod. An opportunity to introduce you as a Scientist, to replace their memory of you as their peer with this fact."

"We can come again." Berk stands and faces Dr. Grenz.

"What if the pod were out here when this happened?" The doctor shakes his head. "It would have been disastrous."

I move farther into the shadows. I cannot be seen, but I do not want to take any chances. I still do not understand what is happening, though.

"We must perform an autopsy." Dr. Grenz's voice is stronger now. Clinical. "Dr. Spires was in good health according to all our data. Obviously something is flawed in our tests. We need to know what happened and why so it does not happen again. We cannot risk any of the citizens being exposed to death. It is too dangerous."

Death.

The word barrels into me. My throat tightens. I am looking at a dead body. I know it is a natural part of life, that it occurs. I have been taught that. But to see it happen. This must be the death of natural causes that I studied. But this is not a lesson on my learning pad. It is real. It is horrible. That man had been walking around just minutes before, his heart beating, mind making plans, solving problems. And now . . . his heart has stopped. Berk said he is gone. But gone where? His body is there on the ground. But it looks empty. Frightening.

Once again, I find myself grateful for the protection the Monitors supply. Will this image ever be erased from my mind? I look at the body—not the man, the Scientist. The body. Its cheeks hang down, its mouth is slack, slightly open. The arms are at odd angles, obviously lying where they were left when Berk began to work on him.

Berk lays one arm on the dead man's chest. Then the other.

"I will get transport." Berk walks on a path that will lead directly to me. I panic. Where do I go? If I move, he will see me. If I don't move, he will see me.

I move.

Slowly. One leg sliding out, the other sliding next to it. Again. Only twenty more of these and I will be back by my pod.

"Thalli?" Berk is in front of me. Why was I watching my feet instead of looking out for him?

His green eyes stop me. They have little specks of gold swimming in them. A lock of hair has fallen in the space between his eyebrows and I can see the little boy he once was.

"Thalli, what are you doing here? Do you have any idea . . . ?" He takes a breath. "How long have you been watching?"

I cannot take my eyes off Berk's eyes. Even though I feel guilty. My punishment is, no doubt, going to be incredibly severe. I might as well enjoy every minute of whatever time I have left. "Long enough to know Dr. Spires is dead and Dr. Grenz is old and you are very important."

Berk closes his eyes. Then he places his hand on my elbow and walks me away from where the light can find us. This feels very different from when the Monitor touched my elbow. This feels wonderful, like his fingers contain heat that drips into my bloodstream, making my arm tingle, my heart race. When he removes his hand, my arm feels like ice.

"How did you get out?" His eyes widen and he looks around. No one is nearby.

I consider telling him that I came here accidentally, that I was walking in my sleep or made a wrong turn on the way to the lavatory. But I cannot tell him that. Not Berk. So I tell him exactly what happened, starting with my being sent to isolation and ending with my seeing Dr. Spires dead.

Berk sighs. He doesn't take his eyes off mine. He is thinking about something, but I cannot tell what it is. I know he is not upset. It is something else. "I always thought you were—"

"Malformed?" I finish his thought for him.

Berk laughs—an odd sound in these circumstances, with a cooling corpse just a few yards away. "No, not malformed."

My eyebrows rise. Why is he trying to spare my feelings? I know there is something wrong with me.

"I don't have time to explain." Berk looks to the pod and pulls out a card. "Follow me."

He steps gently toward the side of my building, slides the card in an opening, and a door clicks open. We are in the storage chamber. "There are clean clothes in there. Change into them and try to find something to wash yourself with. You smell like . . ."

"Garbage?" I spare him the effort of finding a polite word to finish that thought.

Berk shakes his head. We are children again, with me getting into trouble and Berk laughing at me—while at the same time urging me on.

I miss that time. Because, in reality, we are not children, and this is not funny, and I will likely never see Berk again.

This makes me sad. I sigh and Berk seems to know what I am thinking. He pulls me to him and wraps his arms around me. His breath tickles my ear and my knees feel like they are going to buckle. We stand there for several seconds, not speaking, just holding each other. I wonder if he enjoys this as much as I do.

Berk pulls away and my eyes water. I am not going to cry. I am not going to cry. "Thanks." I manage to slip that one word past the huge lump in my throat and then I go. Back to my pod. Back to the darkness. Away from Berk, forever.

Again.

# CHAPTER FIVE

nd why were you placed in isolation?" The Monitor asks
the required question the moment she opens the door.

"I was talking in line." I give the required answer, the
one the behavior-modification module drilled into my brain. I
allow my shoulders to slump. I hope I look contrite. I hope she
cannot see how my mind is racing from the events I saw last
night.

"Very good." The Monitor nods and steps aside as I walk
back toward my cube. Rhen has started on her lesson for the
day. Of course.

"Calculus," Rhen says, her eyes never leaving her learning
pad.

I groan. I'd rather return to the isolation chamber.

"We have a special meeting at ten." Rhen makes the slight noise from her nose like she made before. Her gaze darts toward the door, her hand touches her upper lip. The yellowish substance is back.

"A meeting?" I will not allow her to talk about this. She is fine. The image of the dead Scientist's body flashes in my mind. That will not happen to Rhen. She is not old. She is not malformed.

"Perhaps to discuss the canceled meeting." Rhen leans closer toward her learning pad, and I know I have lost her to vectors and imaginary numbers.

I sit on my sleeping platform. The Monitors have already been in. How they can make the cover lie so smooth I don't know. The corners are folded perfectly, the pillow is in the exact center, no wrinkles. I push the pillow a little to the right, turn it slightly. Imperfection is so much more satisfying. Then, reluctantly, I move to my workstation.

Sitting there, I rush through the calculus lesson. As a Musician, I am not expected to master this. Math with real numbers is helpful—it improves my understanding of music theory. All calculus does is help me write music communicating my hatred of imaginary numbers. I get enough answers correct to be able to close the program and open the program that really interests me—my music.

I want to write what happened last night. I know I cannot use words. But I can use notes. I wish I were allowed to write a full orchestration. A big bass drum to represent the moment the Scientist fell. Cymbals crashing as Berk tried to revive him. In the silence that follows, an oboe plays sad and slow.

My escape would have to be played by a violin. Staccato notes. Berk would be a cello, confident and lyrical. Together, the duet would be heartbreakingly beautiful.

I sigh. I can only write for my violin. Although I have learned to play each instrument in the music chamber, no one else has. Not in this pod. And when I once asked if the Musicians from the other pods could join me, a combined performance, the Monitor said, "That is a waste of time."

"Rhen." Even though I whisper, my friend looks up in shock. "Do you think, before the war, people played instruments together?"

Rhen's eyebrows come together, looking like a quarter rest lying on its side. "I don't understand the question."

"I was just thinking about what life was like before the war, and I wondered—"

"Life before the war was terrible. Chaotic." Rhen repeats the phrases we have been taught all our lives. "Why would you think about that? They were a primitive people."

I sigh. As much as I care for Rhen, I know we are different. She doesn't question anything. She doesn't imagine anything beyond the facts on the learning pad. She is perfect.

I do not doubt the Scientists desire to protect us, and that they want to keep us from returning to the type of people who existed before the Nuclear War. But I sometimes wonder if they took away too much. If there is more. We are, after all, made from those people. We are not a new species. Their DNA runs through us, makes us who we are. They cannot have all been terrible. Maybe, like down here, only some were anomalies.

I wonder sometimes if emotions and curiosity might not

be so terrible. I don't feel terrible, and I have both in me. Often. But maybe it is natural to think the best of ourselves. History teaches us that those who made the bombs that destroyed the earth were doing what they thought was right. Maybe I am so malformed that I lack the ability to understand how detrimental my malformation is.

My thoughts are interrupted by a beeping noise from the speakers. The sign that an important, unscheduled announcement is to be made. I hear silence as my pod mates stop their work and the Monitors stop their rounds.

"Please direct your attention to the wall screens for a special announcement." The Announcer looks somber. His eyes are directed at a point past the camera. He nods, then looks into the camera, his eyes seeming to drill into ours.

"Members of the State, we are gathered today to honor one of our founding members, Dr. Leonard Spires."

The screen changes from the Announcer's face to a young Dr. Spires, sitting behind a desk in the Scientists' laboratory.

"Dr. Spires is responsible for our oxygen system, for the creation of greenhouses, and, along with Dr. Williams, for the implementation of the solar panels."

With each line, the camera switches to what is discussed. They will discuss all his great accomplishments and then they will *announce his death*. How will everyone react? Will they show his body? I don't think I can stand to look at it again.

Suddenly, the camera switches to an older Dr. Spires. Not as old as the body I saw yesterday—fewer wrinkles, less white hair—but old nonetheless.

"My children." Dr. Spires smiles into the camera. "As you

know, life has a beginning and an end. This is natural, and it is right. I have fulfilled my purposes in this life. I have completed the assignments I have been given. I have prepared the next generations to take over those assignments so the State will continue to function and flourish. I am no longer necessary, and what is unnecessary must be set aside to make room for what is necessary. This is natural, and it is right."

I hear my pod mates murmur, "This is natural, and it is right," in response. I refuse to let those words come out of my mouth. What I saw last night may have been natural. What I am seeing now, however, is not right. What are the Scientists trying to do? What is happening?

"And so I tell you good-bye. I have no regrets. I leave behind a State that is filled with people who understand the value of peace, who appreciate the advancement of society. I leave a better world than I entered, and for that, I am content."

With that, Dr. Spires stands and walks away. There is no sound but his footsteps on the concrete floor. When he opens the door at the end of the laboratory, the Announcer's face once again fills the wall screen.

"And so we say good-bye to a great Scientist." The Announcer smiles. An odd sight, considering what just happened. "In other news, last night's moon viewing for Pod C has been rescheduled for tonight."

The Announcer disappears, the pod is silent. No tears. No questions. Rhen returns to calculus. The Monitor walks in and wipes down the shelves with a cleaning cloth. My lungs feel like they are going to explode. *This is a lie. A complete, total lie. Dr. Spires didn't choose to end his life. His life chose to end itself.* I can't erase the image I saw last night, the dead man lying on the ground, Berk trying to revive him. The raised voices, the concern. I have always thought the Scientists were totally in control. Now I know they are not.

But if they aren't, then who is?

# CHAPTER SIX

I can't sleep.

All day I have been fighting emotions I can't even define. I want to throw something. I want to scream. I want to shake Rhen and make her feel this too.

My mind is full of questions I can't ask: Why did the Scientists lie to us? Why did they prepare these "good-byes" in advance? What else do we not know? What really happens after death?

I can't stop thinking of Asta now too, of the questions I had when she was taken away. We are taught that life begins and ends and that is all. But I find I don't believe that. That thought is wrong. But isn't lying to the entire State wrong? Why should I follow the Scientists' rules if they don't follow their own?

I wish I could escape. Not just for the night. Forever. I want to leave. But there is nowhere to go. Aboveground? Never. It is poisoned, decimated. I have no choice. No one does. But no one else seems to care. No one else fights these emotions. Not that I can tell, anyway. Maybe they are hiding their feelings like I am hiding mine. Maybe there are more people like me.

I think of Berk's eyes, his whispered words. He feels things, I know it. He helped me return to the pod when he should have turned me in to the Monitors. His touch was . . . different. But Berk is a Scientist. They are designed differently than we are. He was never reprimanded the way I was, though he did some of the same things. Even when he was very young, the Monitors treated him with respect. Once every six months, he would be allowed out of the pod. He never told me where he went, but he was the only one permitted to leave. And he always came back with extra energy, excitement. I was aware that he knew things about the State none of the rest of us knew. I would beg him to tell me, but he said he couldn't, wasn't allowed.

"I want to tell you," he would say, every time I asked. "But I have to promise not to speak about my training."

"Why?"

"If I could answer that, I could tell you." Berk rolled his eyes. "And you shouldn't be asking anyway."

"Why?"

"Because." He sighed. "You're not supposed to be curious. Musicians don't ask questions."

"I do."

"I know. But you shouldn't. You could get in trouble."

"But I only ask you," I said. "You won't get me in trouble, will you?"

That conversation was repeated a dozen times in a dozen ways. Right before he left, Berk made me promise not to ask any more questions. "No one here can know you have them." I didn't like that, but Berk was so serious, so concerned, I had to agree.

Will he be there tonight? The night I escaped, Dr. Grenz said the moon viewing was an opportunity to introduce Berk to us as a Scientist and not a pod mate. I hope he will be there. My heart races with the thought. From wanting to throw things to wanting to feel Berk's touch—I am very sick. This is far worse than Rhen's dripping. But thinking of Berk calms me. Recalling his touch makes me relax. I finally fall asleep thinking of his eyes. The gold flecks float in my dreams.

::: ::: :::

"You overslept." Rhen taps my shoulder and I jump. Overslept? Rubbing my eyes, I recall my thoughts from last night. I only slept a few hours. My body needed more. Of course I overslept.

"The Monitor is calling for you." Rhen grabs a uniform from my closet. "Hurry. You cannot afford to be late."

I tear off my sleeping shirt and pull on my uniform—the white shirt and white pants I can hardly ever manage to keep clean for an entire day. I think, not for the first time, that the Clothing Specialists would do better to make black or brown uniforms. Not white. But the Scientists love white. The bedcovers, the floors, the walls—everything is white.

"Piano today." I slip on my white shoes and stand as the

39

Monitor enters and hands me a white folder. It is heavier than normal. New music.

Piano *and* new music. My fatigue is replaced by excitement. I am only allowed access to the piano once or twice a month. It is housed with the other instruments in the performance pod. When I was younger and learning how to play the instruments, I was allowed to go there once or twice a week. I love the feel of the piano keys, the rich sound of the magnificent instrument filling the room. I especially love when the Monitors leave me alone. The soundproofed walls afford me freedom I don't have anywhere else, freedom to explore new sounds, new rhythms.

We exit our pod and walk east. The Botanists have planted tulips this month. They line the walkway. One of the Botanists is adjusting the watering system—one of the many inventions Dr. Spires was responsible for. He recognized the need for plants and trees in our State and created a fertile ground so those plants and trees could grow.

We pass Pod B. Our Monitors are from this pod. No longer forced to spend their days with their learning pads, they work. From the panels, I see the gathering chamber filled with desks as the Clerical Technicians complete their task of monitoring and updating the computers that run the many facets of the State. An Announcer stands beside the Pod B greenhouse, speaking to the camera held by a Screen Specialist. I know what tonight's announcement will be about. Everyone is doing what he or she was designed to do. Here in this pod, in ours, in Pod A, and, in a few more years, in the pod that will come after us.

Everything is ordered and smooth. I should find that comforting.

I don't.

We reach the performance pod. The Monitor presses a hand to the screen by the double doors and they slide open. I love the smell of this pod. It is the smell of music—of reeds and oils and brass. The grand piano sits in the far corner. My fingers itch to touch its keys. To my relief, the Monitor excuses herself. She must return to Pod C to accompany Gen to her mechanics class. The Monitor walks to the screen beside the door and types in the command that will lock me in here until she returns. I have no desire to try an escape from here. I would live here if I were allowed. The double doors open and she exits. I am alone with my music.

I place the white folder on a music stand. I will open it later. For now, I flex my fingers and position myself on the piano bench. My feet tap the pedals. I play a simple scale to warm up. My fingers touch every key in a cascade of sound, my hands crossing each other again and again as I go up and down, up and down. Sometimes it feels as if my fingers make their own choices. They go where they wish and I simply follow, allowing the music to speak through me. I play my frustration with Dr. Spires's death and the Scientists' lies in covering it up. I play my longing to see Berk again, to feel his touch on my arm. I wish his hands were the keys of the piano. I play my fear for Rhen, fear that she will speak to the Monitors about her illness and I won't be there to stop her. I play my questions about life and death, my doubts that all the Scientists tell us is true.

I must have played for a long time because I hear the door click and the Monitor returns.

The white folder is still on the music stand. Untouched.

"You are to record this." The Monitor opens the folder and

hands me the music. I rarely see paper music. Usually I am sent music on my learning pad. "This was discovered in the records room. A primitive composer named Bach. He was considered a genius. The Anthropologists want to analyze the composition and see what they can learn about his thinking patterns."

I nod and take the music from the Monitor carefully. It is yellowed and feels as if it could disintegrate in my hands. I lay out the pages in order. I understand most of the words in the title, but I don't understand their meaning: "Jesu, Joy of Man's Desiring." I do not have time to think about those words, though. I need to practice the piece and then record it. I scan the notes on the pages, the song coming to life in my mind.

It is beautiful.

I begin to play and a lump forms in my throat. I know I am playing someone else's feelings. But this composer isn't like me. He isn't asking questions. He is answering them. I am hearing the answers. With every measure, every chord, I hear his thoughts, I hear something I have never heard before. What is it? I don't know. But I do know it's there. The answers to my questions are there, in this music, written by this primitive man so many centuries before this one.

I can't stop the tears from forming. I can't stop my heart from racing. My fingers are playing the notes, and the notes are speaking to me, reaching out from the page and squeezing my heart, my lungs. I can't breathe but I keep playing, from one page to the next. I hear myself sobbing but I can't stop. I can't stop playing, can't stop crying. My tears are cleansing, freeing. They are right. This music is right. I am not here. I am somewhere else. I feel like I am above myself, watching myself play, weep, laugh. This is beautiful, painful. I want it to end and I don't want it to end.

And then it is over. I cannot stop myself. I fall from the piano bench onto my knees. My sobs are absorbed into the cloth walls. The Monitor has left the room. I want to get up, to play more. But I cannot stop crying.

Finally, I am spent, lying on the floor, clutching the music in my hands. I don't even recall taking it with me. A Monitor stands above me. She is joined by three others.

"I suspected she was an anomaly," my Monitor says. The others nod in agreement. I cannot even react to what they are saying. I am still in the music, playing it in my head, trying to translate the answers to the questions.

"Stand up." One of the other Monitors folds her arms. Mine is speaking into her communications pad.

"We need an emergency transport at the performance pod." She speaks quietly. "Code 4."

Asta was a Code 4. I am a Code 4.

Anomaly.

Taken away.

Suddenly, the gravity of my situation invades my mind, pushing the music out. Panic seeps into my bloodstream. I jump up.

"No." I force myself to breathe, to be logical. "Don't take me. It was just a momentary loss of control. It was the music." I point to the papers strewn on the floor, feeling guilty for pointing the blame at something so beautiful. But I want to live. More than anything, I want to live.

"I have been watching you for some time." My Monitor reaches for my arm. "You rush through lessons. You argue. Your emotions are beyond what is acceptable."

The other Monitor nods. "Anomaly."

"No." How can they be so calm? They are sending me away from everything and everyone I know, and they behave as if this is just another assignment. Run the track. Clean the cube. Leave. "Please. I am begging you."

"We do not beg." The door opens and Officers enter.

I will not let them take me. I am screaming, my arms pushing the Officers away. I try to run, but one of the Officers grabs my shoulders. Another reaches into his bag, pulls out a syringe. I fight, twist, yell. But the needle comes closer, aimed at my neck.

Music plays—"Jesu, Joy of Man's Desiring"—and the room spins. I see Berk and Rhen, I see Asta. And then . . . I see nothing.

# CHAPTER SEVEN

You have one hour." The voice seems far away, coming from underneath a pile of bedcovers. I try to open my eyes, but they are too heavy. I lift just enough to see tiny slits full of bright lights. They fall shut.

A hand touches my shoulder. Its fingers feel strange—knotted and curled, like they cannot straighten.

"Hello, Thalli." This is a new voice. I have never heard a voice like his. It sounds like a garden full of rocks. Like speaking requires effort. And yet, the voice seems kind. The touch calms me, loosens the weights on top of my eyes.

"My name is John." His hand remains on my shoulder, but I feel him sit beside me. A chair scrapes against the floor.

I try to open my eyes again. I am able to force my eyelids up, but the lights are so bright. I can't focus on anything. I want to bring my hand to my face, but my hand won't move. I am strapped to this sleeping platform. I kick my legs. They are bound as well. The room comes into focus and I remember everything. The music, the tears, the Officers, the syringe.

"Where . . . ?" My throat burns with the effort to speak. My mouth is dry. So dry. I lick my lips. They feel dry, cracked. How long have I been out?

John's hand rubs my shoulder. "You are in level H of the Scientists' quarters."

My mind reaches back to geography lessons. The Scientists' quarters are located at the easternmost quadrant of the State. Like all of the State, it was built below what was called a mountain in the prewar world. I see the map in my mind. There is no level H. There are levels A–E. Going any farther down is impossible.

"No . . . level . . . H." My throat is on fire. I have so many questions, but I will never be able to ask them all. I try to swallow. Nothing.

John touches a screen by his chair. My sleeping platform inches forward. My head spins with the movement. I close my eyes. I hear his fingers tap against the screen again, then I feel something cool against my lips.

"Just a sip," John says as the water slips into my mouth. I want to grab the cup, gulp it down. But as the water hits my stomach, I feel sick. "Deep breath, Thalli."

I open my eyes again. John is even older than Dr. Spires. His hair is completely white, thick. He has white hair on his cheeks and chin and upper lip. It falls down upon the front of his shirt—a shirt that has a pattern I have never seen, with colors and buttons on the front. His eyebrows are bushy, gray and white. His nose is large and his eyes are so blue they are almost transparent. Every inch of his face is covered with wrinkles. When he smiles, there are even more. I have never seen anything so ugly.

"What are you doing to me?" The water is giving me some strength. I pull against my restraints. If I can get up, I can fight this man. I can escape.

John removes his hand from my shoulder. "I am not your captor."

He speaks with a strange accent. Almost musical.

I look at him again. "Then who are you?"

"I am like you."

"Malformed?"

John laughs. The sound of it hits the walls and echoes back in my ears. I have only heard laughter a few times in my life. I like the sound. "No, my dear. We are not malformed."

"But that is why I was taken away." I am strapped to this sleeping platform because I am an anomaly. Because I am a Code 4. I will be annihilated.

John sighs and places an ancient hand over mine, covering the restraint. "Tell me about yourself."

No one has ever asked me that. No one ever needed to. I have grown up with the same people. I have never met anyone new. Never seen anyone that old. I look into the old man's eyes. They are different. Kind. I have seen that look before—in Berk's eyes. John leans back and waits. He is not rushed, not demanding. He is curious. About me.

My story comes pouring out. My music, my rebellion, even my escape. Berk. Bach. My breakdown.

Through the whole story, John listens, nods. He wipes the tears from my eyes that I cannot reach and that I cannot stop. He doesn't speak. Not with words. But I can tell he is interested in my story. That I am important to him. I cannot imagine why.

When I am done, I am exhausted. I have no more words, no more tears. John's hand remains on mine as I sink into a deep, dreamless sleep.

# CHAPTER EIGHT

S he is scheduled for annihilation tomorrow morning."
The deep voice wakes me, but I don't want to open my
eyes. John's comforting hand is gone. Was it even there to
begin with? Perhaps John was a hallucination, a result of whatever pharmaceuticals were pumped into my body through the
syringe.

The door opens. Footsteps stop just a few feet from my
sleeping platform. I keep my eyes closed. I am sure I will learn
more if they believe I am still asleep.

"I have a request, sir."

My heart begins to race. Berk.

"Yes?"

"I have never seen an anomaly of this type." Berk seems to stutter at the word *anomaly*. Or maybe that is just my imagination as well. It is hard to know what is real and what is not anymore. "Could we postpone her annihilation so I can perform some tests?"

"What kind of tests?"

"I have a theory." Berk's voice is closer. I feel him standing beside me. "I have been testing on mice in the laboratory, and I think I am ready for a human subject."

I force myself not to scream out. Berk wants to use me as a science project? I thought he was an ally. He held me. He protected me from getting caught when I escaped.

"What is the theory?" The Scientist sounds wary.

"I believe we can correct malformations." Berk's finger brushes mine. An accident? "It seems a waste to annihilate those who have been created and trained to aid their pods. Thalli is Pod C's only Musician. I know the benefit of music on the brain and on productivity. What if we can correct her malformation and reintroduce her to the pod?"

"That hypothesis is certainly intriguing. But how many resources would be spent in carrying it out?"

Berk's finger brushes mine again. Definitely not an accident. "I believe the resources spent would be fewer than what could potentially be lost as a result of her absence."

"But if you fail, those resources are wasted."

"And if I succeed, this can be repeated on other malformations. The need for annihilation could be drastically reduced."

I have never heard people discuss different opinions in

this way. That is not allowed in the pods. Arguing is one of the "clues" my Monitors had to prove I was an anomaly. Yet Berk has no problem arguing his position with this Scientist. And the Scientist is not angry. He seems to be actually considering Berk's suggestion.

The Scientist takes a full minute to respond. "I will give you two months. You begin now."

"Yes, sir." I can hear the smile in Berk's voice. I close my eyes to keep the tears contained.

I listen for the Scientist to leave the room. His feet beat a steady rhythm as he walks to the door. When the door clicks shut, I open my eyes.

"Thank you," I whisper, my voice sounding like a broken violin string.

Berk looks at the screen by my sleeping platform. A warning look. "Thalli, you will be undergoing a series of tests over the next few weeks."

The screen is also a listening device. Berk is telling me not to say anything that would endanger either of us. "I understand."

Berk's fingers brush mine. The device cannot see. "We will begin as soon as you feel you are able."

"I am ready now."

Berk smiles. "I'm afraid you are still very weak." He presses the screen to lift the platform and the room begins to spin.

"Yes." I close my eyes to keep from getting sick. "You are right. Of course. How long have I been here?"

Berk's eyes look sad. He traces my jaw with the tips of his fingers. "One week."

My eyes widen. "A week?" What was in that syringe?

"You were considered a threat to yourself and others." He glances at the screen again. "But we are going to fix that."

I play along. "Thank you for the opportunity."

Berk smiles at me. The room is spinning again. "Just doing my job."

# CHAPTER NINE

am in a different room. The restraints have been removed. My sleeping platform is more comfortable, the walls are slightly less white. A tray of delicious-smelling food is beside me. A couch sits against the opposite wall. My violin lies on the couch.

This might be a test: food or music. The Scientists could be watching. I do not care. I sit up, fighting the vertigo, my fingers desperate for my instrument, my mind already creating the music: mysterious, frightening, wonderful.

The violin fits under my chin, my left hand caresses the strings, my right hand holds the bow. I don't think. I just play. Strains of "Jesu, Joy of Man's Desiring" are woven into my song. Though I do not fully understand why, I know that song is for me.

My legs are weak. I sit on the couch. But I keep playing. I play until my arms refuse to hold the violin. Against my will, I lay it back down and return to my sleeping platform. The food is cold, but I have never had a meal that tasted better.

The reality of my situation hits me. I was unconscious for a week. I was going to be annihilated. Berk rescued me by turning me into a science project.

I finish my meal and stand, my legs feeling stronger. I am lonely. I miss Rhen. I never thought about how much we talked until now, when I have no one to talk to. She has always been there, right across the cube. Even though she is perfect, she still treated me like an equal. I am sure she knew about my abnormalities. But she never reprimanded me, never criticized. Why did I not appreciate her more? I wish I could have told her good-bye, thanked her for being my friend. Will I ever get to see her again?

I think of my other pod mates: Lute and Senic and Gen. So many memories. So much I took for granted because we have always been together and I assumed we always would be. Do they miss me? Or do they just go on, the way we all did when Berk left, when Asta left?

I think of Asta. Could she still be here? I walk to the door, look out the panel. The hall seems deserted. No Monitor guards my door. Could I walk out? Look for her? I turn the latch on the door. Of course it is locked. But maybe I could catch it the next time a Monitor comes. Escape—not the building, of course. I know the security here is much tighter than in Pod C. But at least explore. Look for Asta.

I sit back on the sofa, pick at the remainder of my meal. Memories of meals past flood my mind. Sitting at the long table in the gathering chamber with our pod, eating and discussing our lessons. Senic always sharing a riddle he devised and Lute planning a new pastry for our next special event. The silence seems to scream at me in the face of those memories. I wish I could go back to the moment I played Bach and . . . what? Not play it? No. I want to play it. Over and over. But maybe hold in my emotions while I play. Not allow myself to be overwhelmed. To continue to fool the Monitors.

I hope Berk can fix me. I will gladly sacrifice my malformed mind if I can go back to my friends and my pod. I don't want to be alone here, visited occasionally by strange old men.

The Monitor comes and I follow her to the door, holding it slightly open so it does not lock me in. When I am sure she is gone, I peek my head through. No one is in the hall. In fact, I am not sure if there are even cameras in this hall. I step out and see that the walls and floor are different from those in my pod. Older. Everything in Pod C is white and so clean it shines. This floor is gray—I cannot tell if it used to be white and went years without being cleaned or if it was made gray. The walls, too, are strange. I touch them and they are rough, not smooth like ours. There are no panels here either. But John said we are in the lowest level. Perhaps there is nothing beyond these walls. Maybe they only made outdoor areas in the upper levels.

I look in each room. They all look the same as mine—sleeping platform with white covering, white clothing cubicle, lavatory.

Then I see a room that is different: the bedcovering is multicolored and the room looks . . . lived in.

I peer through the door panel. John is sitting in a large, worn chair, his eyes closed. I am so desperate for conversation that I go in, not even concerned that I might be waking him from much-needed sleep.

"You're not a hallucination." I speak softly, not wanting to frighten him.

He opens his eyes, looking wide awake. Maybe he was not sleeping after all.

"I've been called many names in my life. But that one is new."

I walk closer to him, shocked again at his face. "But you are so old."

John laughs. I am amazed at the musicality of his voice. "I am, my dear. In fact, if I'm not mistaken, this will be my nine-tieth year."

"Ninety?" I am sure I heard wrong. "But even the oldest Scientist isn't that old."

"Very true."

I am confused. We have been taught the Scientists are the oldest living beings in the State. Everyone else was destroyed in the war. I sit on the end of John's sleeping platform so I am facing him. I have so many questions.

"You were gracious enough to tell me your story." John leans back and folds his hands in his lap. "Would you like to hear mine?"

"Please." I smile, wanting to know more about this odd man. Ninety years old. He must know so much.

John is thinking. I can tell his mind is reaching back in his past—the ancient past.

"I was born in a different world. A place called California. I grew up right by the ocean. My parents called me a fish. I swam, surfed, had my own sailboat before I could drive."

John's accent is so different from ours, I am having trouble understanding him. And the words he is using: I know the ocean, but only as a contaminated body of water aboveground. Pipes pump the water into the State, and it is put through years of decontamination before we receive it to drink and bathe in. But swim? Surf? Sailboat?

"Never mind about that. Let's just say I had a happy childhood. Fun. My dad was a pastor and my mom taught kindergarten. I was the youngest of five kids."

I put my hand up. "You had parents?"

John shakes his head. "I always get ahead of myself. I forget how different life is for you. Yes, I was born in the way you were taught is primitive."

"You don't think it is primitive?"

"I believe a lot of things the Scientists don't like." John's smile is sad. "That's why I'm here."

"I am sorry. Go on." I want to ask him more—like how can he believe differently than the Scientists and still be alive? How can he have lived so long? What is it like being from a primitive world? I know he doesn't want to keep the answers from me. For once, someone wants to give answers. But I must allow him to give them in his own time, his own way.

"I grew up in a home with two wonderful parents. We didn't have much, but we were loved. My father taught us to know God."

"God?"

John leans forward. He has tears in his eyes. "Yes. The Designer."

"The Scientists are the designers." I think of our genetics lessons. The Scientists worked with the basic ingredients needed to create life. Those ingredients had been gathered years before the war, from primitive humans all over the world. They were stored somewhere in this facility. From those ingredients, the Scientists manipulated DNA so each child would fulfill a particular role. The Scientists determined everything—hair and eye color, height, build, even talents and interests.

"No, my dear. They are not."

No wonder he is here. Speaking against the Scientists is not permitted. I am surprised he hasn't been annihilated for such thoughts. "You cannot say that."

"I've been saying it for most of my ninety years." John rubs his gnarled hands on his knees. "I don't intend to stop now."

I am intrigued. And a little frightened. I have never heard anything like this before.

"The Designer, God, is not human. He is not bound by this or any world because he created everything. He has always existed, he will always exist, and he created humans for his glory."

I don't understand, but I remain silent.

"I grew up knowing this Designer. Speaking to him."

This man is crazy. That is why he is here. The Scientists must feel sorry for him, and that is why he is still alive.

"It's all right to doubt." John seems to be reading my thoughts. "I understand. Now, where was I? Oh yes. My childhood was wonderful. When I finished high school, I wanted to go on and study the Bible—the book written by the Designer—so I went to a special college just for that. I met my wife there."

John stops. Tears flow from his eyes. He doesn't apologize for them. He just waits for the tears to stop before he continues. "Amy. She was the most beautiful girl I'd ever seen, with a voice like an angel. I heard her singing in chapel at school and I was lost. I knew I had to meet her. I saw her sitting alone, outside on a bench by the lake. I pretended not to notice she was there." John laughed. "I asked to sit next to her and she said yes. We started talking and we kept talking. Well into the night. We had so much in common. We both wanted to go into the ministry, we both loved the Beatles, we both thought rocky road ice cream was the greatest dessert in the world. We fell in love and got married a year later."

"Fell in love?" John uses so many words I have never heard.

John stands and walks to me. "Love is the Designer's greatest gift to us. Of all the changes Scientists have made to this world, removing love is, to me, the worst. It's terrible."

"You mustn't say things like that."

"Why not?" John shrugs. "What's the worst they can do to me?"

"They can annihilate you."

"Death is just the beginning."

Yes, this man's mind is completely malformed.

John sighs. "It's hard to unbelieve what you have been taught. How about if I just tell you the rest of my story? We can talk about the Designer later."

"All right. You said you fell in love?"

"I did. Love is a feeling, but it's also a commitment. At least it was to us. Amy and I committed to love each other for the rest of our lives, no matter what. We had a wedding ceremony where we promised that to each other. We promised to help each other, to care for each other, to look out for each other, forever. She was the prettiest bride to ever walk down an aisle. We lived together for thirty-one years. We had three children. Life wasn't always easy, but we made wonderful memories and we never forgot the commitment we made. Amy has been gone for more than forty years, and I still miss her. Still love her."

I cannot help myself. Even though I know he is crazy, I am wishing for something like that. Love. Someone who feels about me the way John feels about Amy. "What happened?"

"The war." John rubs his hands on his legs. "I came out to Colorado to visit my son, James."

"Dr. Turner?" One of The Ten?

"Yes, Dr. Turner. He was too busy to fly out to California to visit us, and it was his thirtieth birthday. Amy and I didn't want him to spend it alone. She was helping our daughter with her baby, our first grandchild. So I went. It was amazing." John motions to the facility. "I had never seen anything this massive. I knew there were rumors of nuclear war, and several countries were threatening to strike each other. But Amy and I didn't think it would happen. Those countries knew that if one struck, the others would follow. Everything would be destroyed. We were sure the threats were empty."

"You were wrong."

John nods. "James was giving me a tour of the State when the first city was attacked. The Scientists didn't have time to bring in the politicians like they'd planned. They only had time to seal everything up and set their plan into motion. I couldn't believe it. I was sure it was a mistake. That only part of the world was destroyed, not the whole thing. But the Scientists had satellites that told them otherwise. The world as I knew it was gone. Amy was gone. My daughters, my grand-child. All gone."

"How awful." No wonder John has lost his mind. I would too, given these circumstances.

"James and the other Scientists had already decided how they would run this State in the event that catastrophe struck. Their plans did not include me—a believer. They wanted to eradicate faith from society. They felt sure that belief in a Designer was one of the downfalls of humanity. It led to con-flict, and they believed that a conflict-free world was the best kind of world. James allowed me to live, but the others insisted I live down here, given permission to speak only to those sched-uled for annihilation."

"That is why you came to me?"

John nods. "But then the Scientists decided you would be spared. So I was not allowed to return."

I think about that. He is locked in a room, alone, allowed to speak only to those who are about to be annihilated. What a miserable life.

"Do you ever wish you had not come to visit your son?"

John reaches out and holds my hand, his thick fingers squeezing mine. "Sometimes, yes. This is certainly not the life I would have planned for myself. But I have a purpose here. For whatever reason, the Designer has chosen me to be his remnant."

"What?"

"The Designer always leaves a remnant to tell others about him. People throughout history have tried to rid the world of their Creator. But that will not ever happen. He ensures his truth will live on. Even if it is just through one old, unworthy man."

I do not know what to say. I am not sure what to think. I barely remember saying good-bye or walking back to my room. I barely remember climbing onto the sleeping platform.

I fall asleep immediately, dreaming of beaches and wars and love.

# CHAPTER TEN

G ood morning, Thalli." It is Berk. Dr. Berk. He is dressed just like a Scientist, with a white lab coat and a passel of Assistants beside him. His eyes seem cautious, clinical. His fingers fly over his pad—not a learning pad, exactly, but similar. A bit smaller. Berk holds it in his left hand while typing with his right, moving images and digesting data.

"Doctor." I follow his example. At least, I hope it is an example. Perhaps I really am just an experiment. Perhaps the touches I was sure were to reassure me were simply an accident. Perhaps I am just a larger, more complicated version of his lab rats. I want to believe Berk is doing this to help me, but along with curiosity comes something else, something other. An uncertainty about everything. Questions. So many questions. And never, ever enough answers.

"We will spend this first week establishing a baseline." Berk looks up from his pad and addresses his Assistants. "From there, we can begin some experimental treatments I have been developing."

The Assistants nod, typing Berk's instructions into their own pads, seemingly undisturbed by the fact that the "subject" is right here, terrified, wondering if this testing might be worse than death.

"Follow me." An Assistant with reddish hair walks out of the door. I do as she says. The other Assistants scatter. I suppose they are each preparing their part of my tests. Berk walks behind me. Silent. I want to look in the other rooms we pass, to examine this level I never even knew existed, but the Assistant moves quickly and I cannot slow down. I look at her hair, perfectly straight, pulled back halfway in an elastic that is wound around her hair in perfect circles.

The elastic makes me think of Rhen. I worry that she will reveal her sickness to the Monitors now that I am not there to stop her. As much as I miss her, I don't want her here with me. I don't want her to be a test subject, a lab rat. I want her to live out her logical life in our pod with all the others.

I do not have much hope that Berk's tests will result in my being allowed back into our pod. Somehow I have absorbed enough of Rhen's logic to know that my return would be more disconcerting for my fellow pod mates than my leaving was. No, the Scientists are just allowing Berk to test on me as part of his training. I am sure of that. But I will do my best, for him.

Even if I am just a project. I am discovering I would rather live than die, no matter what that life may look like.

"Sit here." The Assistant points to a large white box, about half the size of my cube back in Pod C. She opens a door in the box and I see a stool in the center. I sit and the door closes. I am surrounded by screens on all the walls and even the ceiling. They flicker to life and images of a garden pour in. I smell grass and trees.

What are they testing? How should I react? What should I say? Are they reading my thoughts? Are they administering medicine?

I decide to relax and just watch. Berk wants an accurate test, so I must respond accurately. I enjoy this scene. Above me is sky. Just sky. Not a glimpse of the sky through a panel high up at the top of the State, but just blue, with clouds that float along. I twist around in the stool, my neck angled so I can see all of it. I want to lie down and just watch the clouds.

I feel a slight breeze. Not like the forced air that comes out of the ventilation panels in the pods. This is lighter, like a gentle touch. It reminds me of the way Berk touched my face after I saw him with Dr. Spires. I look straight ahead and the trees sway, the grass moves. I wish I could walk into the image. I have always wanted to walk on the grass outside my pod with my bare feet. That, of course, is not allowed. But the desire is still there. I am sure it feels wonderful. So different from the hard, smooth surfaces in the pod.

The screens change to an image of a city. I have seen these pictures before, on my learning pad. But I am not just looking at a picture. I am in the city. The images move as if I am walking. I know, in my mind, that I am sitting on the stool. I am not really moving along the walkway. But I feel like I am. It is a thrilling feeling. It feels like freedom.

I see people. They are dressed so strangely. All different fabrics and colors. I smell something awful. I cannot place the smell, but I hope it goes away quickly. I look down and a man is lying on the ground, a tattered blanket covering his filthy body. It is his odor that has reached my nostrils. I gag.

The screens change again. I cover my nose with my hand to try to erase the smell of the fetid man from my nostrils. Now I am on water, on some type of transport floating on the water. I look at all the screens. I am trapped. There is nothing solid anywhere. The transport moves. Up and down. Up and down. I feel sick. The bread and fruit I had this morning threaten to come back up.

I turn to the screen behind me and see another floating transport. This one is much larger than mine. It is black and has tubes sticking out from all sides. It is far away, so the people on the transport look tiny, like music notes bobbing around. I try to create a song about this, to keep my mind off the moving, endless water. But I cannot create anything. I can only try to concentrate on keeping my breakfast in my stomach.

The tubes on the other floating transport turn toward me. The tiny people see my floating transport. I hear distant shouts in a tone I have never heard. How loud they must be for me to hear them from so far away. One of the tubes erupts. The sound is deafening. Fire spits out from the tube and some type of projectile flies toward me. I panic. I can't escape. I can't jump in the water, can't get the room to move away. Is this experiment trying out new ways to annihilate the anomalies? I am sure there is a better way. I am frightened. I cannot breathe.

Then suddenly, right before the projectile is about to land

in my floating transport, the screens go black. I see nothing. Normally, I would not like this. But darkness is a welcome relief to the alternative. I can still feel the heat of that projectile flying through the air toward me. Still feel the motion of the room going up and down.

The screens slowly come back to life. At first, they just glow, a shade lighter than the black. Then lighter and lighter. From gray to dark blue. Light comes up from a corner of the cube. Daylight. In minutes, I am back in the garden. I see images of birds. I smell flowers. The wind blows through the trees and caresses the back of my neck. I sigh in relief. I wasn't killed. I am not floating on water. This is only a test.

The door opens. Berk stands behind the Assistant. His eyes seem to be communicating to me, *I'm sorry.* Or maybe it's my imagination. Since talking to John, I have felt a greater desire for the love he spoke of. I am projecting that desire onto Berk. That's what Rhen would say. I try to be logical. Try not to let my errant thoughts control me.

"I will debrief her, Sami." Berk dismisses the Assistant. He points to a plastic chair beside him. He sits after me, typing on his pad before looking at me. His eyes lock on mine, then move to a spot to my left. Cameras?

"Let's talk about the first simulation." Berk's voice has no music. Flat tones with a steady rhythm. Different from how I have heard him speak before, with varied pitches, long and short phrases. I am sure, now, he is communicating with me: *We are being watched. I must appear disinterested, a Scientist completing an experiment.*

I nod, a slight movement, just enough for him to know I understand.

"The garden?" I try to speak in flat tones. I sound like the notes on a muted keyboard.

"Yes. What did you see?"

I tell him what I saw, what I smelled, how I felt. Berk reads dozens of questions about the experiment, questions that seem to have no point, although, of course, every question has a point. Everything here in the State has a purpose. What would it be like to do something, to say something, that has no set purpose? Just for pleasure?

I keep that thought to myself. That will never happen. When productivity is paramount, pleasure is pointless. I smile. I like that thought. When productivity is paramount, pleasure is pointless. I could put that to music. Sing it fast, repeat it. That would be pleasurable.

"Were you frightened?"

I should not be smiling right now. Berk is talking about the water simulation. The floating transport with the exploding tubes. I try to change my smile to a grimace. "Yes. That was uncomfortable."

"How so?" Berk is typing onto his pad, recording my words.

"The transport was rocking, and the people on the other transport were shouting. I believe they wanted to hurt me."

Berk looks at me. His green eyes remind me of the ocean. The yellow specks are like the reflection of the sun off the waves. It is hard to concentrate when he looks at me like that. "You were on a boat."

"A sailboat?" I remember John speaking of a sailboat, something he enjoyed as a boy.

Berk drew his eyebrows together. "No. A battleship, actually."

"But you said it was a boat."

"Boats and ships are similar."

"Oh." I am not sure I understand, but I do understand from his tone that this particular line of communication is irrelevant.

"What else?"

"I thought I would be hurt by the people on the other boat."

"Did you want to hurt them?"

"What?"

"Did you think about looking around your boat for something that could hurt the people on the other ship?"

I don't comprehend this question. Why would I want to hurt someone? Berk's mouth tips upward slightly and he moves on, asking me about the city again, the old man, the smells. He keeps asking me what I was feeling. I suppose the cube can only record so much data. It cannot determine how I feel. I am relieved to know that.

And then we are finished. He shuts down his pad and stands. I follow. We leave the room, but instead of turning right toward my room, Berk turns left. He doesn't say anything. Neither do I. I just follow. He opens a door that leads to a stairwell. I have only traveled by elevator in this building. The stairs look even older than the rest of the building. They aren't as clean. The paint on the walls seems dull and there are scuff marks on the floor.

Berk turns and almost runs right into me. He is standing just inches away. I smell the soap on his skin. I see where the beginnings of facial hair are standing out on his chin and his upper lip.

"We don't have much time." Berk speaks so quietly I barely hear him.

"Time for what?"

"There are cameras and microphones everywhere. We are being watched closely."

"But not here?"

"No." Berk is still whispering. "But we can't stay here very long."

"All right." Berk is still close. So close it is hard to think clearly. "What is this all about? The cube and the images?"

Berk looks at me, his eyes saying something I do not quite understand. But whatever it is makes my heart beat faster. "I can't explain right now. You answered well. Keep doing that. Go along with the simulations. Be honest in your evaluations."

"I want to help you succeed in your project."

Berk's hands come to my shoulders. He pulls me close and wraps his arms around me, holding me so tight I can barely breathe. But I don't care. This is the most wonderful feeling I have ever experienced. My head reaches his chest, and I can hear his heart beating. It is beating fast, like mine. He leans his head down, and I feel his breath in my ear, the stubble of his cheek on my cheek. "You are not a project, Thalli."

He pulls away, and I want to pull him back in. I want to stay like this. But he is opening the door, looking out into the corridor, motioning me to follow him back to my room.

And we walk back the way we came. I stare ahead at Berk. I am memorizing everything about him. The way he walks, the way his hair curls over the collar of his white jacket. Too soon, he stops.

"Thank you for your cooperation." He opens the door for me to walk into my room. And then he is gone.

I go to my sleeping platform and lie down. I close my eyes and relive that moment in the stairwell. Feel his arms around me, his whiskered face at my ear. I dream of gardens and birds and Berk.

# CHAPTER ELEVEN

I wake up thinking of John and Amy. And love. I try not to think of Berk and Thalli and love. That is too ridiculous. Primitive. And pointless. As much as I would like to believe otherwise, I know I am scheduled for annihilation. Berk is simply prolonging the inevitable. Because we are friends.

But he doesn't feel like a friend. I have many friends. Rhen, Lute, Gen. All of Pod C. But I don't want those friends to hold me like Berk held me. I don't think about those friends far into the night. I don't crave to be near those friends like I crave to be around Berk.

I expel all the air in my lungs. I need Rhen right now. What would she say if she were here?

"Thalli, you were designed to bring the beauty of music to our pod. You make us productive, you stimulate our brains. How can you do that if your own brain is filled with such superfluous thoughts?"

Rhen is right. And now I have moved from thinking about love to having imaginary conversations with my pod mate.

I go to my violin. I need to play. Even if I am the only one whose mind is stimulated.

I lift up the violin and place it beneath my chin. Just the feel of the smooth wood comforts me. My fingers flex. I need to play something fast, so fast that all I can think about is getting the bow from one string to the next. I want to play something slow, something that reminds me of my "stairwell moment" with Berk.

But I know I should not. Perhaps if I learn to control my emotions, my errant thoughts, the Scientists will allow me to live. I wouldn't even mind if I had to live here, like John, a prisoner of the Scientists. Especially if my captor were Berk.

*Play, Thalli.*

And so I do. I play the difficult pieces I learned as a child. Pieces designed to improve my dexterity and my sight-reading skills. I don't even have time to think about anything else. I close my eyes and forget where I am. I am just playing. I am doing what I was designed to do. I relax. My arm seems to be moving on its own. I listen, enjoying the sounds of the music, the feel of the bow in my hand, the strings underneath my fingers.

But I don't want to play. Not by myself. I think of John, all alone. When was the last time he heard music? No one seemed to notice my previous visit to his room. Maybe this hallway doesn't have cameras, as I suspected. Or if it does, maybe those monitoring them think that I will be annihilated, so talking with John is not a problem.

I take my violin and bow and open my door. The last Monitor did not bother to lock the door.

I go to John's room and show him my violin. "I need an audience."

John rubs his hands on his knees. "I'm thrilled to be your audience, maestro." He smiles. I don't know what *maestro* means, but it seems like something nice. I lift the violin to my chin and begin to play.

I play something slow and soothing for John. He closes his eyes. I have never seen that reaction in anyone but myself. When I play for the pod, they just sit and watch. Sometimes they pull out their learning pads to accomplish a task. But they never really enjoy what I am playing. No more than I enjoy Rhen's logical solutions to problems or Gen's mechanical innovations.

My arm is tired. But John is so happy. I recognize the look on his face. I know it has been on mine. He is lost in the music. It is speaking to him. So I fight through the fatigue and keep playing. With renewed energy, I play the piece that changed my future. I don't know why. I should not like this piece. But I find I need to play it. I must. And though I have only seen the music once, I have memorized every note.

As I begin the first strains of "Jesu, Joy of Man's Desiring," John's eyes fly open. He stands and puts his hand to his mouth. I stop playing.

"No, please." John sets his hand over his heart. I am afraid he is going to die. I don't know what to do. "That song . . . my wife walked down the aisle to that song. Played by a string quartet. Please continue."

I have so many questions. Walked down the aisle? String quartet? But I do not ask. John is transported to another place in time. He remains standing, but his eyes are closed, his hand still over his heart. He is swaying to the music with tears slipping down his wrinkled face and becoming absorbed in the white hair on his cheeks.

I cry with him. I don't know why, but his emotion becomes mine. It is love that makes him cry. It is painful, obviously, but not the same kind of pain as a sore arm or a blistered finger. This pain seems almost pleasurable. He doesn't want to avoid it or seek a solution for it. I slow the tempo, knowing that John doesn't want this song to end. I hold out the final notes, my finger wavering on the string to make the final notes sing with vibrato, filling the room.

And then I am done. John falls back onto the couch. I am sure something is wrong. I go to the wall-com to call an Assistant.

"No," John whispers, like he is forcing his voice past rocks lodged in his throat.

I wait. John wipes his eyes and smiles at me. "Thank you."

"For what?"

"For bringing back a beautiful memory."

"What memory is that?" I sit on the sleeping platform and watch John spin a thin gold band on his finger.

"Do you know what a wedding is?"

I think back to my history lessons, but I cannot recall that word. "No."

John looks sad. "A wedding is a ceremony where two people promise to love each other forever, no matter what. This was something the Designer intended from the beginning of time.

Marriage is a picture of his love for the people he created. His commitment to them. Sadly, that picture grew distorted over time. But Amy and I knew what he wanted. Our wedding was a celebration of what the Designer intended—to care for each other for better or for worse."

"That sounds wonderful." Strange. Impractical. But wonderful. "But you said something about walking down an aisle? And a string quartet?"

John's blue eyes sparkle. "Yes, our wedding was at a church."

"A church?"

John looks like he is going to be ill. "You have never heard that word either."

It isn't really a question but I shake my head. I can see the answer pains him.

"A church is a place where people who want to worship the Designer gather together. We would sing and pray and listen to men speak from the holy book."

I have read about ancient rituals like that. The Scientists tell us those types of gatherings were for people who were incapable of sustained rational thought. They needed superstition in order to function in their society. The need for such ideas has been eliminated with the evolutionary advances made by the Scientists and their predecessors. It is odd seeing someone from this era, someone for whom this superstition is so real. It is fascinating, though.

"So you had a wedding in a church?"

"Yes, we did. I stood at the front of the church and my Amy entered from the back. She was wearing the most beautiful white dress." John can't speak for a moment. I am uncomfortable with so much emotion, but I am also intrigued by it.

"When she walked toward me, a string quartet played 'Jesu, Joy of Man's Desiring.' Amy's mother played violin, like you, so Amy grew up with classical music. Bach was her mother's favorite composer."

"There were four instruments playing this song?" How I would love to play alongside other musicians. I can imagine the richness of the sound, the harmonies and countermelodies that would afford.

"Yes. I can't hear that music without seeing Amy in her dress walking toward me, that beautiful smile aimed right at me, promising a lifetime of love."

A lifetime of love. Superstitious, maybe. Primitive, certainly. But since I am malformed anyway, I suppose I am allowed to long for this. Perhaps I would have thrived in John's time, before the war, when emotions were seemingly encouraged.

Would I have been like Amy and John? The thought fills me with feelings I can't define. "But what does it mean?"

"The music?"

"Yes." I ask him the questions I have had since I first played this song, since I was taken away for the emotion it stirred within me. "I can hear answers in this music. But I don't know the questions. What is it saying?"

John closes his eyes and sighs. "Thank you, Lord." When he opens them, his face seems younger, replaced with a glow I cannot describe. "My mother-in-law, Amy's mother, used to say that the Designer speaks through music. He reveals himself to his people through the notes on the page. She would say that when certain music is played, it is like hearing from the Designer himself. I thought she was crazy." John laughs. "My favorite kind of music was rock-and-roll. I didn't care much for classical music. It had no words to sing along to. But now I see how right Judy was."

"I don't understand."

"Have you ever wondered if there is more than what the Scientists are telling you?"

This is dangerous talk. Even among the condemned.

"It's all right." John senses my fear. "Let's pretend you have had those thoughts. I believe they are not symptoms of a disease. They are placed in you by a Designer far more intelligent and far more caring than the Scientists."

"But the Scientists do care for us." I repeat what I have always been taught. "They give us everything we need and ensure this world is a better place than the one into which they were born."

"I know." John nods. "My James has always had a good heart. And I do believe most of the Scientists have the noblest of intentions."

John is speaking like he knows better than the Scientists. But he cannot. No one knows better than them.

"But in trying to eradicate the Designer from this State, they have committed a grievous wrong. One the Designer will not allow to continue."

My eyes widen. What is he saying?

"I am saying too much, too soon." John folds his hands in his lap. "It's just ... I can tell you are—no. I need to wait. Let me return to the music. The Designer is speaking to you through that music. It is him that you hear. And he promises that those who seek him will find him."

I try to swallow, but my throat is tight. I am either as crazy as John, as unevolved as he is, or everything I have ever been taught about life is a lie. Seeing John, hearing him, I have trouble believing he is crazy. But it is just as hard to believe the Scientists are flawed.

John stands. "I have given you much to consider."

I blink. I am not sure I can even speak. I have never felt so conflicted in my life.

John stands and walks me to his door. "When you have questions, I will be waiting. In the meantime, I will pray the Designer speaks to you in ways you cannot deny."

# CHAPTER TWELVE

A week has passed. Berk must be concerned about the
Scientists watching us because he has been very clinical
with me. Despite his earlier reassurances, I am beginning
to feel like a lab rat. More like a science experiment and less
like a friend. I am run through a different series of tests every
day. Sometimes I am back in the cube. Other times I am put to
sleep with electrodes recording my brain activity. Berk and his
Assistants record everything, asking me about my reactions,
checking my heart rate and blood pressure. I suppose they are
trying to determine where, exactly, the malfunction in my
design stems from so my particular error won't be repeated.

I have not visited John again. I haven't even played my violin. And I definitely don't ask the questions that are burning in my consciousness.

"Thalli?" Berk is in my room. Dr. Berk. The Scientist. As much as I try to resist, my heart always beats faster when he is around. "We are taking a short trip."

"But it is evening."

"I know." Berk releases a slight smile. Just enough for me to see. "You have not seen the moon in several weeks. This is your pod's night. You, of course, cannot join them. But studies continue to affirm that glimpses of the sky are beneficial to the mind and body."

I want to jump up and hold Berk. But I control myself, willing my stomach to calm, suppressing a squeal of delight. A trip to the moon with Berk. What a wonderful thought.

"And bring your violin." Berk motions toward the couch, where my instrument has sat since my last visit with John. "It has been noted that you haven't played in a week."

I place my violin in its case and follow Berk outside. He is silent, so I am too. I'm sure this is just another one of my many flaws, but sometimes I feel like we can communicate even without words, that I know what Berk is thinking. Right now, I am sure he is saying we need to behave as if this were just a Scientist/patient outing, with no hint of friendship so no one will be required to come along with us.

We walk down the hall and turn down a corridor. More empty rooms. Then we come to a large metal door. Berk places his finger on a pad on the wall and the door slides open. We are in what looks like a stairwell, but it has no stairs. A blue bag is against the wall, and Berk hefts it onto his shoulders. He keeps walking and reaches another door, with another pad. This door slides open and we are out in the open.

This is different from the area outside my pod. We have a small garden with grass and flowers, as well as a greenhouse with vegetables and fruits that is used by the Culinary Specialist to make our meals. But this just has patches of grass, remnants of flowers. No greenhouse. No pod nearby. It looks like I feel—missing important pieces. I love it.

"This is the end of the State," Berk tells me as we walk farther away from the door, where the grass disappears and is replaced first by dirt and then with concrete. Looming above the concrete are massive structures.

"The water tanks." I recall seeing pictures of the water tanks on my learning pad, but nothing could prepare me for the reality. Enormous couldn't even begin to describe the size of these tanks. They are so wide that I can't see around them, so tall that I can't see where they end. I look at Berk. "Is this part of a test?"

Berk takes the bag off his back and opens it. He pulls out a bedcovering and spreads it out on the ground. He sets containers of food on top of the covering and sits. "This is a picnic."

"What?"

"It is something the ancients used to do." He motions for me to sit.

I am sure this is something the Scientists would not approve of. "Are we allowed—?"

"We are looking at the moon because you need the boost from that." Berk points to a panel right above one of the tanks. "And we are coming here because you need to be isolated from the other pods. We wouldn't want anyone to see you, you know."

"Of course." I smile. Berk is having fun with me. It is a

wonderful feeling. It reminds me of when we were younger, carefree.

"Sadly, though"—Berk holds out a slice of bread with cheese and a slice of tomato on it—"no cameras were installed out here. It was pointless. There are no pods out here, no citizens."

"But we are permitted to be here?"

"Dr. Spires was out here almost every day so he could check on the tanks." I take the bread from Berk. His fingers brush mine. "Since he is gone, that duty is shared by several of us younger Scientists. Today is my turn. And since you were also in need of some time outside, I requested that I complete both tasks at the same time."

"How very convenient."

"Productive." Berk lowers his voice. "And completely private."

"No cameras?" My heart lightens. I am alone with Berk. Outside of the Scientists' quarters. Beneath a distant glimpse of a full moon. Music plays in my mind, and I don't stop it.

We eat in silence. Once the initial excitement of being alone with Berk wears off, I find myself uncomfortable. I don't know how to behave alone with him. When we can speak with complete freedom, what do we say? Can I tell him about John, or will his training and design as a Scientist rebel against the ideas John has planted in my mind? Will he think that my even considering John's ideas confirms my hopeless status in the State?

Berk looks at me. The gold specks in his eyes seem to be dancing. He does not appear uncomfortable at all.

"Will you play?" Berk points to my violin case. "For me?"

He says it quietly, the words soaking deep into my being. Will I play for him?

I open the case and pull out the violin. I look at Berk and I know he is not thinking like a Scientist. He isn't just looking at me, he is looking into me. Into my mind and my heart, into the secret places where I dream and question and hope. We are more alike than I ever imagined. I tear my eyes from his. I cannot look at him and play, so I close my eyes, position my bow, and begin.

I forget about the testing, I forget my fears. I forget that my life could soon be over. I forget everything but this moment. And I play. I play everything I feel, everything I hope. I play love and a wedding and a world where those things aren't primitive. A place where a Scientist and a Musician can be together, forever, the way John described. My bow glides over the strings of my violin, bringing to the surface everything I have hidden.

When I am finished, I am gulping air. Frightened, excited, completely transparent. I have laid bare everything that is in my heart.

Berk stands. He takes the violin from my hands and places it carefully back in the case. He faces me, his green eyes just inches from mine. He touches my face, tracing my jaw with his finger. Then he pulls me closer and wraps his strong arms around me. His face is buried in my hair, his breath is a whisper in my ear. I fall into him, my head on his chest, my ear listening to his heartbeat. We don't move, we don't speak. But I know what he is saying. And I say it back.

# CHAPTER THIRTEEN

Your dinner." An Assistant comes in with a tray and sets it on my dresser. She leaves just as she came—silently, methodically.

She doesn't see that I am not the same person I was yesterday. I am sure my skin has changed hues. I feel every nerve tingle. I just think of Berk and my heart rate increases, my stomach feels as if it were floating inside me.

I don't need food. I don't want food. I want to go back to the sleeping platform and close my eyes and think of Berk. I want to remember every moment of our picnic, every word that he said. I want to recall the feel of his arms around me, his warm breath in my ear. I think if I tried, I could fly around the room. I want to shout. I want to play. A violin is too soft for how I feel. I need a trumpet to declare these feelings, to fully express what is in my heart.

I do not want food, but the Scientists will be suspicious if I don't eat. I am sure the Assistant records how much I eat and drink and reports that information back to her superiors. I am, after all, simply an experiment.

I walk to the dresser and take a sip of the orange juice. It tastes different from my usual orange juice. Or perhaps my nerves aren't the only things affected by these feelings I have for Berk. Perhaps even my taste buds are altered. Everything in me is different, more alert.

Why would the Scientists want to keep feelings like this from us? This is wonderful.

I am hungrier than I thought. The fruit is not enough. I eat a second slice of the toast. I think of last night. Again. Will I ever stop thinking of it? I hope not.

I get dressed, still thinking of Berk. I wish we could run away—to that patch of concrete and grass—and be there together. Forever. No Scientists, no tests, no annihilation chamber. Just Berk and me.

But, of course, that cannot happen.

The door opens and Berk walks in. I want to rush to him, but I remain where I am. I greet him like a patient would greet her doctor. At least, I hope that is what it sounds like.

Berk nods and holds the door open as I walk out. He is alone. No Assistants with him. Instead of turning toward the laboratory, he turns right. Toward our stairwell. He doesn't speak, but he does walk faster. I have to jog to keep up with his long legs.

When we finally reach the stairwell and the door closes, Berk turns to me. His eyes are different. Serious. He grabs my shoulders and looks at me with such intensity that, for a moment, I am scared.

"I have only been given one more day to test on you." Berk's voice is quiet, but the emotion behind it is not.

I nod, unsure of how to respond.

"I am trying to prove that your emotions can be modified. That's why you have been in the cube. All the testing has been recording your responses, your brain activity, everything."

"What do I need to do?"

Berk sighs and lowers his hands. "When I tested on the mice, I developed a serum that would alter their brain function."

I feel the blood drain from my face. "What do you mean?"

"I can't do that to you, Thalli." Berk runs a hand through his hair. "It would change you."

"So I am going to fail the test?" I refuse to consider this possibility. If I fail, I am of no use. I will be annihilated.

"No." Berk pulls me farther into the stairwell and speaks so softly I can barely hear him. "I am going to inject you with a placebo. But only you and I will know that."

"But how will I pass the test if I don't have the serum?"

"The same way you managed to conceal your emotions from the Monitors all your life." Berk manages a small smile. "You need to think like Rhen for the next six hours. Respond the way she would respond. Don't react to the garden. Don't enjoy the smell. Keep repeating to yourself that you know it's only a simulation. Look at the screens, try to analyze them. The same with the city scene. Don't show disgust or excitement. Try to look as disinterested as you can."

"And the boat?" I don't know if I can pretend I am not sick when it is moving.

"You can be affected by the motion, but not by the attack," Berk says. "Physical responses to outside stimuli are expected. It's the emotional responses you have to ignore."

"What if I can't do it?" Fooling the Monitors was different. Almost like a game. And, usually, the worst that happened if I failed was I was sent to isolation. But this—if I fail this, I am useless to the State. No, more than useless. Detrimental.

"You can do it." Berk takes a step closer to me. I can smell the soap on his skin.

"And if I do? What then?" I don't want to be sent back to Pod C. Not anymore. That would mean never seeing Berk again.

"Then I will go to Dr. Loudin." Berk squeezes my shoulders. "I will suggest that we keep you here. He will want to run some tests too. I'll try to stay a step ahead of them so you know what to expect."

"And then?" I swallow hard. "Am I going to be a science experiment the rest of my life?"

Berk pulls out his pad and steps away. "We have been here too long. I need to get you to the lab."

"I am scared." All the possibilities for failure rush into my brain. If I get caught, the punishment will be severe. If I get caught . . . "You could get caught."

"It's a risk I'm willing to take." Berk stands straight. "You can do it. I know you can."

Berk opens the door and we head toward the lab, toward the future.

# CHAPTER FOURTEEN

The cube test is beginning. I try to imagine myself as Rhen in these simulations. As much as I want to watch the clouds pass, I do not. I glance at them and consider the technology that went into their creation. I breathe in the scent of the garden, but I try not to allow my face to reflect any enjoyment in that. It is just a scent, manufactured to imitate the smells of the plants and flowers that grow by our pods, in our greenhouses.

In the city, I look at the buildings and try to think of the primitive world they represent, not of the height of the buildings, the smells coming from the windows high above the moving sidewalks.

I prepare myself for the boat simulation. The motion does affect my stomach, but Berk said that would be all right. I try not to give in to feelings of fear when I see the other boat, with its tube pointing toward me. I jump at the sound of the first projectile. I hope that is recorded as a physical reaction, not an emotional one.

And then it is over. The cube is dark. I do my best to keep my breathing level normal. The serum Berk was supposed to have given me would make me feel nothing as I wait. So I try to feel nothing. To think about nothing. To be just like everyone else. Berk is right—I have done this for so long, it comes naturally. But, for a moment, I allow longing to fill my being, a longing to just be me and have that be acceptable. But I shove the thought out of my mind. It can't happen. I cannot dwell on it.

The lights come on and I am escorted out of the cube. Berk is remaining at a distance, looking over the data, talking with another Scientist. Dr. Loudin, I am guessing. The one he wants to convince that I should stay. I try to read their lips, but I cannot. Trying to eavesdrop on their conversation is probably not the wisest choice. The serum was supposed to inhibit my curiosity. So I just look straight ahead, waiting for my instructions.

"What did you think of the simulation, Thalli?" Dr. Loudin is in front of me. I think of Rhen. How would she answer that question?

"The technology is quite advanced." I mentally applaud myself for my response. Very Rhen-like. "The images are even clearer than what we have on our wall screens."

"Indeed." The Scientist nods. "We have some Engineers developing software to use those cubes rather than learning pads in education."

I want to say how much I would have loved that—being *in* history rather than just reading about it. And music—writing a composition on the walls and the ceiling rather than just on my pad. But I don't say that. Instead, I say, "Certainly a viable option for the younger generations."

"I find your mind quite interesting, Thalli." Dr. Loudin is looking at me with his eyes half closed, like I am a piece of DNA under a microscope and he is trying to analyze my makeup. "A Musician with advanced logic."

Advanced logic! I want to stand up and shout. But that would not be logical. I do, however, glance at Berk. He smiles slightly, just enough for me to know this is a victory.

"Dr. Berk." Dr. Loudin turns and plants a hand on Berk's shoulder. "Your serum seems to work just as well on humans as it did on your rodents. Well done."

"Thank you, sir."

"I would like to run some tests of my own." Dr. Loudin looks at me with his microscope-eyes again. "You may return the patient to her room. And since this has been so successful, I will be giving you a new assignment."

Berk looks at me and then back at Dr. Loudin. "Sir?"

"Report to my office once you have delivered Thalli." Dr. Loudin walks away.

Berk opens the door and walks down the hallway, turning toward the stairwell. I cannot see his face, but he must be happy. He just cannot show it. Not here. But when the door closes, and we are alone . . .

"We did it." I jump into Berk's arms, but he does not return my embrace. I step back. Berk's face is pale, unhappy. "What is it?"

Berk shakes his head. "Dr. Loudin is reassigning me. He wants to experiment on you, and I won't be there to protect you."

Understanding replaces my joy with fear. "What type of experimenting does Dr. Loudin do?"

"His specialty is brain research. But he does much more. I don't even know half of what he does. So much of it is secret."

Brain research? I fall back against the wall.

"I'll try to talk to him. I'll try to convince him to allow you to work with us, that further experimentation isn't necessary. We need you exactly the way you are."

I hear what Berk *isn't* saying. That this experimentation could be terrible, destructive. That I would be nothing more to Dr. Loudin than an interesting test subject, a human lab rat. That he has no intention of allowing me to stay here with Berk and the others, or even be returned to Pod C.

"Thalli." Berk is standing inches from me. I am hyperventilating. Berk pushes my head down so my breathing will return to normal. He rubs my back as I am bent. Finally, I stand again. I take his face in my hands. The feel of his stubble on my fingers is overwhelming.

"I am all right." I look in his eyes, memorizing every detail of them. "You did everything you could. You made these last few weeks wonderful. The most wonderful of my whole life. I am glad I got caught. I'm glad I got to be with you, to experience this."

Berk closes his eyes. "Don't talk like that."

"It is true." I lean into him, listening to his heart.

"I don't know what to do." Berk leans his head against mine. I don't say anything. I just enjoy this moment, knowing it might not come again.

"Dr. Berk." The voice from Berk's pad sounds like a shout in the quiet stairwell. "You are needed in laboratory M."

"You need to go." I pull away. Berk looks at me, looks into me, and then he sighs. A deep sigh. I understand.

I open the door. I know Berk doesn't want to leave, but it's my turn now to protect him. So I lead the way. Back to my room, away from Berk.

8">93

# CHAPTER FIFTEEN

don't want to wake up. I was dreaming about Berk and me in a city, walking together. No Scientists were around. No cubes. No tests. Just him and me. And freedom.

But when I open my eyes, I am not in the city. I am not with Berk. Berk is an important Scientist, and I am just an experiment.

The door opens and an Assistant comes in. She brings me my breakfast, lays the tray down beside my sleeping platform, and then stands by the door.

I sit up straighter. Why is she staying here? Usually she just leaves my tray and walks back out.

"You have ten minutes to eat and get dressed." She waits until I pick up a piece of fruit. A plum. I bite into it. She doesn't leave until I swallow. I finish the plum without thinking. I take a few bites of the toast, but I can't finish it. I have ten minutes.

I get dressed, pulling the white uniform shirt on, the white pants, the white shoes. The door opens. A different Assistant enters. Who is she and where will she be taking me? What is going to happen to me?

I cannot dwell on that now because the Assistant is talking and I should be listening. Something about a chamber.

"You will remain overnight."

I am listening now. "What?"

"The isolation chamber," the Assistant repeats, never slowing down as she leads me down a hallway I have never seen before.

I stop. "The isolation chamber?" They know. They found out about Berk and me. I am being punished. I don't mind. I was prepared for worse than isolation. But what will happen to Berk?

"Please follow me." The Assistant does not stop.

"But . . . why? I . . ." I have to run to catch up to her. She doesn't even turn around.

"This is part of another test that the Scientists are conducting."

"What is the test?" I slow down and pull oxygen into my lungs. It is a test. Not a punishment. Berk will be all right.

"You are the test subject." The Assistant's voice is almost mechanical. "Your instructions are simply to remain in the isolation chamber until I return for you."

"And when will that be?"

The Assistant does not respond. She simply stops before a metal door and turns the handle. I have been placed in isolation before. In Pod C. The last time was when I escaped to find Dr. Spires dead and to be reunited with Berk. But this is different. This room is spacious. It has coverings on the floor, a large sleeping platform in the corner with four white sticks protruding up from it. The sticks are decorated with flowers and leaves. It is pretty. The platform is covered not with the typical white I always see, but a pink covering that looks soft and thick. There is a chair in the other corner with long, rounded legs and it is covered with padding, also pink.

The dresser is white, with a huge mirror above it. Mirrors are rare. I have seen just a few in my life. The Monitors said they were frivolous accents, remnants from the ancients that we have no use for. The room smells like flowers. I don't have time to think about stopping the door before it closes. I am too overwhelmed with the room to think of anything.

I go to the chair and sit in it. It moves. I lean back and it leans back, in a smooth, soothing motion. I lean forward and it leans forward. I do this several times. I go faster, lifting my feet and using my knees to create momentum so the chair goes so far backward that it threatens to tip. I laugh. And do it again.

When I stop, I decide to walk to the mirror. The image in there is me. I know that. I have seen my image in the reflections of the windows at night. But this is so clear. I see every detail. I see what Berk sees when he looks at me. I take my hair out of its elastic so I look exactly the way I did last night. My hair has more colors in it than I realized. It is brown, but with subtle hints of lighter brown and blond mixed in. It is neither curly nor straight. Somewhere in between. My eyes are bluish-green and large and my lashes are dark. I smile. My teeth are white and straight and I have dimples on my cheeks. When we were little, Berk teased me about my dimples. He said they were indentions left by the Scientists when they lifted me from my birthing pod.

I sigh. I need to stop thinking about Berk. Stop dreaming about him. I will likely never see him again. There is no use longing for something that can never be.

I lie on the sleeping platform. It is so soft, I feel like it could swallow me. I am not tired, but I do not get up. I lie here and think of Berk by trying not to think of Berk.

The door opens. Is my test over already? I sit up and I can't believe what I am seeing, who I am seeing. I can barely get the name past the lump forming in my throat.

"Asta?"

# CHAPTER SIXTEEN

Asta?" I say it again, a little louder. She is still at the door. She is taller. Her face is thinner. But I recognize her onyx eyes and caramel skin. Her dark hair that seems to fall to her shoulders in perfect curls.

She smiles and I know it is her.

I run to her and hug her and cry. I can't help myself. I thought she was gone. And she is standing in front of me. I don't care if the Scientists are watching, testing my reaction. Asta is alive!

"I don't understand." I pull Asta to the sleeping platform

and we sit facing each other, like we used to when we were younger, our legs folded under us. "I thought you were . . ."

"Annihilated?" Her voice sounds different. But then, she is older. I'm sure mine sounds different to her as well.

"What happened?"

"There's so much more going on than you know." Asta's voice is quiet, confident.

"The Scientists . . ."

Asta smiles. "They are good. So much better than you can imagine. They keep things from you for your good. But they are allowing me to tell you some of it."

I am confused. "If the Scientists are so good, why did they take you away because you were just a little sick? Why did they take me away because I cried over some music?"

"They have to retain a sense of order in the pods, Thalli." Asta is speaking to me like I am a child. "But when people are brought here, it is for rewards, not punishments. Differences are good. They just don't want that advertised. Only a few are made to be like us."

"You were made to be sick?"

"No. I wasn't sick. Not really. Just different."

"And I was made to . . . feel?"

"Yes."

I sigh. I am not an anomaly. I was made to be this way.

"Tell me about how you feel."

And so I do. I tell her everything. Almost everything. I can't bring myself to tell her about Berk. Not yet. She says the Scientists are good, that I was made this way. But even Berk wanted to keep our meetings private. Even he wanted us to go somewhere we could not be seen or heard. I must protect him.

But I tell Asta about the music. I tell her that since she left, I learned to play my feelings through my instruments so I wouldn't get in trouble. Asta listens and nods and smiles.

"I don't want to talk about myself anymore." I have too many questions racing through my brain to think about my own thoughts and feelings. "What have you been doing?"

"Living." Asta shrugs.

"I know that." I smile. "But what have you been *doing*? Did the Scientists run you through tests like they did me?"

"Of course." Asta stands and walks to the dresser, her curls bouncing with each step. "They had to make sure my body was well enough for my new life."

"And what is your new life?" Asta seems to take pleasure in making me wait. I remember that about her now. She could be exasperating.

"My new life." Asta walks to me and points up.

"You live in an upper level?" I knew the Scientists' pod had more levels than ours. I have wanted to explore more of their building.

"You could say that." Asta smiles and walks to the door.

"Can I see it?"

Asta's hand is on the doorknob. "Not today. But soon." She opens the door with a finger to the pad.

"Where are you going?"

"These things take time, Thalli." Asta turns to face me. "You always were impatient."

"When will you come back?"

"Later." She puts a hand up. "But you need to keep my visit quiet. The Scientists know about it, of course, but the Assistants do not. They aren't special like we are. They think annihilations really happen and that you really are a danger to the State. And they need to keep thinking that."

"Why?"

"Patience, Thalli." Then she turns back to me with a wink. "You'll know everything. Eventually."

# CHAPTER SEVENTEEN

ime to return." The Assistant opens the door.

I pretend to be waking, although I have actually not slept at all. How could I? Asta is alive. Differences are good. After the testing, I will . . . what? Get to live here in the Scientists' pod? Above with Asta? I have so many questions I feel like I will explode if I don't get answers soon.

"Where am I going now?"

"Back to your room." The Assistant is already walking down the hallway. "You have some lessons to complete before your next round of tests."

Nothing bothers me anymore. Not the tests, not even the lessons. I will do whatever I am required to do so I can complete this testing and move on to whatever awaits. Asta looked so happy, so free. I crave that freedom more than I crave anything. To be able to walk around, to open any doors I wish, to know what only a select few know. To be different and have that be something positive, something special. It almost seems too good to be true.

The door shuts and I return to my sleeping platform. I am not tired, but I have nowhere else to go. I wish someone would come, that I could tell someone—anyone—what I experienced. How can I keep silent about this?

I fall asleep quickly—I did not even feel tired. I wake and immediately think of Asta. Asta!

I need to talk to someone. I will explode if I keep this to myself. But who? Not Berk. I don't even know where he is.

John? I could tell John. He wouldn't tell anyone, I am sure of it. I catch the door after the Assistant brings my dinner. I walk to John's room, my mind reeling with this news.

"John." He is in his chair again, eyes closed but not asleep. "I saw a friend today."

John lifts his head. "Did you?"

"I haven't seen her in several years." My heart beats faster. This still seems so impossible. So amazing. "I thought she was annihilated."

"But she was not?" John seems confused. Even he doesn't know about this.

"No." I can still see Asta in front of me. Smiling. "She has been living somewhere here. She is so happy. So free. She said the Scientists are so much better than we know. She is going to take me to where she lives. Maybe, when the testing is over, I will get to live with her."

John's bushy eyebrows come together. He doesn't speak, but I can tell there is something he wants to say.

"What?"

John shakes his head. "That is certainly interesting."

"You've never heard of this?"

"No." John opens his mouth to speak but closes it again. "This is a good gift for you. I am happy you saw your friend. But is that all?"

I am sure my face is turning red. "What do you mean?"

"I saw you walking down the hall with the young Scientist."

"Berk?" Are my feelings so obvious that John could spot them in the few seconds we spent passing his window?

"I was in love myself once." John's ice-blue eyes moisten.

"In love?" I lean forward. "You've spoken of that before. But what is it?"

John's laugh is low and rough, like a cello being plucked by hand. "Oh, Thalli. How do I define love? It is the Designer's greatest gift to us. It gives us a small glimpse of who he is, how he feels about us."

"You still haven't said what it is."

John laughs again. Louder this time. "You are right. Love is a feeling of connection to another person. You, no doubt, feel love toward your friends—a desire to spend time with them, to protect them, to help them."

I think of Rhen. I feel that toward Rhen. I feel that about Berk too. But there is more with him. "This is what you felt for Amy?"

"It started with that, with a friendship type of love. But it grew into romantic love, then it deepened into a committed love."

"Romantic love? Committed love? What are those?"

John pats my hand. "Romantic love is what I expect you are beginning to feel for the young Scientist. Your heart beats faster, your mind races with thoughts of him. When you touch, you feel like your skin is on fire."

I gasp. How can he know this?

John lifts a weathered hand to his heart. "I may be old, but I hope I will never forget that feeling. It is wonderful. Terrifying at times. Confusing. But wonderful. It is nothing to be ashamed of."

"But the Scientists . . ."

John shakes his head. "They fear those emotions because, unchecked, they can lead to other emotions—jealousy, anger, betrayal."

"So they were right to create us without them?" Most of us.

"No." John closes his eyes. "The solution is not to remove your feelings."

"Then what is the solution?"

"The Designer is the solution." John's eyes open, and I see so much in them. I am sure he is sane. Perhaps the sanest person I have known.

"He did not intend for us to live without feelings. In fact, we are told that he *is* love."

I hear a door at the end of the hallway open. Someone is coming. I need to return to my room.

I dart out of John's room and rush down the hallway.

"Where are you going?" The Assistant is walking toward me. Did she see me leave John's room? Will John be in trouble? Will he tell the Assistant what I said about Asta?

"I . . ."

The Assistant waves her hand. "Dr. Loudin is ready for you. You can explain this to him."

I swallow hard.

I am rushed into the same room with the same simulation cube I was in last time. The Assistant begins to tell Dr. Loudin about the hallway incident, but to my relief, Dr. Loudin refuses to let her finish. "We will begin testing now." He bends down over his communications pad and begins typing. His Assistant walks me to the cube and motions for me to sit.

And now I must focus. This time, in the cube, I am in the dark. I do not like the dark. I begin to feel panic, and then the lights come on so brightly I am blinded, wishing for the dark. The dark is cool, but the light burns me. My skin feels like it is on fire.

Should I remain emotionless like I did last time? But last time I was supposed to have been under the influence of the serum. Today I am not. I am just regular, malformed Thalli who feels more than she should. Berk always said to respond honestly. So I will.

"Stop." I can't help myself. I know it is a simulation. But I am in pain.

The light dims and a slight wind cools my skin. The light gets even dimmer, and I look above me and see the moon. But it is not as far away as I am used to seeing it from the panels. It is closer, larger. And there are sounds around me. I don't recognize them, but I like them. They are soothing. Relaxing. Stars fill the screen above me. They, too, seem closer, brighter. There are so many. It is beautiful. I don't want to leave.

But then the simulation is over and I am out. Dr. Loudin is discussing the simulation, pad in hand. An Assistant records my vital signs and wipes down the cube. How many others are being tested this way? And what is the purpose? I want to ask so many questions. But I can't. The Assistant is watching. The cameras are watching. I have to concentrate so I don't allow my mind to wander to what I would say and do if no one were watching.

And then I am back in my room. I should be exhausted. But I am wide awake. I eat the food left for me on my tray. I am not very hungry either, but I know I must finish it all. I must do what is expected of me so I can be done with these tests and on to—what?

I try to close my eyes when the door opens and I see Asta.

"Follow me."

# CHAPTER EIGHTEEN

Where are we?" The elevator has gone farther up than I have ever seen it go. Asta has access to places I didn't even know existed, and she gets there with just a tap of her finger.

"Patience." Her white teeth flash as she winks at me, mocking my impatience.

"You're not going to tell me anything?" She comes in and completely rearranges everything I know, then smiles and winks about it like it's all a game? Emotions I haven't felt since I was a child well up. But they disappear when the elevator doors open.

"Wh—" I can't form a complete sentence. I am not even sure if I am awake. Surely this is a dream. The building, at least I think that's what it is, is falling apart. The walls have large pieces that have just fallen off to be left lying on the floor. The floor appears to be a hundred years old. It looks like it may have contained many colors, but now those colors have faded to a uniform yellowish-brown. And the panels—they are so large. I walk over to one.

"What is out there?" I see dirt where there should be grass. And it goes on for as far as I can see. There are no other buildings. Above it is gray.

"I told you I live above."

"Above?" I hear her, but I am sure I do not comprehend. "This is . . . ?"

Asta opens a large door. It groans with the effort and I scream, "No! It's poisonous."

Years of history lessons pop into my mind. The Nuclear War destroyed everything on the earth and it destroyed everything above the earth. The atmosphere became toxic. Our air, like our water, is purified before it ever reaches our lungs. It has to be or we would all die horrible deaths, like the ancients did. Yet Asta pushes the door open more and more.

This is how I am to die.

I don't want to die. I lunge at Asta, shove her out of the way, close the door, and block her from it. My leg hurts from running into the corner of the door. But it is closed. I am alive. Asta looks up from the ground, wiping remnants of the floor off her shirt.

"I live out there." She stands and shoots me a look filled with a mixture of annoyance and fatigue. "It isn't poisonous."

"You live . . . there?" How much do I not know? How much has been kept from me?

"Yes." Asta grabs my arm gently and pushes me aside. "They test us to make sure we have the physical and emotional capacities to survive."

"But . . ." Will I ever be able to speak a complete thought again?

"The air is no longer toxic." Asta eases open the door. I hold my breath, still wary. "Several of us have returned to try to cultivate life. Follow me."

I have to breathe or pass out. I choose the former. I gulp a lungful of air and find, to my surprise, that I do not die. It is different from what I am used to breathing. It seems dirty, like my mouth is being coated with the dust that is all over the ground. Is that dust going into my lungs? Will death come slowly, over time, as the dust builds up until I can no longer take a breath?

"Thalli." Asta is holding my shoulders. I am gasping for air but I can't get enough. This is the end. Asta forces my head down. I can breathe again.

"You were hyperventilating," Asta says, her black eyes boring into mine. "Maybe we should come back another time. This is too much."

"No!" I push her away. "I'm fine. You are going to show me around."

"You always were stubborn." Asta laughs. "That's good up here. All right, let's go."

The dust is fine, and with every step, it flies over my shoes, onto my legs. I can't help myself. I bend down and touch it. We have dirt below—we use it to grow plants. But it is thick. This is dust. It seems to serve no purpose whatsoever. I pick up a handful and it floats away, leaving my fingers brown. What did this used to be? Am I touching the remnant of a building? A tree? A human? That thought forces me up. I wipe my hands on my pants and shudder.

"Where do you live?" As far as I can see, there is nothing.

"At the bottom of the mountain." Asta begins to run. I look around. Until now I have focused only on the ground directly in front of me. But farther ahead the ground slopes downward. I hear Asta laugh, and when I find her, she is sitting on a sheet of plastic, skimming down the mountain.

"Come on." Asta points to a pile of plastic sheets held captive under a rock. She is already halfway down. I don't want to lose sight of her, so I pull a sheet out, sit on it, and push. Nothing happens. I lift the front edges slightly and then I take off. I lift my legs and go faster.

"This is fun," I shout, my eyes half closed against the dust.

"Turn left," Asta is yelling. I grab the sheet and pull up on the right-hand side. "Excellent."

I am filthy and panting when I reach the bottom. But I don't care. I have never experienced anything so exhilarating. And when I stand and look around, I am silenced.

Pods are everywhere. Dozens of pods. "How many of you are there?"

"There is much you don't know." Asta cups her hands around her mouth. "Visitor."

The pods open to reveal people of all ages. They smile at me and nod. Their faces are different from ours somehow. Darker, with more wrinkles. Their clothes aren't the uniforms of the pods but a mismatched conglomeration of fabrics and colors.

"Welcome." A woman at least two generations older than me reaches for my hand. Hers feels rough, but her eyes are kind. "This is Progress."

"Progress?"

The woman motions me inside her pod. "Yes, that is our name for this city."

The pod is far different from what we have inside. This resembles what I have seen of John's room and the pink isolation chamber I was sent to. The walls are covered in a light blue, the floor in a striped pattern of blues and greens. It is large—more than one room. I am standing in what seems to be the main room, and there is seating for five or six, comfortable seating that looks worn.

"My name is April."

"April?" I look into this woman's eyes. They are hazel, kind, and they wrinkle at the corners when she smiles. We are all named after elements in the periodic table. Not after months of the year.

April sits and I follow. "We choose our own names here in Progress. We are no longer bound by the rules of the Scientists."

"But you said the Scientists are good." I look to Asta, who has taken a seat across from us.

"They are." Asta leans back in her seat. "The rules are necessary below, but not up here. Those of us who are different are given more freedom."

"So you choose your own names?" I look at my friend. "Then what is yours?"

"Hope."

That is a good name.

"What do you do here?"

"We live." April leans forward and places her hands on her knees.

"Asta." I shake my head. "Hope. What do you do?"

"We all use our abilities, just like you do below." She glances at April. "We just use them a little differently."

"Like what?"

"Below," April explains, "I was the pod Dietician. I still do that here. Which is why my kitchen is larger than the others'. Would you like to see?"

"Yes."

We stand and walk through a doorway into a kitchen that is quite similar to ours below. The requisite heating and cooling appliances are in place, along with counters and tools to prepare meals. But it looks different. Less precise somehow. Cloths lie on the counters and the appliances have smudges of food caked on them. That would never be allowed below. Lute kept the entire room pristine.

"I love to experiment with food." April opens the heating appliance and pulls out a white pan filled with some type of pastry. "Try one."

I do, and it is delicious. Flavors I have never experienced touch my tongue. "What is this?"

"I'll take you out to my greenhouse later and show you." April hands me another pastry. "For now, just enjoy."

A door opens and footsteps lead into the kitchen. A boy my age enters. He is slightly taller than I am and has much the same coloring as April, dark hair and eyes, olive skin. His smile isn't as white as ours below, but it is kind.

"Stone." April nods in my direction. "This is Thalli. She is visiting."

"First timer?" Stone's eyes are bright and inquisitive. There is something different about him.

"Yes." I shake his hand. Like April's, it is rough but firm. He keeps my hand in his a little longer than is necessary for a greeting.

"Stone is my son."

# CHAPTER NINETEEN

almost choke on the pastry. "Son?"

"She really is a first timer." Stone's laugh is kind, but I barely hear it.

"Let's return to the front room." April links her arm through mine and walks me back.

"I don't understand." John spoke of having children, but he was from primitive times. The Scientists eradicated that form of procreation. It was a danger.

We sit and April turns to me. "The Scientists never intended for life to be as it is below forever. That was simply necessary until the earth once again became habitable."

"And it is habitable now?"

"Not entirely." Stone shrugs. "But we are working on it."

"We receive aid from below," April says. "And occasionally we receive people like Asta—and hopefully you—who can help us as well."

I feel like my entire world is tilting. Strong arms—Stone's—hold my shoulders and I fall into them, unable to right myself. He smells like flowers. His chest is hard. I blink a few times and regain my balance. "I am sorry."

"This is a lot to take in." Stone's arm is still holding me. "Why don't I take you back? You can return another day."

"To live here?" I'm not sure I want to live here.

April laughs. "It will be several months before you are given the choice to live here. It is a monumental choice. And it is yours to make. You will not be forced to come here."

"But if I don't?" Will I be annihilated? Or relegated to a solitary room like John?

Stone helps me up. "Don't worry about that now. You are safe."

I look into his eyes and I know he is sincere. We walk without speaking for a long while.

"The mountain." I look up and it seems impossibly high. Sliding down on plastic was easy. But how do we get up? It will take hours.

"There's a shortcut." Stone takes my hand and squeezes it. "This way."

We walk past several more pods. Some are larger than others. A few have little gardens in the back. I stop when we pass a small child. I have never seen a child before. In the State, ours is the youngest generation. This child is dark, with huge brown eyes and the curliest hair I have ever seen. I want to sit and stare at her. I have never seen anyone so adorable in my life.

"Hi, Summer." Stone tousles the girl's hair and she grins and runs off. I still cannot move. Stone turns to me. "You've never seen a child before, have you?"

I shake my head, still watching the little girl run off, her chubby legs churning up dirt behind her. "Children here are ...?"

"Born." Stone looks at me, his eyes saying something I don't understand. "You were taught that way is primitive. But up here, it is as natural a part of life as eating and sleeping."

I don't know what, exactly, he is talking about, but I find I can hardly think clearly with his eyes on me like this. Berk flashes into my mind and I look away, feeling guilty. I shouldn't be speaking to Stone this way, shouldn't be letting him touch me so much. Or should I? If I move here, I can start a new life, and Berk can know I am safe. He can concentrate on being a Scientist and not on trying to save me. Or does Berk even know about Progress? I am so confused.

"It's all right, Thalli." Stone's hand is on my back, rubbing circles. "You can visit as often, or as seldom, as you want. And you can always choose to stay below."

Stone is facing me now, his hand on my cheek. I don't know what to think, what to say. He seems so confident, so kind. But he is a stranger. One who lives above, in a primitive way, with a mother, surrounded by children and dust and ... what else?

"I hope you'll choose to stay, though. There aren't many others our age. I have been hoping someone like you would be sent to us."

"You have Asta—I mean, Hope." It is odd to call her by that name.

"No, Xander has Hope." Stone shakes his head.

"What do you mean?"

"I'll explain more later." Stone keeps walking. "I don't want to overwhelm you on your first trip up."

We continue on, past the last row of pods and beyond a large building with a huge window that houses items for the pods. The sign on the front reads Progress Store.

"Here we are." Stone stands aside and points to a door leading into what I assume is the State.

"Are you not coming?" I don't want to be alone, don't want to walk back into the Scientists' quarters by myself. I am frightened.

Stone takes a step back. "No. I don't like it in there. I was born here, free. This is where I belong."

I nod.

"This door will take you to level C." Stone puts his hands in his pockets. "Just walk straight until you come to a metal door. It is unlocked. Walk through and then you'll be in a washing room. You can shower there. Hope has laid out clean clothes for you to change into."

I look at my clothes, layered in dust from the earth.

"We don't want anyone to become suspicious," Stone explains. "I know Hope told you this, but you really must be silent about our existence. Those below cannot know. It would cause turmoil."

I wonder again if Berk knows about this place. But I can't speak Berk's name in front of Stone. "I won't say anything."

"Good." Stone steps forward and brushes my cheek with his lips. The sensation is wonderful. "I look forward to seeing you again."

Stone looks at me in a way that makes me feel both shy and wonderful at the same time. And he is not hiding it. He is not embarrassed. He is not concerned someone will see us. This is so different from below. There is so much more freedom here.

I open the door. This looks like the room Asta took me in when we were at the top of the mountain. Old and yellowed, with windows. But now I feel like I may have trouble breathing because I am in and not out. The air feels heavier, the walls so close. But I walk on. I find the washing room and am amazed as the floor turns from white to brown as the water washes all traces of Progress from my skin and hair.

It cannot, however, wash away the memory. I go to the sleeping platform and dream of children and gardens. And Stone.

# CHAPTER TWENTY

hardly remember returning to my room last night. I know I did. The washing room was in the far corner of a stairwell that led to level C.

The stairwell makes me think of Berk and I feel guilty again. But I don't know why. Can I not enjoy the attentions of more than one boy? I'm not sure why I am conflicted.

The day goes by quickly. I don't see Dr. Loudin. Just Assistants who prod and poke me. I spend my allotted time in the exercise chamber, but no one is there. I miss conversations. I miss Rhen. I miss the routine of life in Pod C.

My violin is on the couch. I know I am changing when even

the sight of that does nothing to me. How do I play these feelings? I would need several instruments, playing at different tempos in different keys, to express my mind right now. I wonder if Progress has a Musician, if they have instruments. Could I teach others to play, have something like the string quartet John spoke of? That would be wonderful.

I close my eyes and play music in my mind. Berk is a cello, solid and deep. Stone is a French horn, complex but beautiful.

The door opens and Dr. Loudin walks in. I sit up straight, frightened. Why is he here? In my room? When he has so many more important things to do?

"Good morning, Thalli." His voice is higher than most men's voices.

"Sir." I don't trust myself to say more than one syllable. I stand, unsure where to go or what to do. What is the etiquette when one of the founders of the known world enters your cube?

"Relax, my dear." Dr. Loudin sits on my couch and motions for me to return to my sleeping platform. I sit on the edge, my back straight.

"Is something wrong?" Maybe I wasn't supposed to go up last night. Maybe Asta lied to me and they are a rebel group. Maybe he is here to personally escort me to the annihilation chamber.

"Nothing is wrong." Dr. Loudin's hair is an odd mixture of blond and gray. His eyes are small and hazel and they are constantly moving. "I have been monitoring your testing, as you know, and I am quite impressed."

"Thank you."

"What did you think of Progress?"

I exhale, not realizing I have been holding my breath. "It is astonishing."

Dr. Loudin smiles. "I'm glad you feel that way. I think you would be a fine addition to that community."

I nod.

"Of course, you still have several more weeks of testing to undergo."

"Of course." And what if I fail those? What does failure look like? All I am doing is talking and being prodded with machines whose functions I don't understand, being placed in simulated situations that make no sense.

"You have many questions."

"I'm sorry." I swallow hard. Am I so easy to read?

"Don't apologize." Dr. Loudin's tiny eyes stop for just a moment as they lock on mine. "Up there, curiosity is necessary."

*Then why is it treated as an anomaly down here?* I want to scream. *Why have I spent seventeen years suppressing it?*

Dr. Loudin leans forward. "As you know, your friend Berk is quite a promising Scientist."

"Yes." I am sure his mind moves as fast as his eyes.

"We are in the process of testing him as well."

"Testing Berk?"

"He is one of the brightest Scientists we have ever seen." Dr. Loudin leans back. "He will likely be one of The Ten who replaces us. But we need to make sure he is capable of such a responsibility. We need to know he will not be distracted from his duties."

Understanding hits me. Dr. Loudin knows Berk and I have spent time together. He knows we have feelings for each other. He is telling me that I am distracting Berk. That I could prevent him from becoming one of the next generation of leaders. That is why he moved Berk onto another project. That is why he wants me as far away from Berk as possible.

"Do we understand each other?"

"Yes, sir."

"I am certain you will do all you can to help your friend prepare for the important task he was designed to accomplish."

"Of course, sir."

"You are a bright girl too, Thallium." Dr. Loudin stands and I follow. "Continue to focus on your testing. You will be finished soon, and then you can choose where you would like to stay."

And what choice is that? Here in captivity, able to be near Berk but not to be with him? Or above, where I can forge a new life?

"Good morning to you."

Dr. Loudin leaves and I lie back on my sleeping platform. I can never see Berk—no more picnics or clandestine meetings on the stairs. No more music between us. Even if he tries to see me, to rescue me, I cannot let him. He is a Scientist. He will be—should be—one of *The* Scientists. I cannot hold him back from such an honor. I will not be the reason he loses such an opportunity.

I want to run back to Progress and stay there. Why do I have to wait? Why should I wait? What will they do if I just abandon the tests and make my choice now?

I gather my belongings and go to my door. I am not locked in. I will soon find out.

# CHAPTER TWENTY-ONE

I am locked in.

My room is the only door that is open. Every other exit is locked tight. I cannot leave this hallway. Is this another test? If it is, I am tired of them. I am tired of trying to pass inane tests that serve absolutely no purpose. I want to throw something, to yell at the top of my lungs.

I have decided that the Scientists are right—feelings *are* destructive. I wish I didn't have them. I cannot stop thinking about Berk, but I know I can't think about Berk. I *can* think about Stone, but I do not want to. Why do I want what I can't have?

Feelings are terrible things.

I am wandering the hall now. There is nowhere to go. Surely one of the Assistants will find me and make me return to my room. Or better yet, to the isolation chamber with the pink sleeping platform.

I lean against the wall. I need to talk to someone. John. I do not realize that in my wanderings, I have brought myself right to his door.

I open it and peek my head in.

"Come in." John walks over to me and opens the door wider for me to enter. His room smells like the Cleaning Specialists have not visited in several days.

I sit on the chair in the corner. It is so worn that I sink down farther than I expect and my feet fly up.

"I apologize." John pats my hand and walks to his couch. "I have not redecorated in years."

"How can you stand this?" I can't stop crying. I don't even care that the tears are dripping off my face and falling onto my shirt.

"It's not so bad." John rubs the arm of his couch. "James has offered to get me new furniture, but this reminds me of the old days. I need reminders."

"No, not the room." Although it could certainly use a good cleaning and, at the very least, some new fabric. "This. Life. Being cooped up and told what to do and who to talk to and who not to talk to."

John leans forward. Yesterday I would have found his slow movements endearing. Today they are just frustrating. Everything is frustrating.

"Did something happen?"

I laugh. The question isn't funny, but the laugh escapes anyway. "I found out there is a whole community of people living aboveground, and that if I care anything at all for Berk I can never see him again, and if I'm really good maybe I can go above and be completely removed from him forever. That's all."

John's thick white eyebrows come together. It's an odd sight. "There is a community aboveground? Are you sure?"

"Of course I am sure." My mind flashes to the dust, the pods. Asta. Stone. "It's . . . nice. Different."

"A community aboveground." John isn't talking to me. He is somewhere else, lost in memories I can't even imagine. "What does it look like?"

My frustration melts away. He is so eager, so hungry for news of the world he once knew. "I didn't see much. Just some pods and gardens. And a child."

John sucks in a breath. "A child?"

I see the little girl again. Summer. Her dark hair and eyes. Her tiny hands. "She was beautiful."

"What I wouldn't give to see a child again." John sighs. "The only time I see children is . . ." He shakes his head, unable to complete the thought.

"I also saw my friend Asta." I know Stone said not to speak to anyone down here about Progress, but this is John. "We were told she was annihilated several years ago. But she wasn't. She is alive."

"Asta?" John's face changes. "Was she a young girl when she was brought here? Eight or nine?"

"Yes."

"I spoke to her." John puts a hand over his heart. "All she had was a little cold. Just a cold. And they—"

"They took her above." I try to comfort the old man. "She is fine. Happy."

John shakes his head. "No. I walked with her to the annihilation chamber. I prayed with her."

"The Scientists must have taken her from there." I am sure there is a simple explanation. "She wasn't annihilated. They allow the ones who can survive above to live there. They even allow them to have children that are . . . born."

John stands. I have never seen him so agitated. I stand to walk to him, but the door opens.

"Thalli, you should not be here." My Assistant is at the door, motioning me to follow. She gives me no time to comfort John or even to say good-bye. She is walking down the hallway, and I know I need to stay with her. I look back and John is still standing, his eyes wide, blinking away tears. I wouldn't have told him about Progress if I knew it would upset him so much.

"You must eat." The Assistant opens the door to my room, where a tray with food that seems even more unappetizing than usual sits. "Then I will return to take you to isolation."

She expects me to object. I should not disappoint her. "Isolation?"

The Assistant raises her hand to stop me. "Leaving your room without permission is not allowed. And that man—"

"His name is John."

"He is dangerous."

I want to defend John, to argue with this Assistant that there is nothing dangerous about John, that he is the only one down here—other than Berk—who treats me like a human. But I don't say anything. Because she is taking me to the isolation chamber. And that is where Asta found me. Perhaps Dr. Loudin is allowing me to go to Progress again. But this Assistant cannot know that.

"You must eat," she repeats. I realize she will not leave until I do.

I swallow the food—a vegetable patty with sourdough bread and apple slices. I barely taste any of it. My mind is in Progress. I want to see more of it this time. Last time I was so shocked, so overwhelmed, I could barely take anything in. Not now. My curiosity—it is still hard to believe that is a positive trait—drives me to see more, to explore.

The Assistant opens the door. "Isolation."

I haven't heard music in a while, but it is there again. A flute plays staccato notes, trilling, skipping up and down the scale. I wish I could take out my pad and type this out. The music of Progress. Of hope.

I sit in the white moving chair and wait.

I barely have time to close my eyes before the door opens. Asta pokes her head in.

"It's about time."

# CHAPTER TWENTY-TWO

I am having trouble seeing. Everything looks white. My eyes water. The last time I was in Progress, the sky was darker, closer to evening. But it is daytime now. And it is bright. So much brighter than what we have below. Even with our artificial lights and our panels, our world is darker. And the sun—I can actually feel it. It is an amazing feeling. Like nothing I have ever felt before. I blink a few more times and my eyes begin to adjust.

"Stone insisted that he get you all to himself today," Asta says as we continue walking.

Stone is smiling, two sheets of plastic in his hands. "I would have come to get you—"

"He is scared of the inside." Asta smiles at me. "He thinks he'll get stuck in there and not be allowed out."

Stone rolls his eyes. "No. I just prefer the air out here."

"Right." Asta laughs and walks off. I have never seen people interact like this. So . . . not serious.

"Ready?" Stone hands me a sheet of plastic and I begin to follow Asta. "No, not that way."

"What?"

Stone takes off in the opposite direction, to the other side of the building. "You've already seen that part of Progress. I want to show you the west side." He turns to look at me and bends down, his face inches from mine. "Plus, I want to have you all to myself. I haven't been able to stop thinking about you since you were here."

I don't know what to say. I said those words about Berk just a few days ago. Is it wrong to accept them from Stone now? But Berk has to remain in my past. Stone could be my future. I am confused. But I don't have time to think about it because I am sitting on the plastic, careening down the hill. I don't even think about the dust. I just enjoy the speed and the rush of movement. I could do this all day.

It is over and we are at the bottom of the mountain. This looks similar to the other side. Dust as far as I can see. But this side has no pods, no people. Stone holds his hands out to help me up. Instead of letting go when I have risen, he pulls me closer, wrapping his arms around my back. I lean into him, enjoying the feel of my face against his chest, his breath in my ear.

"I have missed you."

I pull away, but Stone keeps his arms around me. Our faces are so close that my eyes struggle to focus. "Why?"

Stone lets go of me and laughs.

"What's so funny?" This response seems quite strange. Everything about Stone is strange. I find myself almost as curious about him as I am about Progress itself.

"You are so innocent." Stone shakes his head.

"Innocent?"

Stone takes my hand and we begin to walk. "It isn't a bad thing. It's just so different."

"Different?"

"Out here, feelings are encouraged." Stone squeezes my hands. "Lots of feelings. We get angry. We get excited. We love people and we miss people."

My heart is beating faster. "I have heard of love."

Stone stops and turns to me. "What have you heard?"

I am embarrassed to tell him about John and Amy. Will he think I am feeling that way about him?

"It's all right. We don't have to talk about it right now. We'll have plenty of time."

I sigh. I am relieved that he isn't pressing this. We walk again, and I see something in the distance. "What is that?"

"A building." Stone smiles and pulls me along, moving faster.

"Building?" I recall that word from my history lessons. "Built by the ancients?"

"Exactly."

I cannot believe it. "But I thought everything was destroyed."

"*Almost* everything."

"But our lessons said that nothing was left standing. That our community only survived—"

"Because of the reinforcements put in place by the Scientists?"

"Yes." I am surprised he knows that.

"Some of the newcomers have brought their learning pads with them." He shrugs.

"So the Scientists lied?"

"The Scientists really are good, Thalli." Stone stops and looks at me. "But they can't let everyone know everything. Sometimes it's best to withhold the whole truth in order to protect people."

"I suppose."

"Not everyone is like you and me." Stone moves closer to me. Our shoulders bump as we walk along. "The others down there, they are programmed to be productive. To help the State survive. They don't need to know there have been some unaffected areas in order to do that."

"But it's okay for you to know that?"

"And you." Stone motions behind us. "The original settlers of Progress broke free from the programming and they raised us the same way. And the Scientists recognize that is good. We will be the ones to move our generation on to bigger and better things."

Stone is so confident, so inspiring. So sure. I am still struggling to understand that I am really not malformed. It's a wonderful thought, but it's also a little frightening. How much of what I was taught is false? How long will it take me to unlearn what I have learned?

"Have I lost you?" Stone stops again.

"I am sorry." I keep walking, my eyes looking down at my feet. "I was just thinking."

"About what?" He grabs my hand again, this time fitting his fingers in between mine. "I want to know what you're thinking."

"I don't like feeling so unsure. Just a few weeks ago I thought I knew everything. Now I don't know what I know."

"That is one of the beauties of living on the outside." Stone releases my hand and places his arm around my shoulder. "You don't have to know everything. You *can't* know everything."

I feel like I want to cry. But I don't know why. I look up and realize we are almost there. "The building!"

"Cinema Royale." Stone points to the faded letters above us.

"How do you know that's what it was?" All I see are a few scattered letters, some barely hanging on.

"Come inside and I'll show you." He pushes aside a sheet of plastic, like the ones we came in on, and I am in a massive room. Bigger than I have ever seen before. "Welcome to Cinema Royale" is written in huge, sparkly letters on the wall to our right. I can tell people have visited this place often because it is free of dust. But it is so strange. "What is that?"

"The concession stand." Stone steps behind a long counter and pushes a button that brings a machine to life. In minutes, the machine makes a horrible noise but emits a wonderful smell.

"A concession stand?" I reach toward the machine, but Stone pushes my arm down.

"Don't. It's hot."

"Oh."

"And that isn't a concession stand." He points to the machine. "That is a popcorn machine. This whole thing is a concession stand. People who worked here would sell all kinds of things. Most of it requires ingredients we no longer have. But this"—he opens a small door and fills a metal bowl with some of the contents of the popcorn machine—"this we can use."

"Is it safe?"

"Of course." Stone takes a handful and stuffs it into his mouth. "Try it."

I lift just one piece to my mouth. It dissolves almost immediately. "It's good."

"I told you."

"But how does it work?"

"I'll explain it to you later." Stone leaves the concession stand and walks in the opposite direction. "But there's something else I want to show you."

We walk down a dark hallway where I see half a dozen rooms. Stone leads me into one of them. It is even darker than the hall. Chairs are in there, strange chairs whose bottoms are folded to meet the backs. Stone folds one down and tells me to sit.

"I'll be right back."

I am too overwhelmed to say anything. I am in a building. Eating popcorn. I feel like I have jumped into one of the lessons on my learning pad. I lean back and the chair follows. It doesn't move like the white chair in the isolation chamber, but it does move. My eyes adjust to the darkness and I can see art on the walls. Cloth pictures of strange people wearing strange hats and clothes. I want to get a closer look, but then the wall in front of me blinks on. Then I hear music. Amazing music. Instruments I cannot identify, all playing together. I have always wondered what that would sound like. I close my eyes and just listen, picking out the violins and flutes, percussion and piano. So many people playing.

"Don't close your eyes." Stone is sitting next to me. "You'll miss the movie."

"Movie?"

"It's an ancient form of entertainment. My father and I want to reinstate it. We just haven't quite figured out how. But we did find a few old movies hidden away in this building. This one is my favorite."

His father. He says that so casually. I want to ask what it was like to grow up with a father and a mother. With children of different ages. But I don't have time.

Images fill the screen, and I see places that are beautiful. Cities filled with buildings that are new, with a ground that is clean. People who had no idea their world would be destroyed. But I can hardly concentrate on what they are saying because underneath almost all their talking is music. I wish I could turn the voices off and just hear the instruments. I wish I could play with them. I can hear a part for my violin, a harmony that could be played just under the melody.

I feel Stone's gaze on me. "You like it?"

"Yes."

I am captivated by what I see. It's like the simulations, only better. I am part of the story, but I only observe. The people on the screen speak only to each other. Their accents are different. Like John's.

As the story progresses, I grow uncomfortable. I feel like I am watching someone's private interactions. I see two people go out together alone, like Berk and I did on the picnic. But they are in a building filled with tables and flowers and Assistants who bring food to them. Afterward, the couple walks on the shore of an ocean. The man takes the woman in his arms and puts his lips on hers.

Stone is looking at me again. I feel his arm brush against

mine. The music is swelling to a crescendo and my heart beats in time to the music. I feel dizzy and scared and ... wonderful.

"Are you all right?"

I look back up at the screen. "I'm sorry. I need to go."

I rush out of the room, out of the hall, all the way back outside. I finally stop and I am panting, gasping for air.

Stone rushes through the plastic at the entrance. He pulls me to him in a tight embrace. "I'm sorry. I'm so sorry. I thought you'd like it."

"I did." I pull away, needing more air in my lungs. "I do. It's just ... so different from anything I have seen. The music. The places. That couple—"

"They were in love." Stone smiles at me. "Many of the films we have found are about love. That is one part of the Scientists' formulations I don't understand. Why eradicate love? It's beautiful."

I think about John and Amy and I must agree. Love doesn't seem like something that would create division. Could it?

"Do you want me to take you back?"

I can only nod, grateful for his understanding.

"You know"—Stone takes my hand again as we follow our footprints back to the base of the mountain—"if my dad and I can figure out how to make movies, we will need a Musician to create the background music. Do you think you might be interested?"

My heart beats faster. Make music like that? "Oh, Stone. Yes. But I would need others."

"We have some you could train. Or we could record you playing each instrument, then play the recordings together. You could be your own orchestra."

We spend the remainder of the walk discussing movies and music and techniques and plans. It is wonderful. I can hardly believe when we are standing at the door.

"You don't have to go." Stone takes a step closer to me, his hand grazing my cheek, then cupping my neck.

I see the couple from the movie in my mind. I am scared. Stone steps back. "It's all right. We have plenty of time. I'll see you soon?"

I can only nod and rush back inside. I am barely inside the isolation chamber before I collapse on the sleeping platform, exhausted.

I do not dream at all.

# CHAPTER TWENTY-THREE

I am back in my room. I vaguely remember being escorted back here earlier. I am holding my violin. So many notes are bombarding my brain I don't even know where to start. I try to erase those notes from my mind. To just play what I feel. My fingers reach for my bow, and I place the instrument in the familiar spot on my neck and close my eyes and play.

I play my walk with Stone. I play the movie. I play the feel of Stone's hand in mine. I play the fear at his closeness. I play the music of Progress. So different, so free. Scary and inspiring and hopeful. I play my sadness at the thought of leaving this place forever. Never again seeing John. Or Berk. I try not to play

Berk. His future is planned. And it is a future without me. But I cannot stop myself from playing. I see his face in the young man's from the movie yesterday. I am the woman. He puts his hand on my face, just like Stone did. But with Berk, I don't pull away.

I open my eyes.

Berk is standing there.

"Don't stop." He moves to sit beside me. "Please. I love hearing you play."

I jump up and walk to the other side of the room. "You shouldn't be here."

"I know." He walks to me. I am frozen. I have missed him. So much.

"The cameras." If Dr. Loudin or one of the others sees him here, what would happen?

Berk shakes his head. "No cameras right now. They have been shut off for the next thirty minutes because of some testing going on in level H."

He pulls me to him and I cannot resist. I rest my head on his chest, hear his heart beating loudly against my ear. How I have missed him.

"Are you all right?" he whispers into my ear, still holding on to me. Or am I holding on to him? I don't know.

"Yes." My head is still against his chest.

"They have me working on something else." He pulls away and looks at me. "I tried to stay with you, but—"

"You are too important to waste your time with me." I move away, my words reminding me of Dr. Loudin's admonition.

"No." Berk is beside me again. "There's just a lot going on."

"I know." I want to talk to him about Progress, but I can't.

It feels wrong to tell him about Stone. He would be hurt if he knew.

"I am trying to keep them focused on you, though." He is speaking so softly. "I am doing everything I can to keep you from being . . ."

Berk believes I will be annihilated? He must know I won't, that I will be sent to Progress.

Unless I am not good enough for that either. Maybe the Scientists have been watching me up there, seeing how cowardly I am. Maybe my introduction to the city was a test and I failed it. I begin to cry. I was so sure I would live.

He pulls me to him again. But this time I resist. I know how it feels to lose someone. I felt it when Asta was sent away and when Berk left to be a Scientist. I don't want him to feel that.

"You were designed to be a Scientist." I try to speak with as little emotion as possible. "You cannot forget that. I have enjoyed your friendship. But you have more important work to do than to help me. I will be fine."

I open the door, refusing to allow him to speak or hold me again. I can only resist so much. He walks out. I see sadness in his eyes, and I do not like that I am the cause of it.

But this is how it must be.

As soon as the door shuts, I fall to the floor and sob.

# CHAPTER TWENTY-FOUR

I cannot stay in here, cannot keep thinking about Berk.

I need to see John.

I walk to his room, then open the door. He is sitting in his chair, eyes closed.

"Thalli." John opens his eyes and smiles. "I have been thinking of you often. The Designer has had me praying for you every day."

"Why?"

John's ice-blue eyes look distant, like he is seeing something beyond this room. "I don't know exactly. But I know that you have a purpose. A great purpose. And he wants me to help you fulfill that."

I am not sure what to think of this. "Of course I have a purpose. I am a Musician."

John motions for me to sit. I go to the couch. He continues, "The Scientists designed you to be a Musician. And you are a beautiful Musician. But the Designer has plans that go beyond that. He has chosen *you*."

"Chosen me?" Again I am reminded of how old John is, how strange. His mind is weak.

"Yes. I am sure of it." John leans forward. "Listen for him, Thalli. He will speak to you if you listen for him."

I do not know what to say. We are silent for a moment.

"I also wanted to speak to you more about Asta." He takes a deep, labored breath.

"She is happy." I place my hand on his arm. "She loves living in Progress."

"I would not hurt you for anything." John shakes his head. "And I have been thinking and praying about that young woman. I am old. My memory isn't what it used to be. I know that. But as much as I have tried to reconstruct those events, I am certain that she was annihilated."

"No." I don't want to argue with John, but I know she wasn't annihilated. I have seen her. Touched her. "She is alive."

John leans back. He grimaces as if he is in pain. "Tell me about your trips to see this community aboveground."

"I take an elevator to a top level."

"What level?"

"I don't know. We take an elevator I have never seen."

"Have you tried to find it on your own?"

"Once." I think of that time. "But all the doors were locked. I couldn't get there."

"So who takes you?"

"Asta," I say. "She has access to all the doors."

"You cannot get there on your own?"

"No." I lean back. "I can't get anywhere on my own."

"And she comes here?"

"Well . . ." A terrible feeling begins to take root. "She usually comes to the isolation chamber."

"The isolation chamber?" John's eyebrows draw together.

"Yes. It's nice. Pink and white. I actually enjoy spending time there."

"A room that is pink and white?"

I realize again how little John knows, how little he has seen. No wonder he is partially crazy. He has lived here, alone and trapped, for forty years. "Yes. I believe I am taken there so the others do not see me going above."

"What others?" John asks. So many questions.

"I do not know." I shrug. "I just know that the existence of Progress is kept secret from most people."

John takes a long, shaky breath and then looks into my eyes. "Thalli, are you sure this community is real?"

"What?" I feel almost nauseous. How could he ask that? What is he insinuating?

"The Scientists' technology is quite advanced." He hesitates. "Is it possible that what you have experienced isn't actual reality?"

"No." I stand and walk to the other side of the room, images of Progress flooding my mind. "It has to be real. I can smell things there, touch things. I have eaten there. I get dirty there and clean up here."

"In your room or in the pink room?"

I cannot remember. I don't want to remember. "It's impossible. John, why are you saying this?"

"Because you have a purpose. And you need to be fully aware of what is real and what is not when it is time for you to accomplish that purpose."

John is scaring me. I feel light-headed.

"I'm sorry." John crosses to me and places his hands on my shoulders. "This is too much."

Stone said those words. Stone. He is real. I felt his arms around me, I heard his heartbeat. I looked into his eyes. No technology could reproduce that much detail, that much humanity. Could it?

I suck in a lungful of air. "No. Progress is real. I know it is real. You are mistaken about Asta. You saw her go into the annihilation chamber, but then she was taken from there. People down here had to believe she was annihilated. But she wasn't."

"I didn't just see her go into the annihilation chamber. I went with her. James allowed me to stay with her until the end." John shakes his head and leans forward, a pained look in his eyes. "I saw Asta die, Thalli. I stayed with her body."

"No." The room is spinning. "You just thought she was dead."

"I stood by when she was placed in the incinerator."

I am going to be sick. This cannot be true.

"Asta is dead."

Those are the last words I hear. Then the room goes black.

# CHAPTER TWENTY-FIVE

My eyelids feel like they are made of lead. I try to open them but I cannot. I hear voices, but they sound so far away. I cannot understand what they are saying.

I must have fallen asleep. The voices are gone now, and I feel a sheet draped around me, all the way up to my shoulders. I try to open my eyes again. I can get them halfway up. I am in a medical chamber. Through tiny slits I see a medical wall screen with data I don't understand. I close my eyes again.

The next time I wake up I can open my eyes all the way. An Assistant enters the room and taps something onto the wall screen.

"What happened?"

"That's what we are trying to determine." I wish Assistants had a little more emotion. I am scared and her cold demeanor only increases my fear.

"How did I get here?"

"You were found in your room." The Assistant doesn't even look at me. She just examines her pad. "You had passed out."

I remember now. I was in John's room. He told me Asta was dead. He hinted that Progress was not real. That Stone wasn't real. And I passed out. But how did I get back to my room? He couldn't have carried me. But he knew I would be reprimanded if I was found in his room. I don't understand.

"Everything looks fine, though." The Assistant offers at least one bit of comfort. "I will tell the Doctor."

I go back to sleep. I am either exhausted or I am being sedated. The fatigue is too complete for me to think through which it might be.

"Thalli." A hand is on my shoulder. I open my eyes and see Dr. Loudin sitting on a stool beside my sleeping platform.

I want to sit up straighter, but I can't move. My body feels so heavy.

"You frightened us, young lady."

"I did?"

"Yes." His smile looks forced. He is worried about me? "You had been doing so well. But maybe we pushed you too far too quickly."

"What?"

"Stone didn't have permission to take you to the cinema the other day," Dr. Loudin explains. "That long walk along with all the new sensations from the movie was too much for you,

I'm afraid. He is so excited to have you there all the time that he rushed the process."

"Stone?" He *is* real? Of course he is. I knew it.

"You know, of course, that we monitor all the rooms." Dr. Loudin speaks quietly. "I reviewed your conversation with John."

That is how I got back to my room. They saw me in there. They heard us. They have heard everything?

"He said Asta was dead." I swallow past a lump in my throat. "He saw her. He watched her go into the incinerator."

Dr. Loudin runs a hand through his thinning hair. "No, Thalli, he didn't see any of that."

"He didn't?"

"John is getting older." Dr. Loudin's smile is sad. "He has a hard time differentiating between reality and his imagination."

"Why would he imagine that he saw Asta annihilated and incinerated?"

"Minds and bodies deteriorate as they age." Dr. Loudin purses his lips. "John has not been completely lucid for years. We have tried to convince James that it is in his father's best interest to be annihilated. But James insists we let John live out his years."

"He cares very much for his father."

"Yes." Dr. Loudin nods absently. "But we will have to monitor him more closely. No longer allow him to have access to others."

I want to defend John, but if Dr. Loudin is right, then John could be a danger to himself and to others. To me.

But he has never seemed like a danger. And he certainly appears lucid every time I have seen him. Of course, what do I know? Dr. Loudin is a Scientist. And he is very kind to take time to come here and speak with me. Like a friend, not a patient or test subject.

"I want to keep you here one more day, just to make sure you are well." Dr. Loudin stands to leave. "Then you can be released. We have almost concluded with your testing. Another week, perhaps two, and you can choose whether or not you'd like to live in Progress."

Dr. Loudin leaves, but his words linger. *"You can choose whether or not you'd like to live in Progress."*

I know John isn't entirely whole, but his words linger too. *"You have a purpose. You need to know what is real and what is not."*

Which words do I believe? Or are they both right? Is John, in his haze, still speaking truth to me? Perhaps I do have a purpose greater than I imagined. And perhaps that purpose is in Progress.

# CHAPTER TWENTY-SIX

Thalli." My name is spoken so quietly I can barely hear it. I open my eyes. I see green eyes through the slight opening in the door.

"Berk?"

He motions with his head for me to follow him. I crawl out of my sleeping platform. Whatever medicine I have received is still working its way through my body. I feel so heavy.

"Hurry," Berk whispers. "We don't have much time."

"Time for what?"

Berk doesn't answer. He is scanning the hallway. He grabs my arms and propels me into the last room on the right. It looks just like mine.

"What is going on?"

Berk is out of breath. He closes the door and checks the wall screen. It doesn't work. "The Scientists are dealing with a crisis right now."

"A crisis? What is happening?" I realize this room is silent. Completely silent. Usually there is some type of noise, the ticking of the medical monitors, the hum of the wall screen.

Berk turns to me. "We're safe."

"Safe from what?"

Berk's eyes are on mine. "Are you all right?"

"What?"

"When I heard you were here—" He takes a deep breath. "I am talking with the Scientists, trying to convince them you are too important to lose."

"What?" I step back. "I am here because I passed out. That is all."

Berk shakes his head. "Do you not know where you are?"

"I am in a medical chamber being treated. Dr. Loudin just came in and told me I would be released soon."

The muscle in Berk's jaw flexes. "He said you would be released?"

"Yes." His tone is scaring me.

"We've got to get you out of here." Berk is pacing.

"What? Why? What is going on?"

Berk stops and puts both hands on his head. "Dr. Loudin is preparing you for annihilation."

"No." I don't realize I am yelling, but Berk's hand is on my mouth. He looks at the door and then back at me. "That's impossible. He said as soon as I finish my testing, I'll get to choose whether or not I want to live in Progress."

"Progress?"

"Surely you know," I say. "The community above."

Berk's face is a mask of confusion. "Above?"

"Yes." Berk is being prepared to take over as one of The Ten and he hasn't been told about this? "People have been living there for at least twenty years. There are families. Babies."

Berk shakes his head. "Impossible."

"It's not impossible." I do not like that Berk doubts me. "I have been there."

"Above?"

"Yes. Twice."

He sits down on the sleeping platform and I sit beside him. I tell him about Asta, about going to the top level. I tell him about the dust and the pods and the children. I don't tell him about Stone, not exactly. But I do tell him I have made friends. That I saw a movie and ate popcorn.

When I am done, Berk has his face in his hands, his elbows resting on his knees. "I can't believe it."

"I thought you knew." I want to comfort him. He seems so . . . sad. "I'm sure they were going to tell you. You are being prepared for something great. Dr. Loudin told me so himself."

Berk slams his hand against the wall screen. It pulses blue and purple, then returns to black. "Dr. Loudin is lying to you, Thalli."

"What?" I grab the end of the sleeping platform for support.

"He is testing you."

I have never seen Berk so angry. "Of course he is testing me." I put a hand on Berk's arm, but he pulls away. "He is making sure I am capable of surviving outside."

"There is no outside, Thalli." Berk's voice is quiet, but sadness lies underneath it.

I start to speak, but Berk lifts a hand to stop me.

"Sit down." He guides me back to the sleeping platform. We sit. He rubs his palms against his blue pants. "Thalli, Dr. Loudin is experimenting on you."

"Experimenting?"

"I had no idea," Berk says. "I promise you. The tests I was running were meant to demonstrate your superior intellect. I was trying to prove that annihilating you would be a loss to the State."

"But you stopped testing me."

"Because I was forced to." Berk rubs his temples. "The other Scientists saw that I was getting close to you. But I was assured they would continue running the same types of tests. I told them with your talents and intelligence, you could stay here, work with us. We haven't tried to connect music with technology, but I was sure we could. We could do so much. Together."

"But Dr. Loudin told me I was distracting you."

Berk lets out a loud sigh. "You are not a distraction, Thalli. But I was—am—getting close to you. That's why he warned you away."

"So what kind of experiments was I being used for?" I have a sinking feeling as Berk takes my hand.

"Remember I told you Dr. Loudin's specialty is the brain?"

"Yes, but he has just done what you did—tested me in the cube, with different simulations. In the last few days, he hasn't even tested me at all. He has been allowing me to visit Progress instead."

"He has been testing you, Thalli." Berk rubs his temples again.

"No, that's impossible. He has just talked to me, that's all." I don't remember having anything ever hooked up to my brain. Every other part of my body, but not that.

"I didn't know this was happening."

"You didn't know what was happening?" My heart feels like it is being squeezed. Berk won't even look at me. He is staring at the ground.

"It's new. I've only heard discussions about it." Berk is speaking slowly, like he doesn't want to have to say the words. "Dr. Loudin thought he had come up with a way to create a virtual reality that involved all the senses. He was trying to develop scenarios, places, people with histories and personalities, all within a computer program."

"A computer program?"

"Dr. Loudin spends a lot of time in his laboratory." Berk shakes his head. "A lot of time. He doesn't really say much about what he is doing. I've just heard bits of conversation from some of the younger Scientists like me. He doesn't allow anyone in to see what he is doing. But we hear hints every now and then, when he gets stuck on something and needs to ask advice from one of the other Scientists. When I was working with the cube, I heard Dr. Williams mention that Loudin was close to completing his project."

"But it can't be this." I can barely speak. "You have to be mistaken. You said yourself you only heard hints of it. You've never seen it, right? Never been in his laboratory?"

"No, but Dr. Williams confirmed what I've heard—that Dr. Loudin is working on a complex simulation, one that would engage the whole mind. It would transport the person so she wouldn't even know she was in a simulation."

"No." Progress couldn't be just a computer program. I would know. I would be able to tell.

"I'm so sorry, Thalli." Berk finally looks at me. I look away. The pain in his eyes is too much. I cannot believe what he is saying. I won't believe it.

"Isn't it possible that Dr. Loudin knows about the community aboveground and just doesn't want to tell you? Maybe he is making you think he is creating this so when people like me come back from it, you'll just *think* it isn't real."

"Why would he do that?"

"Why would he create a virtual reality?" I argue. "What is the point of going to all that work?"

"I don't know."

"Isn't it possible that the air above isn't toxic?" I twist my hands in my lap. "Isn't there a chance that people could survive aboveground?"

Berk closes his eyes. "That's what the Scientists are discussing now."

"So it is possible?"

"We don't know, Thalli." Berk's voice is loud. I know he isn't upset with me, but he is upset. "That's why they are testing. To see if the air is less toxic. But no one even knows that yet. And even if it is less toxic, people can't live there right now. We are just hoping we can use more of the atmosphere from there quicker."

"Why?"

"We are running out of some of the necessary ingredients to allow for continued growth here. If something isn't done soon, we will have to eliminate people."

"Eliminate?"

"There isn't enough oxygen to sustain all of us." Berk frowns. "Not unless the Scientists can uncover a new formula using what we already have."

"So why would Dr. Loudin be working on this mind experimentation when that is going on?"

"He started it years ago. It was originally intended as a learning module. Rather than reading about history, you experience it. Scientific testing could be completed without using up resources here. It is brilliant."

"But Progress doesn't do any of that. In fact, they live without adhering to many of the rules here. They don't even always agree with the Scientists."

"That is strange."

"Maybe it's real, Berk." Hope begins to surface. "Why would Dr. Loudin go to all the trouble to create a place like that, when it has no value? Why, especially if he is just going to annihilate me, would he waste his time on it?"

"I don't know. He has to test on someone."

"But if you are right, those tests would be academic." I am growing more confident.

Berk stands. "Then let's conduct an experiment on our own."

"What kind of experiment?"

"Play along with the Assistants, the Scientists, everyone. Try to return to Progress."

"All right."

"When you're there, take something with you." Berk is speaking quietly. "Something small. Put it in your pocket."

"But I always change clothes before returning—so no one sees the dirt."

Berk looks at me. I know what he is thinking. But I refuse to believe Progress isn't real. I will prove it to him.

"Keep it in your hand, then. Or on you. Maybe you can take something that will stick to your skin."

"All right."

"But be subtle about it," Berk says. "If they are watching and know what you are doing, this won't work."

I nod.

"If it is there when you are back in your room, then we'll know it's real."

The wall screen flickers to life and Berk rushes me out the door. He points to my medical chamber and disappears down the hallway. I lie down and close my eyes. But I cannot sleep. I keep replaying our conversation, hoping that Berk is wrong. That Progress is real. That I am being prepared for a long life aboveground.

Because the alternative is too horrible to even consider.

# CHAPTER TWENTY-SEVEN

You haven't eaten." The Assistant is back in my room. I can't tell her that I don't want to eat because my world has just been turned upside down. "You must finish this to be released."

I sit up. I will eat.

I swallow the bread and fruit, barely tasting it. I keep thinking about Progress. And Berk and Stone. I am so confused. It is a strange feeling. But I am also feeling something else. Something new. I can't define it. Knowing I am the only one who can uncover whether or not Progress is real is frightening and exciting at the same time. I will do this. I will bring something back, and I will prove that Progress is not a cerebral simulation concocted by Dr. Loudin. And then ... what?

Will I finish my testing, as Dr. Loudin said, and live above? Leave Berk?

But what if Berk is right, that Progress isn't real? That I am going to be annihilated?

I close my eyes and lean back on my pillow. Life was much easier when my biggest difficulty was trying to complete a lesson on my learning pad.

"Time to go." The Assistant comes. Not the one who has been in my medical chamber, but the one who comes to take me to the isolation chamber. I try not to smile. I am going to Progress.

Same hallway, same door, same pink room, same white chair. And then ...

"Stone?" I can't believe he has come down here. "I thought you never came below."

Stone reaches me in three huge steps, kneels by my chair, and cups my face with his hands. "I couldn't wait to see you. I was so afraid you had changed your mind and weren't coming back."

I want to tell him about my conversations with John and Berk. But I can't. I don't want Stone to know about Berk. Not yet. And if there is the possibility that he isn't real, that he is just a technical construct, then everything I tell him goes straight to Dr. Loudin. I don't want to take that chance.

"Thalli?"

I shake myself from my thoughts. "I'm sorry. It is good to see you."

Stone stands. "Something has changed."

"No." My heart beats faster. I must be careful not to be so obvious. "I have just been a little sick."

Stone kneels again, his eyes searching mine. "Are you all right?"

I place my hand on his face. I feel the stubble on his cheek, see imperfections on his nose. He has to be real. "I am fine now. Don't you ever get sick up there?"

"Of course. But I didn't think that was allowed down here."

I think of Rhen. "It isn't, normally. Not in the pods. And I wasn't ill, just feeling a little strange."

"Too much popcorn?" Stone laughs and I know the subject has been successfully navigated.

"Perhaps." I stand and Stone walks behind me, out the door and into the hall. "I don't feel much like sliding today. Could we just go out the way we come in?"

Stone's face registers something like shock. "But you love sliding."

"I know, but I just don't feel like it right now."

"Oh, all right." Stone steps in front of me. "It's this way."

We go down two levels and walk through the washing room, where my clothes for the return are laid out.

"Who does this?" I point to the clothes.

"What?" Stone is opening the door that leads outside.

"Who puts clothes out for me?"

"My mother."

"Oh," I say. "Why?"

"That is her job." Stone smiles. "One of them, anyway."

"And what are her other jobs?" I want to know more about life here, life with mothers and fathers and children.

"Why don't I take you to see her and you can find out for yourself?"

We walk into the town, past Stone's pod to a large building.

It has many rooms. April is in one of the last rooms. She is sitting at a machine. It looks somewhat familiar.

"This is the textile department." Stone smiles and April looks up from the machine.

I am amazed again at how similar April and Stone look. The same dark hair and dark eyes. Their olive skin isn't identical, but it is obvious they are related. The idea of it still seems so primitive. Strange.

"You make clothes." I realize the machine is an older version of what we have back in the pods. Bhor is responsible for making our uniforms. But those are white, plain. April is making colorful clothes. She is combining different fabrics. I look around the room and see her creations hanging on racks. What would Bhor think of this? Would he enjoy working with all of these colors? Would his brown eyes light up at all of this fabric? Longing for my friends at Pod C clogs my throat.

"What is this?" I need to think about something else. I touch what looks like a long shirt that gets fuller at the bottom. The top part is made of a bright-green fabric. It reminds me of Berk's eyes. The bottom has several fabrics, with many different colors in each. It is lovely.

"This is a dress," April says. "Would you like to try it on?"

I look at Stone.

"Go ahead." He takes the dress down and walks me to a small room where I can change.

I slip the dress over my head. It doesn't feel like the material we have below. It is coarser. And when it is finally on, it comes only to my knees. I have never walked out in public without wearing pants. I am a little embarrassed to be doing so now.

"Is everything all right?" April calls out.

"Yes." I am still frozen in place.

"Then come out." Stone laughs. "I want to see it."

I open the door and step out, the air feeling strange against my bare legs.

April claps and pulls me into a hug. "You look beautiful. Come see."

She leads me to a tall mirror mounted on the wall. She removes the elastic from my hair and it falls to my shoulders, thick and wavy. I see so much more of myself than I am used to seeing. I cannot stop looking.

"You are a wonderful Clothing Specialist," I say to April.

"We call her a Seamstress."

"Seamstress." I like that word. It sounds more worthy of a piece of clothing like this. "I should change."

"No." April fluffs my hair. "It's yours."

I look down. "I can keep it?"

"Certainly you may." April's smile is so much like Stone's, kind and open. "Of course, they won't allow you to wear it below. But I will have it cleaned and ready for you every time you come to Progress."

"And when you live here"—Stone puts an arm around me— "you can have a whole room full of dresses. Right, Mother?"

I suddenly remember my task today. In the joy of trying on the dress and being with Stone and April, I had forgotten that they might not be real, that I need to discover whether or not this place actually exists. Watching them interact, seeing them, smelling the fabrics in this room, I am sure they are real. I just have to prove that to Berk.

"What would you like to do today, Thalli?"

"I want to know more about Progress. Can I see what's in the other rooms? What the other jobs are?"

Stone smiles. "That sounds like the request of someone who is thinking of joining our community."

Stone doesn't give me time to respond. He just takes my hand and leads me into Progress.

# CHAPTER TWENTY-EIGHT

A nd this is the technology center." We have visited every room in the large building. Stone pushes the door open. "My father works here."

I see a large man, larger than any I've ever seen, sitting behind a huge machine. He is wearing thick, protective glasses and using an instrument that makes a loud, squealing noise.

"This must be Thalli." Stone's father stands, and I have to stop myself from gasping at his height. He is a full head taller than Stone, who is a head taller than I. "I am Miller."

His hand swallows mine. He is darker than Stone but has his dark eyes. Miller, however, has no hair at all. He is older than

April, and his eyes wrinkle at the sides in a way that reminds me of John. "I hear you enjoyed my movie theater."

"Your theater?" Stone lifts an eyebrow and his father laughs—a deep, loud laugh. The sound—and his size—remind me of a tuba.

"All right, *our* theater." Miller puts a large hand on the machine below him. "And I am close to getting this to work—it is another film. It was damaged pretty badly, but I was able to bring it back to life."

I think of the film I saw with Stone. My cheeks heat at the memory.

"My father's main job is to keep Progress running. He and his team keep the electricity going and the machines working properly. But films are his love. He has missed many meals working on this." Stone motions toward the equipment.

Miller pats his ample stomach. "I haven't missed that many meals."

These two are so comfortable with each other. So different from the way we interact with our Monitors. They enjoy being together. They appreciate each other. They love each other. This is what John was talking about. He had this with his wife and children. With his son. Is that why Dr. Turner was not able to send him to annihilation?

"We'll let you get back to work." Stone grabs my hand. "I have one more place I want to show Thalli."

I wave good-bye and try to keep up with Stone's long strides. "Where are we going?"

"Be patient." He smiles at me and keeps moving. We have left the town and are walking toward what appears to be a greenhouse. I don't want to disappoint him by telling him I have seen this before. Each pod has its own greenhouse. But he isn't walking there.

"So your... parents?" I ask the question that has been burning in my mind. "How did they choose to—" I don't even know how to phrase this question. It is so strange, so uncomfortable.

Stone stops and looks at me, his eyes dancing. He sits on the earth and motions for me to join him. "My parents were some of the first to be allowed up here. The Scientists allowed forty people from below to try to begin this new city. They were about our age when they arrived."

"Why did I never hear of this?"

"Only those who were chosen were told."

"But surely not everyone wanted to go."

Stone shrugs. "The State can be very persuasive."

They weren't really given a choice. Of course. That is the way of the State. "So how did your parents survive?"

"Each of the members chosen had training that would help up here." Stone stretches out his legs. "And they went through a few months of training below. It was hard the first few years, but the Scientists helped as much as they could. And our founders were strong and resourceful."

"I can see that." Knowing this place was made from so little, in such a relatively short time, is amazing.

"But back to my parents." Stone smiles. "They knew each other, of course. And they talked. But there weren't really any feelings yet."

"They were designed without feelings?" I think of my malformation. "But that changed? Did the Scientists adjust their makeups?"

Stone laughs and I marvel again at his smile. So open.

So relaxed. He stands, helps me up, and we walk again. "No. Something about being out here, in this air, changes everyone. It's like a child who goes from a liquid diet to a solid. They learn to chew and to swallow. People here learn to feel and to think. It is encouraged."

I don't want to tell Stone I don't know anything about children. But he is lost in the story and doesn't seem to notice my ignorance. I am grateful for that. He would never finish his story if I asked every question that came into my mind.

"A few other couples were joining together and beginning to have children."

"They were married, right?" I am happy to know at least one of these words.

"Married?" Stone seems confused.

"They had a wedding? April walked down the aisle in a white dress?"

Now it is Stone's turn to need an explanation. I tell him what John told me, about weddings and love and commitment.

"No, we don't have that here." Stone blinks a couple times. "But it sounds nice. Some couples here stay together awhile—like my parents. Others go on to pair with someone else."

"Oh." Was John odd, even among the anomalies?

"Anyway, my parents found that they were attracted to each other, so they chose to be together. I was born a few years later."

"The sky is getting darker." I have been so busy listening to his story that I didn't notice. I realize I spend little time noticing the sky at all here in Progress. I rarely look up. There's no need to below, except on our moon-viewing days. And usually when I am here the sky is so bright, I don't want to look up. "It is beautiful."

I have to stop. The sky is blue and pink, and I see the moon, although it is almost translucent. I wish I had my violin with me. I would like to play this beauty. I wish I could capture it on my learning pad and look at it again. But it wouldn't be the same. My little rectangle on the pad couldn't truly display the grandeur. I can look in all directions and see the sky. Part of it is blocked by mountains, but it is never completely blocked. This is so much more amazing than seeing the moon through the panel.

"I had no idea the sky was so huge. Why have I not seen this before?"

"You were too busy looking at me." Stone is laughing at me. It is a kind laugh, and it makes me feel good. Happy. "We're here."

I tear my eyes away from the sky and I am shocked by what I see.

"A river." Stone points to the water.

Water! "I thought—"

"It was all destroyed? Toxic?"

"Yes." I think of the huge tanks we have below, tanks that bring in ocean water from far away. The tanks I sat by when Berk and I had our picnic. "Can you drink it?"

Stone shrugs. "I suppose. But we usually filter it first."

"So it *is* toxic?"

"No, it's perfectly safe." Stone scoops a handful of the brownish water into his palms. "Our Water Technicians devised a way to remove the contaminants before I was born."

I look at the water in Stone's hands. Amazing. I have only ever seen it come from a faucet, never straight from the earth.

"I'll show you what I like to do in it." Stone kicks off his shoes and then lunges toward the water. He puts his hands over his head and jumps in, submerging his entire body in the water. "Come on in. Give it a try."

I step away. I cannot go in there. I don't care that it is safe. What would I do? I'd sink in that much water. But Stone isn't sinking. He is kicking his feet and moving farther in.

"Come swimming with me," he shouts.

I swallow hard. "Swimming?"

Stone comes out of the water and grabs both of my hands, walking backward and propelling me toward the water. "Don't worry. I'll show you."

I reluctantly take off my shoes and follow Stone into the water. The ground feels so soft, so strange. The footprints I leave are deep and some of the water fills in the spaces where my toes and heels have been. I want to examine that, but Stone won't let me stop.

"Just step in to your knees." Stone is still walking in front of me. As the water gets higher, I slow down.

"I'm scared." My dress feels heavy where it has gotten wet.

"It's all right. We can stop here for now. Just get used to the feel of it."

I close my eyes and focus on the water. It isn't cold, exactly, but it feels good. I move my toes and the ground below shifts. I feel Stone step closer to me and I open my eyes.

"You are beautiful, Thalli." He runs a hand over my hair and leans close. He smells like the fabric from his mother's textile room mixed with the scent of the outside. He steps closer still. His face is inches from mine. Just like in the film. The image of that couple fills my mind and I turn away.

"I need to go back."

Stone grabs my arm and turns me to face him. "What are you afraid of?"

My heart is beating fast. I am afraid of so many things. I am confused about so many things. Stone tells me there is a place for me here. Berk tells me this might not even be real. John tells me I have a great purpose. Until a few weeks ago, I was sure I was an anomaly. And I might still be. I don't know. Until a few weeks ago, I knew nothing of love. And now?

I look into Stone's eyes. Could I love him? But what about Berk? When I am with Stone, I cannot think about Berk, and when I am with Berk, I cannot think about Stone.

I must be an anomaly.

"It's all right." Stone lets go of me and we walk back to the ground. "We have plenty of time."

We are sitting on the grass. Stone lies back and I follow. The sky is now a dark blue. The moon is bright and white against that backdrop, and as my eyes adjust, I see stars. So many stars. Far more than I knew existed, than I could see from the panels.

"This is so beautiful."

"Yes, it is." Stone isn't looking at the stars but at me. I don't know how to respond.

I sit up and my hand touches the ground. We have grass below, but this feels different. Thinner. Less perfect. It reminds me of the patches of grass I saw when Berk took me on our picnic. I smile at the memory, then I remember—I need to take something from Progress, to see if it is still with me when I return. Something I can stick to my skin. I could bring grass, but we have that. If Dr. Loudin is constructing this, he is also watching. He could place a blade of grass on my arm when I am sleeping.

The thought that this might not be real, that Dr. Loudin could be watching, causes me to stand. "I should go back."

I can tell Stone is confused. I look at him. "I'm sorry. I will explain everything the next time I come."

"Why can't you explain now?" He stands beside me, wiping wet dirt from his pants. "Why all the mystery?"

I shake my head. "I'm sorry."

Stone doesn't speak as we walk back. He is upset. If he wasn't real, would he be upset? Am I ruining our friendship by choosing to believe he might not actually exist? Will he speak to me when I return?

I want to throw my arms around him and tell him everything. I want him to laugh at me for thinking that any Scientist could ever devise this place, with all its beauty and wonder and eccentricities. But I can't. I have to know.

I am at the washing room before I realize that I haven't taken anything with me.

"Good-bye, Thalli," Stone says, his voice sounding more like an oboe than his usual upbeat trumpet. I have hurt him.

He closes the door and I remove my dress, admiring, once again, its vibrant colors. I want to take it with me, but it would attract too much attention below. I see a string hanging from the bottom. I pull it. It is bright pink with one small section that is blue. I pull it off the dress, cover one hand, and, as subtly as possible, tie it tightly around a hidden finger.

I hope it will be there when I wake up.

# CHAPTER TWENTY-NINE

I open my eyes and see John. He is sitting on the edge of my sleeping platform. His eyes are closed, but his mouth is moving.

I clear my throat and he stands slowly. He looks older every time I see him and his eyes seem so weary.

"I was worried about you." He sounds tired, like his vocal cords are tied in knots. "I'm so sorry."

"It's all right." I sit up, rubbing my eyes. "But what are you doing here? How did you get out of your room?"

Then I remember my finger. The thread. I am afraid to look. If the string isn't there, Progress isn't there. Which means my future is here. And I am an anomaly. I will be annihilated. I keep my hand down, under my bedcover. I cannot look while John is here.

"I have told you that you have a purpose."

I nod. John is kind, but he is old and his mind is decaying. I remember what Dr. Loudin said.

"I do not think I have much more time here." John leans closer, his voice barely above a whisper. "But you do."

"Don't say that." I may not have any more time than he does. But I do not want to tell him that.

"I am at peace." John smiles and closes his eyes. "Death is only the beginning. I want you to know that."

I sigh.

"You do not believe." A tear forms in the corner of John's eye. "I understand. This seems strange, right? Talk of a Designer?"

I think of the sky I saw last night. The music that placed me here. Of love. "Not as strange as it used to seem."

John smiles. "Good. He is showing himself to you, isn't he?"

I wonder again at John's perceptiveness. What must his mind have been like when he was young?

"His Word tells us that if his people don't praise him, even the rocks and the trees will cry out the glory of his name."

I see the blade of grass in my mind. It is perfect in its imperfection, replicated a thousand times over at the edge of the lake. I think of the mountains. Where did they come from? Not even the Scientists claimed to have developed the earth. If they didn't, who did?

"The Designer reveals himself to his children in so many ways."

"His children?"

"'Yet to all who received him, to those who believed in his name, he gave the right to become children of God.'"

"What is that?"

"His Word."

"What does it mean?"

John smiles. "It means that you can be his child through faith."

"Faith?"

"Believing in who he is."

"But I don't know who he is." I blink away tears. "I don't know if I want to believe."

John pats my hand. "Ask him to show himself to you, Thalli. Ask him to show you he is real."

"And if he doesn't?"

John stands. "'If any of you lacks wisdom, he should ask God, who gives generously to all without finding fault, and it will be given to him.'"

I watch John leave, his words ringing in my mind. But unlike the words of Dr. Loudin or Stone or Berk, John's words don't frighten me or make me nervous. They make me feel calm. John is so sure. Strange, yes. Old, certainly. But so sure. And so kind. For his sake, I will ask this Designer to give me wisdom.

I close my eyes, like I have seen John do, and I ask.

Nothing happens.

I open my eyes and remember the string.

Slowly, I pull my hand out from the bedclothes. I don't look. I am afraid to look. My hand is on top of the covers, but my eyes are squeezed shut.

I take a deep breath and open my eyes.

My finger is bare.

# CHAPTER THIRTY

throw the bedclothes down and search every inch of them, every inch of the floor. I search the sheets, the pillow. I throw my sleeping shirt off and search it.

Why did I bring back something so small? Of course it would get lost. A blade of grass would have been better.

I sit on the floor, trying to catch my breath. I lift up my finger, looking for any sign that the thread had been there. I tied it tightly. I should see the impression of the string on my finger.

Nothing.

The thread does not exist.

Progress does not exist.

I fall down on my bedclothes, grabbing a handful to muffle sobs I cannot prevent. I am crying so hard I can hardly breathe.

Progress isn't real.

I don't realize until this moment how desperately I wanted it to be real. Not just so I could avoid annihilation, but so I could live. Really live. In a community with people. Families. Breathing air, looking at the stars, swimming and laughing and loving.

I don't even care anymore that I will be annihilated. I wouldn't want to live down here anyway. I wipe the tears from my eyes and begin to dress again, to replace the sheets and bedclothes.

No, life here isn't life. There is no freedom. No laughter. Only a ridiculous desire for perfection at all costs. Costs like Asta.

The tears come again. Asta is truly dead. The hope that I had when I thought she was alive is crushed. She never came to my door. She never showed me the outside. Never introduced me to Stone.

Stone. How do I even grieve someone who never existed? I feel foolish for missing him. But I do. I learned more from him than I ever learned in the pod. I can still see him, his olive skin and dark eyes. I can feel the rough stubble of his cheek. I can smell the water on his skin.

I want to throw something. Break something. I hate this place. I want to scream for an Assistant to come and send me to the annihilation chamber now.

I take in a shuddering breath. Maybe that's the purpose of the simulation. Maybe Dr. Loudin, in some twisted form of kindness, wants to make those of us who are anomalies eager to die.

If that was his purpose, he was successful.

My door opens. Berk is standing there. His face is as white as the walls. I can tell he has been crying—the whites of his eyes are pink, making his eyes almost seem to glow.

"I know." I want to spare him the pain of having to say it.

Berk crosses to me and crushes me in his embrace. I can hardly breathe. I am limp in his arms.

"I saw you—" He can't continue. I see anger on his face too. He pulls away and rakes a hand through his hair, already tousled like he hasn't slept. "Hooked up to Loudin's machine. Like some lab rat."

I snap out of my apathy. "You saw me?"

"I had to find out. I needed proof. I watched Dr. Loudin all day yesterday."

I need to sit. I walk to the couch and Berk joins me.

"Are you sure you want to hear this?"

"Of course I want to hear it." I rub my hands on my knees. "But what about the cameras?"

"Disabled." Berk's jaw flexes. "I turned them all off, every one of them on this floor. Turned everything off. The Assistants have no idea who did it or how to fix it. They will be working on it all morning."

That explains how John was able to come without being caught. The doors aren't locked and the cameras aren't on. John must have thought it was a sign from the Designer.

"Yesterday"—Berk leans back—"I placed cameras on Dr. Loudin's and his Assistant's jackets."

"Cameras?"

"They are very small." Berk shrugs. "The kind we use to monitor the pods."

I knew there were cameras in the pods, but I thought they were part of the wall screens. "We have no privacy." I am hating this place more and more.

"I attached them to their lapels in the morning."

"How did you watch it without being caught yourself?" I do not mind knowing that I will be eliminated. But I can't bear the thought that something will happen to Berk. "Aren't there cameras watching you too?"

Berk laughs, but it isn't a joyful sound. "It is something I have been working on."

He reaches into his pocket and pulls out a clear disk. "This is a screen I can place right in my eye. I can see everything, and no one knows."

"Tell me what you saw."

"He spoke to his Assistant." Berk sighs. "She brought you your meal."

"My meal." How could I be so stupid? "No wonder she always insisted that I eat everything."

Berk nods. "The drug they used caused you to be mentally unconscious but physically awake."

"What?"

"She waited about five minutes," Berk says. "Your eyes . . . changed. I can't quite describe it. I've seen this given to people scheduled for annihilation. It makes the process easier." Berk closes his eyes.

He has seen people being annihilated. I can't imagine anything more terrible.

"She took you by the hand and led you down the hall. It looked very normal, like you were going to a regular test. She even passed people on the way. No one looked twice at you."

I hate that I don't remember this. That someone has that much control over me. "I remember her returning later to take me to the isolation chamber."

Berk clears his throat. "That was the first simulation. You were strapped into a chair with a probe inserted into your skull."

"My skull?" My hand goes to my head. Berk moves my fingers to the crown of my head where my hair is the thickest. With two fingers, he makes a part and guides my finger to a tiny bump. "There?"

"Yes."

I feel the bump with my finger. I scrape it with my fingernail. There it is. A tiny hole. I would never have noticed it.

"Once the probe was in place, he began the program. Everything you saw was projected on the wall screen."

I feel sick. "Everything I saw?"

"It's all right, Thalli." Berk puts a hand on my knee. "You have nothing to be embarrassed about. Dr. Loudin was cruel to put you through that, to make you think that was real."

"So it was all there?"

Berk pauses, his eyes scanning the floor. "I saw Stone."

I want to run out of the room and hide. "I'm sorry, Berk."

"You don't have anything to be sorry about." Berk turns my face so I am forced to look into his eyes. I can hardly stand it, knowing he saw me look into Stone's eyes yesterday. It must have been so painful for him. "You thought it was real, and you thought you would be starting a new life up there."

I think of holding Stone's hand, embracing him, sharing moments in the water and on the shore, talking about the future. "But I hadn't decided yet. Dr. Loudin said I had a choice. I kept thinking of you, even when I was with him."

"Thalli." Berk releases my face. "Loudin was manipulating you. And he is an expert. I am not upset. It's all right. And if it were real, I'd have wanted you to go with him."

"You would?"

"Of course." Berk looks at me again, his eyes searching every part of my face. "I will do anything in my power to see that you are safe and happy."

I don't like the implications of those words. He can't sacrifice himself for me. He needs to let me go quietly. He has the potential of a future. A great future. I do not.

"You are a good friend." I stand. "But I knew when I came here what would happen. I have been fortunate to have as much time as I had. But my time is up."

"No." Berk stands with me, his hands on my shoulders. "I'm talking with the other Scientists. I am working on some possibilities."

"I don't know if I want possibilities. They would just prolong the inevitable. Dr. Loudin's simulations have made me long for something that will never be. They have made me dissatisfied here. I don't want to stay here below. I don't want to be used for more experiments."

Berk drops his hands. "Don't give up. Please."

I close my eyes. As much as I want to spare Berk, I know the pain involved in losing a friend. I lost Asta. Twice. And even though he didn't really exist, I lost Stone. The pain of those losses is terrible. I wish Berk didn't have to go through it. But he does. So the sooner I can be out of his life, the better for him.

"I am going to ask to be annihilated tomorrow." I raise my hand to stop Berk's protestations. "Do not argue with me."

Berk holds me again, and I feel his chest rise and fall heavily.

I rest my head on his shoulder, memorizing the feel, the smell. I lift my head and touch my lips to his cheek.

"I am not giving up," he says. Then he walks out.

Before I have the chance to think about my decision, to change my mind, I open my unlocked door and walk down the hall, around corners, until I find an Assistant sitting at a desk.

"Please inform Dr. Loudin"—I keep my voice as quiet and calm as I can—"that I wish to be sent to the annihilation chamber tomorrow."

"Very well." The Assistant's voice doesn't even register surprise.

# CHAPTER THIRTY-ONE

I play the piece again. I have memorized the notes. I close my eyes. I beg the Designer—if he does exist—to show me, to explain what this means.

It is only fitting that the song that began all of this should be the last song that I play.

When I played it in the pod, I cried, knowing the answers were here but not knowing what those answers were. I am closer to the answers now. I can feel it. But they are still just out of reach. So I play it again and again. I will be annihilated this morning. But I refuse to go with unanswered questions.

The notes wash over me, reach into the deepest part of my being. But what are they saying?

A knock on the door breaks my concentration.

John enters. As soon as I see him, the tears I have been holding back are released. I don't try to stop them. I don't think I could even if I tried.

John takes my violin and places it on the couch, then he holds my hands. His feel so soft, so old. Like they could break if I held on too hard.

"Tell me what it means," I beg. There is no time for intellectual discussion now. No time for debate. No time to question the sanity of this man.

He leads me to the couch and we sit. He closes his eyes and begins to sing. His voice is soft, but the notes are sure. And the words water the dry places in my heart.

> *"Jesu, joy of man's desiring,*
> *Holy wisdom, love most bright;*
> *Drawn by Thee, our souls aspiring*
> *Soar to uncreated light.*
>
> *Word of God, our flesh that fashioned,*
> *With the fire of life impassioned,*
> *Striving still to truth unknown,*
> *Soaring, dying round Thy throne.*
>
> *Through the way where hope is guiding,*
> *Hark, what peaceful music rings;*
> *Where the flock, in Thee confiding,*
> *Drink of joy from deathless springs."*

We are both crying when he is done. "'Drink of joy from deathless springs,'" I repeat.

"'Jesu' is Jesus—God's Son," John begins. "Jesus brings the salvation you have been longing for."

*Salvation.* The word sounds so primitive. A few days ago I would have scoffed at its use. But if John reflects the primitive and Dr. Loudin is the modern, I want to be primitive. "He is the joy of man's desiring. He is the uncreated light."

"The Designer made us with a longing for him. Yet we deaden that longing or ignore it. In recent years, we have 'reasoned' it away. But it is still there. And you, my dear, are proof of that."

He says that as if I am not an anomaly, as if I am . . . special.

"God sent his Son, Jesus, into this world to save the world," John says. "The world rejected him. They killed him."

"I can identify with this Jesus."

John smiles. "But he did not stay dead."

I want to disregard this. But I know not to. As outrageous as this sounds, I know it is true. I feel its truth in me. "He lived?"

"He *lives.*" John wipes a tear from his eye. "He is not just God's Son, he is God himself. God in the flesh. His death paid the penalty for our sins—for all the wrongs we have ever done. And his rising from the dead allows us to live forever with him."

"Live forever?" I am overwhelmed with a hope like I have never experienced.

"Yes, in a place called heaven." John's face looks like it is lit from within. "A perfect place where there is no pain, no death, no tears."

Those words hang in the air. I find my violin and lift it to my chin, closing my eyes. I play the song. And this time, I understand. Cleansing tears pour down my face as I play. This Jesus is the joy of my heart's desiring. He was speaking to me in the pod when I first played this music. He was speaking to me through John's words and actions. He was speaking to me despite my doubts, despite my condescension, despite my feelings of superiority. He was speaking.

And now, finally, I answer. I pour my belief into each note. My song becomes a prayer. And I know I am ready. Death may come. I am not afraid. Because death is only the beginning.

# CHAPTER THIRTY-TWO

Come with me." Berk is in my room. He is gathering my belongings in a canvas sack.

"What?" I had fallen asleep on the couch, my violin cradled in my arms. He takes the violin and places it back in its case. He pulls me up.

"You are returning to Pod C."

His tone doesn't match his words. This should be wonderful. Why, then, does he seem so sad?

"I will explain on the way."

"Does Dr. Loudin know?" Perhaps Berk is trying to hide me. But he must know there are no places to hide here.

"Of course." I have never seen Berk like this. He is so angry. He won't even look at me.

"Have I done something wrong?"

Berk stops and his shoulders slump. "No. You have done nothing wrong."

"Then why are you so agitated?"

He has finished my packing and opens the door. "Let's get out of here and then I'll tell you."

Something bad has happened. But I cannot imagine what would be worse than my annihilation. Although now, knowing about Jesus, even that doesn't seem so awful. Nothing seems awful anymore.

I am almost out of breath as I rush to keep up with Berk's long strides. We are out of the Scientists' pod in minutes, on the walkway toward Pod C. Berk slows but he doesn't speak. We pass Pod A before he stops. He turns toward the path that leads to the viewing panel. We go behind Pod B, past their greenhouse and their recreation field. Berk finds a spot in the grass and sets my bag and case down.

"I was able to talk Dr. Loudin out of annihilating you."

I want to be relieved, but something in the way he is behaving cautions me, frightens me. "Why do you sound so upset then?"

"I'm not upset about that." Berk's jaw flexes. He is barely controlling his emotions. So unlike him. "But it comes at a cost."

My stomach tightens. "What kind of cost?"

Berk closes his eyes. He sighs. "We should sit."

I follow Berk as he lowers himself to the ground, his long legs stretched out in front of him. His eyes are far away. He is trying to determine how to tell me what is on his mind.

"I looked at Dr. Loudin's charts. As I suspected, your intelligence levels are superior. Even more than what was intended for you. And your intelligence has actually improved since you've been here. I told Dr. Loudin that you are too valuable to eliminate. Your potential is too great."

"And he agreed?"

Berk's nod was slow. "He is very concerned about living conditions here. With the increase in population, the oxygen requirements have risen beyond what we are capable of producing."

"Didn't they prepare for that when they increased the population?" The first generation was barely halfway through their allotted life cycle. Surely they couldn't have made such a simple error as this.

"To say it was a miscalculation seems like a gross understatement. But that's exactly what it was."

"And now?"

"He is eliminating people." Berk raked a hand through his hair.

"But he is not eliminating me?"

"No." Berk looks at me. There is such pain in his eyes.

"Just tell me." I need to know what is causing this pain. "He is allowing me to live as, what, a project?"

"Kind of."

"It's all right, Berk." I want to comfort him. "Things have changed. I am not afraid."

"He is going to erase your memory."

I am sure I heard wrong. He couldn't have said that. "What?"

"He agreed with me that your intellect is valuable." Berk swallows hard. It takes a moment for him to be able to continue.

"But your memory is not. He wants to eliminate what he sees as your flaws."

"My flaws?"

"Your curiosity." Berk looks at me. "Your feelings."

"He wants to erase all of that?" Will I forget Berk? Will I forget Jesus? Can Dr. Loudin erase my faith? Who will I be if I do not have those things?

"But why are we going to Pod C?" I try to think of something else—anything but the fact that my memory, my essence, is going to be annihilated. "The Scientists removed me so I wouldn't cause them unease. Wouldn't seeing me, devoid of any memories, be difficult for them?"

Berk closes his eyes. "No."

I grab Berk's face with my hand. He won't look at me. He can't even speak. "Why, Berk? What has happened?"

"Pod C"—he speaks so quietly I can barely hear him—"has been eliminated."

# CHAPTER THIRTY-THREE

run. I don't care that my lungs are burning and my legs are aching. I don't care that people in the other pods might see me. I don't care that cameras positioned who knows where will record this. I run because I need to see for myself that Pod C is empty.

Surely Berk is mistaken. Surely Dr. Loudin wouldn't do something so terrible. Annihilation of any kind seems awful to me, but annihilation of a whole pod? Unthinkable. Cruel.

I run to the front entrance. The door is open. A gaping hole revealing nothing.

Nothing.

No one is here. Not even the furniture remains.

I look in every room. The group areas, the cubes, the kitchen, even the isolation chamber. I look out the back, to the recreation field and the greenhouse.

Nothing.

My legs refuse to keep moving. I will them to walk back to my cube. Where Rhen and I lived and talked and learned. It, too, is empty. Our sleeping platforms are gone. Our dressers are gone. Even the smell is different. Like someone has taken what used to be Pod C and replaced it with something else. Something other.

Berk comes in. He is out of breath. I realize I am too. I am panting, gasping for air.

"No." I can barely speak. A thought enters my mind. "This isn't real."

"What?"

"This isn't real." My confidence grows. "This is another simulation."

"Thalli." Berk sounds sad.

I walk into the bathroom and look into the mirror. "Look at me, Dr. Loudin. I am not fooled. I know this isn't happening. I know I am really sitting in a chair in your laboratory. Unplug me. Stop testing on me. Annihilate me, like I asked. I am done being your lab rat."

My voice echoes in the small room. I stare into my own eyes, knowing that Dr. Loudin sees what I see. I want him to see that he has failed. That I will no longer be part of his ridiculous experiments.

Berk is behind me. He is looking at me, but I don't look away. I will stare at my reflection until Dr. Loudin ends this. He will not win.

I don't know how long I stand there. Minutes, hours. Berk has left and returned.

He places his hands on my shoulders and forces me to turn. "I wish you were right. I can't tell you how much I wish you were right."

"I am." I pull away. This isn't Berk. It is just some computer program that looks like him.

"This is real, Thalli." Berk's eyes are red-rimmed. "I am real."

I look at him, at the vulnerability on his face, and I think for a moment that maybe he is real. But I don't want him to be real because if he is real, then all this is real.

I need to ask him something that Dr. Loudin wouldn't know. "Where did you take me on our picnic?"

"To the moon-viewing panel beside the water tanks." He doesn't even pause. The answer is immediate and correct. This is Berk.

"Then you are here with me," I say, refusing to believe this is real. There has to be another explanation. "In the simulation. We're both trapped. Think about how you found this out, your talk with Dr. Loudin. Are any pieces missing from the last time you saw me until now?"

Berk closes his eyes. "This isn't a simulation."

"How do you know?" I am yelling but I don't care. "I didn't think Progress was a simulation either. I could see it, smell it, touch it, even taste it. Do you think you know more than I do? That I am easy to fool but you're not?"

"Of course not." Berk stays rooted to his spot on the floor.

"Do you have proof?"

Berk sighs. "Yes."

I blink. "You do?"

Berk nods. "I was hoping you were right. I'd give anything for this not to be real. So I checked something."

"What?"

"Come here." Berk takes my hand and we walk through the pod into the group chamber. "Remember when we were kids and we scraped our names under the couch?"

Of course I remember.

"It's there." Berk points to a spot on the now-bare floor.

I kneel down, hoping Berk is wrong. Praying Berk is wrong.

I trace his name with my fingers.

This is not a simulation.

# CHAPTER THIRTY-FOUR

M y friends are gone. Eliminated. And why? Because the Scientists made a miscalculation. It is so unfair. So terrible.

I think of Rhen. My beautiful, logical friend. I can imagine her reaction when this news was delivered. Ever practical, she probably pulled on her blond ponytail and nodded, agreeing with the decision. "Better to eliminate a whole pod together than take a few people from each pod," she would say. "That way no one will really have to know."

Or did she fight? When faced with actual death, would her logic have failed her? Would she have used it to reason with her killers? To explain that, with a little more research—aided, of course, by Pod C—a solution to the problem could be found?

Or did they drug them all, like they drugged me, making them unaware they were being eliminated? Did they all just walk peacefully outside? Like they were going to a moon viewing or on a field trip?

I need to know. "How?"

"I don't know exactly."

"What do you know?"

"Dr. Loudin informed me your surgery would take place here." Berk stares at the wall screen. "He said that Pod C was no longer needed for habitation, so it was being transformed into an extra medical facility."

"A medical facility?" I feel sick, leaning my head against the wall, my hand tracing our names over and over again as Berk goes on.

"Dr. Grenz was quite upset at Dr. Spires's untimely death, you know." Berk swallows. "So he is conducting experiments on some of the members of the State—even some of the other Scientists—to try to prevent something like that from happening again."

"And I am going to be one of his experiments?"

"No, Dr. Loudin wants to use you." Berk rubs his eyes. "But he needs your memory to be erased first."

"So why not do it there?" I stand. "Why bring me here? If my memory is going to be erased, why do I have to know what happened to my friends? It is cruel."

"I agree." Berk stands beside me. "It is cruel. And I asked him the same thing."

"What did he say?"

"He said that in order to make sure the surgery is success-ful, he wants you to be in a place you know well." Berk walks to the other side of the room. "With someone you know well."

"You?" For the first time, I think about how difficult all this is for Berk. I have been selfish, thinking only of my own pain.

"When you wake up, he will gauge your reaction to me and to the pod. He will allow you to stand and walk around. If you walk like someone who knows where she is going, he will know the surgery failed."

"So there is a chance it will fail?" A tiny sliver of hope—translucent like the moon I saw in Progress—breaks through.

Berk hangs his head. "This surgery has never been attempted."

"Oh." And the moon disappears.

"The simulations were a kind of pretest." Berk leans against the far wall. "Dr. Loudin was able to successfully create memo-ries. Using the same technology and the data he gained from that cerebral intervention, he feels that he has a 90 percent chance of success."

My memories will be erased. I almost hope it does work. I don't know if I can live with the feelings I have right now. My friends are gone. Eliminated. But I, who was supposed to be eliminated, am alive, walking around the pod where they walked, where they breathed and ate and learned and did everything they were told.

I am angry again. Angry at everything. Angry that Berk has to do this. Angry that there is no escape, no chance to say no. I could kill myself. I have that power over the Scientists.

No, I cannot. Something within me warns me against that.

"Dr. Loudin told you all this?"

Berk rakes a hand through his hair. "This morning."

"And when will the surgery take place?"

"Tomorrow," he says, barely above a whisper. "Your memory will be erased tomorrow."

# CHAPTER THIRTY-FIVE

Assistants pour into the pod. They bring machines and sleeping platforms and plastic medical equipment I have never seen before.

The transition from Pod C to medical facility has begun.

I want to push them back out, to throw the machines to the ground and trample them.

Then I hear John's voice in my mind: *"You have a purpose, Thalli."*

I want to scream, to cry, to give in to all the raw emotions simmering beneath my skin. But there would be no purpose in that. No benefit. I know from experience that giving in to those emotions does not bring satisfaction. I cannot fall apart. I need to think of Berk. I need to help him, make this as easy as possible for him. And I need to remember all that John has told me. His words bring me peace. They make me feel stronger.

I have a purpose. I laughed at him the first time he said it. But everything has changed now. I believe him. I do have a purpose. I am a child of God. A child of God! And one day I will drink from deathless springs. But until then, I must follow John's example. I must pray. I must talk to the Designer. I do not know my purpose, but he does.

I walk out the front door of the pod and around the back. Assistants and Technicians continue to enter the building. Berk remains behind, knowing I need to be alone.

I enter the greenhouse. I was rarely allowed in here during my seventeen years in the pod. I wasn't the Horticulturalist or the Dietician, so I had no need to enter. Only during the times we were studying botany was I brought in. But never alone. I always wanted to come in here alone.

It is warmer in here, more humid. Rows of all kinds of plants fill every space, with just a slight walkway between each one. It smells of dirt and flowers. I touch the leaf of an apple tree. The Scientists may have developed the technology that allowed this tree to grow here, but they did not create the tree.

It is the same with me. I am not created by the Scientists. I am created by the Designer. The truth of that fills me with joy.

"I don't want to forget," I say quietly. "Please, God. I don't want to forget." I am talking to the Designer. And though it sounds crazy to me, I feel that he is listening. And I know what I want to ask, what I need to ask. Not to be saved from annihilation or rescued from testing. All I want is to remember what has happened. Everything that has happened. I want the surgery to fail. I ask the Designer to allow that. I ask without words, my throat too tight to speak, my heart too heavy to form any coherent thoughts other than, "Please, God, I don't want to forget."

A calm washes over me. I pluck an apple from this tree and look at it. I have taken so much for granted. I turn it over in my hand. Have I ever really looked at an apple? Have I ever considered its intricacies, its complexity? The one who designed this designed me. He loves me. He has a purpose for me. I am amazed at the thought. I place the apple in my pocket. I will share it with Berk. I will tell him what I know about the Designer.

I continue walking through the greenhouse. The sights and smells bring back memories. Memories of my friends who are gone.

I think of Rhen. When we visited the greenhouse on a research trip, she asked so many questions of the head Horticulturalist. She wasn't content to know the basic information like I was. She wanted details. I could almost see her processing the information, like a computer, filing it away in its proper place. She loved learning.

And now she is gone. Rhen is gone.

I ask God to help me spare other pods. I don't know how I could do that, but I can't stand the thought of any more mass annihilations simply because the rest of us are in need of the oxygen they consume.

The door opens. Berk has come.

"I need to make sure you're all right." He stands at the far end. I can tell he is unsure if I want him here.

I walk to him and stand on my toes so my lips can touch his cheek. "Is it possible to be sad and happy at the same time?"

"I suppose so." Berk turns his head to the side. "If that's what you're feeling right now."

"Such a Scientist." I smile. I reach into my pocket and pull out the apple. It is time to tell Berk about the Designer.

I tell him everything—I tell him about the music and about John, about the one who created everything. I tell him about Jesus, that he is alive, and I tell him about faith.

I cannot look at his face as I speak. I'm afraid of the doubts I will see, the skepticism. I know John saw all that on my face. But he is older, stronger in the faith than I am. I just look at the apple, turn it over and over in my hands. By the end, I have squeezed it so hard that it is soft under the skin. Finally, I lift my eyes. Berk isn't looking at me. He is looking up, through the clear roof of the greenhouse.

"I would like to meet this John," he says after a long silence.

My heart swells with joy. "I would like you to meet him too."

And that is all. He needs to process the information, to consider what I have said.

He takes the apple from my hand and looks at it, then at the tree from which it came. He lays the apple on the moist soil and takes my hand.

As we exit, I see that Pod C's transformation is almost complete. I pray again for the calm I experienced while in the greenhouse. I can't help thinking how different my life is today than it was yesterday. And I can't help worrying what my life will be like tomorrow.

# CHAPTER THIRTY-SIX

"The patient has been prepared for the procedure, Doctor."

*Prepared for the procedure.* I say that in my mind over and over, popping the p's and laughing at the alliteration. *Prepared for the procedure.* I have the faint impression that I might not be thinking clearly, but I don't have time to think about that.

Berk is standing over me. He is handsome. I think I might love him. Do I love him? I love his hair and the way it always looks just perfect. I love his eyes. So green. When we are close, I can see little specks of gold in them. I like it when I can see those specks.

"Can you feel this?"

Berk sounds very far away. Like his voice is on the other side of the room but his body is right here. I love his arms too. They are so strong.

"Thalli?" Why is his voice so far away? "Can you feel this?"

I try to shake my head but it won't move. I am stuck. I suppose I need to speak, but the words don't want to come out. I can see them in my throat. No. I do not feel anything. Wait, I do feel something. I feel love. I want to tell Berk that. But I can't.

"Use something with a sharper edge." That is not Berk's voice. His voice is smooth and deep, like a cello. That voice sounds like a clarinet with a broken reed. Must be Dr. Loudin. I do *not* love him. Now that I think of it, he looks a bit like a clarinet: tall and dark, with a big head and little body. And his reed is most definitely cracked.

"Nothing," Berk says. I love his voice.

They start speaking in Scientist language. I don't love Scientist language. I hear words like *cranium* and *probe* and somewhere in the back of my mind I seem to remember that this is about me. They are doing something to me. And I should remember what it is.

But I can't. Berk is getting farther away, smaller and smaller. I want to reach out and make him stay, but my arms won't move. Nothing moves. And then everything gets cloudy and gray. Now I feel like I am getting smaller and smaller. I am going to disappear. I think that is good. Berk is small too. We will find each other. We live hidden away, underneath a couch somewhere, and no one will ever find us.

: : :

My head hurts. I cannot open my eyes. My eyelids feel like steel doors. I couldn't lift them if I wanted to.

Where am I? I move my fingers a little. Even that hurts. It isn't just my head. Everything aches. Why am I in pain? What happened to me?

"She is waking."

The voice sounds distant. Vaguely familiar, though I can't place it exactly. I try to think, but my head hurts too badly.

Someone touches my arm. The hand feels soft. It squeezes my wrist, then it is gone. I wish it would stay. It felt nice.

"Her vitals look good," the voice says.

Another voice speaks. This one is even farther away than the first. His words sound mumbled. It would take too much energy to try to concentrate on what he is saying. I don't have any energy. I am so tired.

: : :

"She is moving again."

I keep hearing that voice. I hear it, I feel a touch, and then I go back to sleep. I should wake up. I have the idea somewhere in the back of my mind that I should be doing something. But my head hurts and my body feels like all the muscles have been replaced with concrete. Could I move even if I tried?

I think of my pinkie. I could try to move that. I picture my shoulder, my arm, my wrist, my fingers. Just lift the pinkie. Nothing else. Up.

"Her heart rate is increasing." His hand is on my wrist again. He needs to remove it. I can't move my pinkie with his hand there. "There, it's going down again."

His hand is gone. I hold my breath and concentrate on moving the pinkie. It is so hard. I can't do it. I release my breath and moan.

"Thalli?"

My body seems to soften just a bit. Thalli, he said. Thalli. I feel like I should know what that is.

"If you can hear me, blink once."

I want to laugh. Blink. Right.

I hear a door open and then close. I feel the hand again, on my shoulder this time. There is a light pressure and then I hear the voice whispering in my ear.

"Do you remember who you are, Thalli?" The breath in my ear is hot. "Do you remember anything?"

He sounds so sad. I don't want him to be sad. But even if I could move, I couldn't give him the answer he wants. *Do* I remember anything?

Images pop into my mind. Strange images: a piece of string, an apple, an empty room. I can see them, but I don't know what they mean. And I am too tired to think about them anymore. I feel the hand leave my shoulder. I hear a ragged breath. Too tired to think. I wish I could tell him that. But I can't say anything. So I just let the room go black and hope that the next time I wake, things will be better.

# CHAPTER THIRTY-SEVEN

My throat feels like it is on fire. But my eyelids aren't quite so heavy, and with a little effort, I can move my pinkie. Is that enough to signal someone? If I could just get some water. Just a little, to soothe this burning.

I open my eyes. It is difficult. I am blinded by the lights. I have to close them again. Why are the lights in here so bright? And where is "here"? What is going on? Why am I lying on this sleeping platform? Why can't I stay awake? Why is it so hard to move?

I try to say "water," but only "waaa" comes out. And even that sounds odd, like it's from someone else's mouth and not mine. I don't sound like that, do I?

"Thalli." That voice. He is always here. His hand is on my arm again. "What did you say?"

"Wa"—I take a breath. I can do this—"ter."

"Water?"

I lift my eyes slightly, enough for him to see my response, then I close them quickly. It is so bright.

I hear his feet move away. The door opens and shuts. Silence. The burning in my throat intensifies. I hope he hurries.

The door opens again. His feet are coming closer. I feel the sleeping platform lifting my head up. I am dizzy, but I try not to pass out. I need that water.

A cup touches my lips and I open my mouth, ready to gulp it down, to quench the fire in my throat.

"Easy, my dear." This is a different voice. "Just a few sips to start."

I close my lips and the water slides across my tongue and down my throat. I wish he would give me more. I try to open my eyes again. But the lights are too much for me. I can't keep my eyes open.

"Extinguish that lamp, Berk," the voice commands.

The lights go out and I attempt to raise my eyelids once again. A soft light comes in from the side of a room—a panel, perhaps?

My eyes are open, but I only see blurry shapes. I blink again and the shapes begin to come into focus. An older man is standing over me, cup in his hand.

"Better?"

I nod. "More?"

He places the cup back to my lips and more liquid goes down this time. I close my eyes in relief.

"Stay awake now," the older man says. "We need to ask you some questions."

I open my eyes and see another man has entered the room. This one is much younger. Dark hair and light eyes—eyes that are locked on me, like he is trying to communicate something. What?

"I am Dr. Loudin." The old man sits on a stool beside my sleeping platform. "Do you know who you are?"

I am distracted by the young man in the back. He is shaking his head, his eyes wide. He looks afraid. Why is he afraid?

"I-I'm not sure." I look back at the old man.

"Do you know where you are?"

"Medical facility?"

The old man looks at the younger man. "Verbal skills seem to be intact. And she knows the terminology. Good sign."

What is he talking about? "What happened?"

"What is the last thing you remember?"

The younger man is shaking his head again.

"A headache."

The old man laughs. It wasn't a joke but I smile anyway.

"Before that?"

What do I remember before that? A piece of thread? An apple?

The old man shines a small light in my eyes. My eyes water and I close them. My arms are too heavy to bring my hands up to wipe away the tears. And I am so tired.

"We will talk more later." The old man stands. "You should feel much better when you wake."

I open my eyes in thanks and close them again.

"Wean her off the sedative and continue giving her water,"

he tells the younger man. "Unless you'd rather have an Assistant do that."

"No," the younger man responds quickly. "I will stay with her."

"Very well."

"Was it"—the young man clears his throat—"successful?"

"We won't know for sure until she is fully conscious. But yes, the procedure appears to have been quite a success indeed."

# CHAPTER THIRTY-EIGHT

open my eyes. It isn't difficult. The lamps are off and only the slightest bit of light is coming through the window. I turn my head and find my muscles don't feel like concrete anymore.

The young man is asleep in a chair next to my sleeping platform. I look down and see that he is holding my hand. I look at his face. It is so familiar. The dark eyelashes, the straight nose, the white lab coat. I have seen him before. Where?

The fog that has filled my brain is beginning to lift. I think again of the piece of thread, the apple, the empty room. I know those images mean something. I force my mind to focus. I need to remember. I know it is important.

The young man's eyes open. I know those eyes. He leans closer, his eyes searching mine. He moves his hand to my face. "Thalli?"

And suddenly, I remember. Everything. It all comes back so quickly that I can hardly breathe. The thread: I was tricked into believing there is a community aboveground. The apple: I am a child of the Designer. The empty room: All my friends have been eliminated.

All but . . . "Berk."

He places a hand on my face. "You remember."

I swallow. I was supposed to have my memory erased. "I knew it wouldn't work."

"How?"

"I am an anomaly, remember?" I try to laugh, but nothing comes out.

Berk takes his hand from my face and walks to the end of the room. I try to sit up, but I am too dizzy. I lie back down. Berk returns with a glass of water. He lifts my head and helps me sip.

"Thank you." I picture the empty pod. My friends—Rhen—removed because the State needed their oxygen.

Berk leans close and I can smell the soap he uses—I remember that scent. Spicy and masculine. Berk. His nearness is making my mind fog again. I turn my head away from him and look out the panel.

"Are there cameras in here?"

"They were removed."

"Are you sure?"

Berk raises his eyebrows. "I removed them myself. We need power in here for so many things, and we can't afford to waste power, so I took out everything that was unnecessary in order to keep the rest working all the time."

"We can't let Dr. Loudin know the surgery did not work."

Berk releases a slow breath. "You're right."

"Tell me what he is expecting when he sees me." I take another sip of water.

Berk spends the next ten minutes explaining how I am to respond to everything from my first walk to my first meal to my first set of tests. I should be unsure, ask questions—but not too many questions. I should know the words for basic items but need help with the more technical terms. Staying silent is always better than speaking.

"What about my music?" Would the new Thalli know how to play still? Could I live the rest of my life without that gift?

"You were designed to be a Musician." Berk smiles. "It is part of you."

I sigh in relief.

"But maybe you could mess up a few notes, your first time."

I do not even know if I can do that. "Mess up some notes? Unthinkable. That is one thing I cannot remember doing."

Berk laughs. "All right. Maybe not."

"Will you stay?" I look at Berk again. He leans forward and hides my hand in both of his.

"I will never let you out of my sight again."

# CHAPTER THIRTY-NINE

Pretending to know nothing is much harder than it might sound.

The first day after I "woke," Dr. Loudin came in and asked me questions. Silly questions. But I wasn't sure which to answer correctly and which to pretend I didn't know. Thankfully, I am only one of his projects so he leaves the bulk of the work to Berk. Dr. Loudin only comes in now in the evenings for an update and, I suspect, to see how Berk and I are interacting with each other. Berk determined he should look sad—Dr. Loudin knows Berk has feelings for me, and he would naturally be upset at seeing me as the shell of the girl he knew.

My heart breaks every time I think of all my friends from Pod C. I see them in the rooms here in the pod, doing their work or viewing the wall screens. They should still be here. But I cannot bring them back, so I will work to help Berk uncover a solution to our State's oxygen problem so no more pods will have to be eliminated. And I try to keep my face from revealing what is in my heart. I do not want Dr. Loudin to come in unexpectedly and find me crying over the cooking appliance.

So far I have learned our State's history. Again. And I have spent several hours studying the science of our Society. Not as terrible as history, but I do long to hold an instrument in my hands. Any instrument. I do not ask, though. I don't know if the new Thalli is supposed to ask those kinds of questions.

"Time for a field trip," Berk announces.

"Should I bring my learning pad?"

"Not necessary." An Assistant works on a communications pad in the corner of the room, so I try to behave as patient-like as possible.

I put on my shoes and Berk stands at the door. We walk in silence. We pass the technology center, with its gleaming white walls. I have only been in there a few times, but the visits were fascinating. The Technology Specialists work to create updated versions of our current equipment and to develop new equipment as well.

But we are walking too far past that for it to be our destination. I can't stand the suspense any longer.

"Where are we going?"

"I have told you that your memory was erased," Scientist Berk explains. Perhaps concerned that there are cameras on the outside of the building, watching us? "But I haven't told you that before your surgery, you were one of the most accomplished musicians in the State."

I feel a new emotion. I can't quite describe it, but it feels good.

"Was I?" I am Patient Thalli, whose mind is a blank learning pad waiting to be downloaded, who does not feel emotion at this information.

He turns again and we are on a path leading to a large building I know well. I force myself not to run or shout or jump.

"And what is this?" I ask.

Berk turns to me and his lips turn up slightly. He is just as happy for me as I am. "This is the performance pod."

"The performance pod?" We enter the familiar room and I want to cry. The instruments have all been cleaned and are hanging in their slots along the wall. I want to play every one of them.

"We want to see if your musical memory is intact. We have a recording of you playing from before your surgery. We would like to see you practice that piece and record it again. Then we will analyze the similarities and differences."

"I see." I know which piece it is. It is the one I wrote for the night of our moon viewing. The one I wrote when I was supposed to be completing a history lesson. Memories of that day flood my mind. I see Rhen showing signs of some type of sickness. The Monitor came in and I covered for her, refusing to allow her to turn herself in. I feel tears threaten to spill. I swallow hard. I miss her so much.

That was also the day I was sent to isolation, the day I snuck out, the day I saw death. And the day I saw Berk. But I didn't know any of that when I wrote that song. That was the last song I wrote before all of this happened.

I look at Berk and I know he sees the panic in my eyes.

He closes his eyes once, slowly, our signal that everything is going to be all right. "Choose a violin and come into this practice cube."

Am I supposed to know what a violin is? Will I give anything away if I walk right over to it? Berk said my musical memory was being tested, so maybe that means that Dr. Loudin purposed to leave that part of my brain the way it was before the surgery.

Berk nods and I know I am right. So I walk to the wall and I slip a violin from the slot. It is not my violin. Mine is three slots away. I can feel it calling to me. But I know I should not choose it. I should not know it. The new Thalli can know music, but she cannot have attachments from her old life.

Berk opens the door to the practice cube and we enter. The walls, ceiling, and door are all covered in a soft white film that completely insulates the sound. How many times have I sat here practicing while my pod mates were sitting in the main chamber, waiting for me to come out and perform? I hear the door shut with a soft click.

"We can speak freely in here." Berk removes the violin from my hands and sets it gently on the ground.

I look around. "Are you sure?"

"I checked the blueprints." He nods. "There are no cameras in here."

I sigh. Freedom.

"You are doing wonderfully." Berk leans against the wall. "It appears that music isn't the only thing you can perform well."

"Thank you." I bite my lip. There is so much I want to know. "So what, exactly, are Dr. Loudin's plans for me?"

Berk crosses his arms. "Today, his plans are that you play this song so he can compare that to your previous performance."

There is something Berk is not telling me. I can tell by the way he is standing, arms crossed, on the other side of the cube. "What are his ultimate plans for me?"

"He wants to see if you can help solve the oxygen problem."

"And?" I know there is more.

Berk sighs and drops his hands. "He wants to continue to experiment on your brain."

My heart squeezes. "What?"

Berk rushes to me, his hands holding mine. "Which is why we have to prove you are too valuable."

"And how do I do that?" I feel like the walls are closing in on me. "I'm not valuable."

"Yes, you are." Berk's hands are on my face. "Don't worry."

I step back. "Don't worry?"

"I shouldn't have told you." Berk rakes a hand through his hair. "I'm sorry."

"Of course you should have told me." I hold in a groan. "But why do I even bother trying to complete all these tests if all I am is just a lab rat?"

"You're not a lab rat, Thalli." Berk's hands move to my shoulders. I know he is sincere. But he doesn't have any power to stop Loudin. "I have been praising your intelligence every day. I have told him ideas I have to use you as part of the scientific team."

"I am not a Scientist."

"Exactly." Berk begins to pace. "My theory is that we are

handicapping ourselves by only having Scientists work on the team. We need other minds, other ideas, if we are going to move forward. I believe having the same type of people in each different area worked in the past, but we are ready to move on from that."

He is so animated. I want to believe him. But even with his energy and ideas, can Berk really change the minds of men like Dr. Loudin?

"All right." I am going to choose faith over intellect. I am going to trust in the Designer that John is right—that I was created for a purpose. I am not going to live in fear of what might happen. The worst they can do to me is kill me. And, as I have learned, that isn't the worst at all.

# CHAPTER FORTY

have recorded the song. I tried to think only about the notes and not about the last time I played it. But now I am thinking about it. I am thinking about my friends, sitting in the performance pod watching me that last time. Smiling, nodding, working.

"Can I play another instrument?" I need to get my mind on something else.

"Certainly." Berk looks up from the recording equipment. "I need to compress this file and deliver an electronic copy to Dr. Loudin. It will take a few minutes."

I walk to the slots. Which one? The flute? The trumpet? The trombone? None of them are speaking to me.

Piano. That is what I want to play. I walk to the instrument, shiny and black, sitting in the corner of the room. I pull the bench out and sit. I tap the pedals with my feet, play a scale. I close my eyes and the richness of the sound washes over me. I need to be careful. I know there are cameras here. I shouldn't enjoy this *too* much. But I was designed for this, to play, to know these instruments.

I begin slowly. I play what is in my mind, something the old Thalli wouldn't have learned. I don't want Dr. Loudin to click on this scene on his wall screen and become suspicious. I start out staccato. I miss a few notes, on purpose, though it kills me. But I am supposed to be blank, relearning what I know. I stop and play chords. Then I add in the staccato notes with my right hand as my left hand plays the chords. The notes clash, they stumble over each other.

This is my life right now. The old clashing with the new. The sharp pain and the soothing calm. And then my right hand finds a new melody, one that no longer clashes. This is the music of the Designer. It makes sense of what is messy. It fills the room. Sometimes it is loud, sometimes it is quiet, sometimes the melody is barely there. I want to cry. I haven't played the melody of the Designer before, yet this melody seems to have always been with me, waiting to come out.

I close my eyes and play on. Part of me remembers that I must not appear too emotional. That is part of the old me. So I open my eyes. I play a prayer that God helps me be this new person I am supposed to be, that I find a way to help others, so no other pod faces the destruction Pod C faced. I channel my prayers into my fingers and my feet.

Berk has walked over to me and watches me play. I glance

at him and see him smiling. He knows what I am doing, what I am playing.

I finish and pull my hands away. They are still tingling with the music.

I want to tell Berk what I am thinking and feeling. I want to go back into the practice cube so we can have more time alone, unwatched.

But Berk goes back to the work area. He sits back down and taps his fingers across a screen.

"Are you still not finished?"

"I am finished with the first recording," he says, still tapping. "But I am working on the second."

"The second?"

"The one you just played."

"You recorded that?" Something in me says this is not good.

Berk leans back in his chair. "I have a theory I want to test."

"A theory?" Scientist Berk is back. He is tapping into the screen again. "What theory?"

"I want to dissect your music."

I bristle. Music isn't to be dissected. It is to be enjoyed. It enhances and promotes productivity.

"I am working on adapting a program I wrote last year." Berk is still tapping while he talks. "That program was a linguistic analysis. But I think I can develop it into a musical analysis."

I am confused. I can tell by the way he is smiling that something else is going on. But I have no idea what.

Berk groans and stops tapping.

"What?" I walk to him.

"I don't know the musical terminology." He raises his eyebrows at me. A slight rise, but it is conspiratorial. "I need to know the names and values of the notes if the program is going to work properly."

He is trying to prove my usefulness to Dr. Loudin. "I see."

"This will take some time." He stands and walks to the door. "I will speak to my superior this evening. I think this program could greatly benefit the scientific community. If we can decode the language of music, we could potentially unlock parts of the brain that we currently know little about."

Brain studies. Dr. Loudin can't resist that. Berk is a genius. I want to run up to him and wrap my arms around his neck. But I don't. I follow him out like an obedient patient.

We are outside and it is almost dark. I didn't realize how long we had been in the performance pod.

"Have you seen the moon, Thalli?"

I think for a moment. I must answer like the new Thalli, just in case Dr. Loudin is watching. "I have seen the images in my learning pad. I just read about it today in science."

"But you haven't seen it through a viewing panel?"

"Not that I recall." I try to sound as serious and innocent as possible.

"I believe we have some time," Berk says. "And we are near the panel with the clearest view this evening. Follow me."

We walk behind the performance pod. The grass abruptly stops and there is only the hard ground—concrete—that lines the outer edges of the State. I have only seen the ground like this once before: the last time Berk took me to see the moon. But that was by the water tanks. All I see here is what appears to be the wall of a massive pod.

"What is this?" I put my hand on it. It is made of the same concrete that lines the ground. It feels gritty, not like the smooth surfaces I am used to feeling. I look up and it continues, as far as I can see.

"This is the end of our world." Berk places his hand over mine. I jump back. "It's all right. We're safe."

"You're sure?"

Berk takes a step closer in answer. I can feel his breath on my face, and my heart beats so fast I am sure he will be able to hear it. "I'm sure."

His nearness is clouding my thoughts. I step back, my curiosity peaked. "The end of our world? What do you mean?"

"Just that." Berk puts his hands in his pockets and leans against the wall. "You know the State was built inside a large mountain decades ago. This is the northern perimeter."

I place both hands on the wall. "So the other side of this is . . . ?"

"Earth."

I lay my face against the wall and close my eyes. Even though I know it wasn't real, I picture Progress. The pods and the people, the children. I think of the images I have seen in my history lessons. Buildings and roads. I think of John's stories. Oceans and houses and families.

"We might be able to go there."

I pull myself away and feel my head. Is this another simulation? I feel the hole. I hear Berk laugh.

"The Scientists have sent probes above. There are some places where the air is no longer toxic. They think, in a few years, they can send a colony up there."

"Like in the simulation?"

Berk smiles. "Possibly."

"So was I tested to see if I could live there?"

"I have not been told anything about that," Berk says. "But it would seem so."

I place my hands on the wall again. "I could live there? I might not be annihilated?"

"I am doing everything in my power to convince Dr. Loudin that you are necessary." Berk walks closer to me, then leans against the wall and faces me. "I am also trying to convince him that I am the right Scientist to live above."

"So we could go there together?" I pull my hands away and lean into the wall, facing Berk.

Berk stands up straight and looks above. I follow his eyes to the panel above us. The moon is bright, full and clear. "I have been visiting John in the evenings." Berk looks at me. I see peace in his eyes.

"You have?"

"John is an interesting old man. I go to conduct research, of course." Berk smiles.

"Of course." He would not be allowed to visit otherwise. He has to go under other pretenses.

"And he has told me some things you don't know."

I fold my arms in mock protest. "What?"

"Stories from the Designer's book." Berk's eyes are dancing. "He is starting at the beginning and telling me all he remembers. It is very interesting."

I pull Berk down so we are both sitting. "Tell me."

And he does. He tells me about a garden and about the Designer creating a man and a woman for each other. To take care of the earth, to fill earth. To love.

"He told you about love?" I am sitting, my back against the wall, holding my knees to my chest.

Berk is looking at me and I am embarrassed suddenly. "He told me that the Designer created love. It's a gift from him to be shared with others."

"That's not what the Scientists think." I turn my head slightly, enough to see Berk's face in the moonlight, but my back stays against the wall, my knees to my chest.

"Who are we going to believe?"

I release my arms and turn my body to face Berk so our knees are touching. I reach out and hold his face in my hands. "I think love is real."

Berk leans forward slowly. His hands are around my waist and I close my eyes, a feeling like I have never experienced washing over me. His lips touch my forehead and I melt into him, my arms around his neck, my lips on his cheek.

"Me too, Thalli."

# CHAPTER FORTY-ONE

I don't want to wake up. I don't want to move. How can I go through the day acting like everything is normal when I know it isn't?

Berk loves me. And I love him. Love is from the Designer. Berk told me the Designer's Word says that we love because he first loved us. The thought is overwhelming. I want to go with Berk today, above, to start a colony on the earth. We can bring John. He can teach us, help us. We can allow him to live out the remainder of his years where he started.

But reality breaks through the fog that is my mind between waking and sleeping. I am still a project. I am still being monitored. Berk and I must still act like strangers. And if we are to maintain this carefully constructed façade, trips to camera-free zones must be seldom taken.

I walk to the sink to splash cold water on my face. But I can't move my left arm. Did I sleep on it wrong? I try to shake it, but it's just hanging there, useless.

I examine it in the mirror. It looks fine. But it won't move. I try to move my fingers, my wrist, my elbow, my shoulder. Nothing.

I don't know what to do. I don't know what is wrong. I pinch my arm and feel nothing. I bang it against the sink. Nothing.

I can feel myself hyperventilating, but I cannot stop. I want to call for someone, but no one is here yet. Berk won't arrive for another thirty minutes. I try to calm down enough to reach the emergency screen. But I am breathing so fast that when I move, I feel dizzy.

Deep breath in. Deep breath out. I have to calm down.

I start walking again. I make it out of my cube, down the hallway. I can see the emergency screen. I try to concentrate on it and not on the fact that my arm is hanging at my side, dead-weight, slapping against my body.

I am finally there. "Help." I throw my right palm against the screen. "Help."

"Thalli," the voice responds. "Musician of Pod C currently undergoing testing. Please confirm."

"Yes." My whole body is leaning into the screen. Everything but my left arm.

The wall screen flickers to life and a Medical Assistant is peering into the room. I pull away from the emergency screen and move so I am standing directly in front of her.

"I can't feel my arm."

The Medical Assistant's eyes widen, then return to her normal blank stare. "Go on."

"That's all." I want to scream at her, but a display of emotion compounded with a medical malfunction would surely get me sent straight to the annihilation chamber. "I woke up and couldn't feel my left arm. I shook it, poked it, nothing worked."

"Can you move your fingers?"

I have to force my face to remain passive. I can't let her see how unbelievably frustrating such a useless question is. "No. I cannot."

"Are you experiencing any pain?"

"Could you send Dr. Berk here?" I can't take this anymore. "He is assigned to my case. I'm sure he can help diagnose the problem."

The Medical Assistant looks down. She picks up a pad and types in this request. I pray that Berk answers quickly.

It seems like hours, but I am sure it is just minutes later that the Medical Assistant looks up and announces that Dr. Berk is on his way to Pod C.

"Thank you for your assistance," she says, then the screen is black.

I am still in my sleeping clothes. I return to my cube and pull the shirt over my head, the task taking twice as long because my left arm won't cooperate and I have to pull my right arm and head out first. Putting my uniform shirt on is difficult, but pants and shoes are almost impossible. I am sweating and out of breath by the time I have finally finished.

I lie down on my sleeping platform to rest, hoping this is

just a dream. I reach up and feel my head, praying that this is a simulation. I feel the tiny hole. This is real.

The door opens and Berk calls my name. He is trying to sound professional and detached. I hope whoever is with him doesn't know him as well as I do. The fear in his voice is obvious. I need to sit and remain calm so he doesn't give us away.

"I'm here."

"What happened?" His hand is on my arm, holding my hand. I don't feel any of it.

I tell Berk the same thing I told the Medical Assistant.

He takes a needle out of his bag and pokes my hand. "Do you feel that?"

"No." He just stuck a needle in me and I don't feel anything. I want to cry but I won't. I focus on the tiny bubble of blood that is drifting up from where Berk stuck the needle.

"This?" Berk sticks my forearm, my elbow, my upper arm. When he sticks my shoulder, I wince.

"I feel that."

He sticks the needle an inch lower. "That?"

"No."

Berk lifts my arm, turns it over, raises it above my head. He feels the pulse in my wrist.

"What is it?" I don't like the look on Berk's face.

"I don't know."

"What do you think?"

"I don't have any idea."

I force him to look me in the eye. "You have some idea."

"You have had invasive brain surgery." Berk sighs. "You have also had cerebral manipulation. This could be a result of either of those."

"So this could be permanent?" I can feel myself beginning to panic. I try to slow my breathing.

"I don't know." Berk takes my other hand, the one with functioning nerve endings. "I really don't. But we don't have the equipment here that is necessary to make an accurate diagnosis."

Berk walks to the emergency screen and places his palm on it. "We need an emergency hover cart at Pod C."

"A hover cart?" I have only seen those three times in my life: when Gen broke her arm, when one of our Monitors fell and passed out, and when Dr. Spires died.

"It's all right." Berk puts sealant on the dots on my arm where the needle has been. "It's just a precaution. I don't want you walking all the way back to the Scientists' pod."

"The rest of me is fine."

"We don't know that," Berk says quietly.

I close my eyes. I don't want to think about the possibility that there is more wrong with me. That the neurons in my brain are misfiring. Why is this happening? Yesterday my life was better than it had ever been. Why couldn't it stay like that, just for a little while?

I want to pray, but I have no words for the Designer right now. If he is love, like John says, if he is good, why would he do this to me?

"Time to go." The door opens and two Medical Assistants carry in what looks like a large cocoon. It is white and thin, and they unroll it on the floor. Berk helps me lie in the center, and the Assistants take one side each and wrap me in it. The cocoon seems to suddenly come to life. I hear beeps and feel heat. Only my head is exposed—the one part of me that needs to be looked at—while the rest of me is bound in this strange contraption.

"This tells us all the pertinent medical facts," Berk explains as the Assistants lift me and walk me outside. "It also stabilizes your body so when we get to the medical pod, we can immediately take you to be diagnosed."

I am sure this is supposed to comfort me. But lying in a medical blanket while being loaded into a hover cart because my left arm has no feeling leaves me little room for feeling anything but fear.

# CHAPTER FORTY-TWO

B eing on the hover cart is strange enough. But being on a hover cart while wrapped up and being monitored is awful. I am not used to being off the ground. But as soon as I am loaded, the cart lifts straight up, above the pods, then floats off. If I weren't wrapped up, I might enjoy it. But all I can think about is that if I were to roll off, I would end up with far more damage that just a dead arm.

But the Assistants are posted at each corner of the cart, standing with one hand on a pole that sticks up from the bottom of the cart. The one at the top right is moving his feet, I suppose to direct the hover. The one behind taps on the screen of his pad every time my cocoon beeps.

Berk is not here. He promised to meet me back at the medical chamber. I can tell he is worried. He doesn't want to alarm me. But he was about an hour too late for that.

My stomach feels like it is going to burst out of me. All the motion, combined with the fear, is making me nauseous. Then I see we are landing. The cart is being lowered, and the Assistant to the right leans forward and places a hand out to his left. We are back on the ground. The Assistants walk me through the hallway and into a white room with screens on two sides. They place me on a sleeping platform and leave the room.

The screens flicker on, but they are not like the wall screens we have at the pod. They are machines. Diagnostic machines? A red laser darts out from the center of each screen, one coming to my right temple, the other to my left. Out of the corner of my eye, I see an image of my brain on the screen. Parts of it are blue, other parts yellow. I want to look more, but the cocoon tightens around me, crawling up my neck to move my head so I am staring at the ceiling.

I remain like this for several minutes. There is no sound, even the cocoon has gone silent. Then the door opens.

"Thalli." It is Dr. Loudin. I recognize his voice. Clarinet with a broken reed.

The cocoon loosens its hold on me and the sleeping platform is raised. I don't look at Dr. Loudin. I look at the screen. At my brain.

"What is wrong with me?"

"Let's not use the word *wrong*." Dr. Loudin's smile looks unnatural. "Your brain is a fascinating organ, my dear. This little challenge is just an opportunity to study it some more."

Little challenge? He thinks my being unable to feel my arm is a "little challenge"? He walks to the screen on the right side of the room and touches the image. That portion expands and Dr. Loudin touches it again. He is deep inside my brain. I want to stay angry, but this is too interesting for me to think about that. I am seeing *inside* my brain.

"Ah, there." Dr. Loudin points to a tiny line in the center of the screen. "Some scar tissue built up around the site of your last surgery."

"Scar tissue?"

"Nothing to be concerned about." Dr. Loudin looks closer, moving the image around. "This is not unusual. We can go back in and clear out the damaged area. We'll have you better in no time."

Go back in my brain? The last time I was supposed to have my memory erased. What if this "corrective" surgery actually accomplishes that? Or what if more scar tissue builds up and I lose feeling somewhere else? Or everywhere else?

"I'd like to take you back to my laboratory." Dr. Loudin is talking to the screen, not to me. "This facility isn't really equipped for brain surgery."

He is turning my brain around on the screen. I want to know what he is seeing and thinking but I am afraid to ask. I don't know if the new Thalli would have those questions. And I don't know if the old Thalli really wants the answers anyway.

Dr. Loudin taps the screen and the image is gone. "My students will benefit from observing as well."

Wonderful. I will have an audience present. I close my eyes and sigh.

"Prepare her for transport," Dr. Loudin tells one of the Medical Assistants. "And you may remove the diagnostic blanket. She is stable."

Dr. Loudin taps on his pad and my cocoon opens. An Assistant removes it, rolling me on my side to get it out from underneath my back. I stretch my right arm, scratch an itch on my nose, and roll my feet. "Thank you."

Within minutes, I am back on the hover cart and on my way to Dr. Loudin's lab. I am allowed to sit up this time. I look down. Even though we are only a few feet in the air, I am amazed at the difference in perspective. I have only seen the world from the ground. I have never seen the roofs of the pods. They are round and white, with panels stretched across them—our source of electricity, soaking in rays from the solar panels above.

I see the Scientists' pod and realize just how massive it is compared to all the other buildings. I can't see its roof, nor can I see the other side. It looms above us and far out to the side. I crane my neck, but all I see is the white exterior. What else is hidden in there? I am sure I have only seen a fraction of this monstrosity.

My stomach lurches as we are descending. I am allowed to walk out. I am even going to be allowed to return to my room.

"Your surgery is scheduled for tomorrow at noon," one of the hover cart drivers says.

I wave my good arm and walk through the hallway with one of Dr. Loudin's Assistants. I wish I could be allowed to walk unescorted back to my room, but that is not permitted here. I will never be able to explore this building the way I'd like.

We walk in silence. I am trying not to think about why I am

back here, what could happen. Trying not to think about the arm that still hangs like a weight from my left shoulder. The Assistant opens the door, and I discover I am actually happy to see this room. Having watched Pod C turned into a medical facility, I realize this is the only home I have now. When I see my violin in its case on the couch, all happiness is gone. My heart sinks. My throat tightens. I can't play it. I don't even think I could lift it to my shoulder. What if the surgery doesn't work? What if this condition is permanent? What will I do?

The Assistant leaves without a word. I am just a patient— and an anomaly at that. I am not even worthy of a parting farewell or a smile. I am just a job. Deliver the brain-injured girl to her room and return to your important duties.

I stare at the door because I cannot continue to stare at my violin. I didn't hear the normal click that signals the door has locked. So I step forward and check the door to see if it is unlocked. It is. I close my eyes and sigh. I want to see John. I need his reassurance that everything will be all right. I walk toward his room, hope filling the places deep inside that were beginning to die. But then I stop in the middle of the hallway.

I can't go there. The new Thalli doesn't know John. If I were to be seen talking with John, the Assistants would report it to Dr. Loudin. He would know his surgery failed. That I lied to him. That Berk lied to him. I cannot go.

My heart is heavy and I turn back, trying to appear disoriented in case someone happens to be monitoring the hallway. For added believability, I pass my room and open the room three doors from mine.

My intention is to open it, see that it isn't my room, and then shut the door. But when I open it, I gasp. I cannot stop myself. I can't believe what I see. Who I see. I turn around and shut the door quickly. But it is too late. She saw me. She is coming to the door, calling my name.

I have to ignore her voice, get back to my room, not appear at all shocked that there, three doors down, is Rhen.

# CHAPTER FORTY-THREE

crawl onto the sleeping platform, making a show of yawning. I act cold and wrap the blankets around my shoulders, shiver, then place them over my head. I feel my skull for the hole. Surely this is another simulation. There is the hole. This is real?

No. It can't be real. It is an advanced simulation. The Scientists recreated this level, this room, Rhen, and they programmed me to be able to feel the tiny hole in my head so I will believe this is real. But it can't be. It's impossible.

Rhen is dead. She was annihilated, along with all of Pod C. Unless that isn't true either. Maybe I have been in the simulation since I came here. Maybe all of it is false. Progress, Stone, the destruction of Pod C, the problem with the oxygen. The surgery to erase my memory. John. Jesus. Berk.

Did falling in love with Berk happen under simulation? Did knowing Jesus happen under simulation? Tears roll down my cheeks and I hold the blanket closer, trying to keep my breathing steady so those watching the cameras will think I am asleep and not know that I am falling apart.

I try to think back to when I discovered the simulation wasn't real. I couldn't find the thread. But how did I know Progress was a simulation? John and Berk told me. What if Progress is real but the Scientists don't want me to know, so they simulated those conversations with John and Berk?

But why would they simulate conversations about the Designer? About love? They are opposed to those ideas. But why would they simulate an entire world above either? None of the scenarios seem to make any sense. Nothing seems to make sense anymore.

I want to pray. But if none of this happened, if none of this is real, then how do I know there is even a Designer to pray to?

I close my eyes and sense him there. He *is* real. Even if the conversations with John and Berk weren't, I know this is. I know it in a way that is beyond logic. In a way Rhen would never understand.

Rhen. My body stiffens.

If she is alive, everything that came before was a simulation. If she is not alive, then this is a simulation.

I reach for my arm. Still lifeless. Maybe the simulation just started this morning. I try to remember what I ate last night. Something that put me to sleep so I could be transported back here, be made to think my arm is dead, that I am having brain surgery, that I saw Rhen? But why? What would the purpose of that be?

The door opens. I remain still, hoping I appear asleep so that whoever is there will leave.

"Thalli?" It is Berk. But the new Thalli doesn't know him, except as a Scientist. If the new Thalli is real, if she isn't part of a simulation. Which, of course, I don't know. Because, apparently, I don't know anything. I can't even tell the difference between reality and simulation.

I hear Berk again. Calling me. The cameras are watching. What do they expect to see? Do I know him or not? "Are you awake?"

I feel Berk settle on the edge of my sleeping platform. His hand is on my calf. I lower the blanket slightly, my eyes peering out, wondering how to respond.

"It's all right," Berk whispers. "The cameras in this wing are experiencing some technical difficulties."

I wrinkle my brow. "What?"

"We can talk." Berk pulls the covers off my head. "I shut down the cameras."

I scoot away from Berk, my back pressed against the wall, the covers clutched in my right hand.

"What's wrong?"

I bite my lip. He looks so real. I want to tell him everything. But Stone looked real too. So did Rhen. How do I know this isn't a test, with Dr. Loudin watching from his pad deep inside his laboratory?

Berk leans forward. He looks just like Berk, even the gold flecks in his eyes are right. He smells like Berk's soap. I want to reach out to him. But I can't. My whole body feels as dead as my arm. I feel so frightened. So alone.

Berk places his hand on my arm. "Rhen is alive."

My heart races. I want so much to believe this is true. But if this is a simulation, then neither she nor Berk is real. This is just an experiment. A test.

"I saw her." I refuse to look Berk in the eye. "But I don't believe she is real."

"Of course she's real." Berk's hand reaches for mine.

I pull away. "How do I know?"

"What?" Berk looks confused, hurt.

"How do I know Rhen is real?" I am fighting tears, fighting a desire to fall into Berk's arms. I use my good arm to pull my knees to my chest and make myself as small as possible. "How do I know this isn't a simulation?"

"A simulation?" His voice breaks. I am hurting him. I don't mean to. But I have to know the truth.

"Yes." I pull my knees in tighter. "The last time you said I was in a simulation, in Progress, it all felt real. Just as real as this. But it wasn't. So how do I know this isn't just another simulation?"

"You think I am a simulation?" Berk's face falls. But I can't give in.

"I know there is a real Berk. But I don't know which memories are real and which are fake."

"I am real, Thalli." Berk inches closer, his hands on my face. "We are real. This is real."

I don't want to cry, but I can't help it. "How do I know?"

Berk wipes a tear from my eye and then stands, pulling out his pad. "Give me a minute."

He is tapping, tapping. His face looks sad, resigned. The wall screen in front of me comes on and I see Progress. The town, the people walking around. The view changes and I see the mountains, the movie theater in the distance. I smell the popcorn. Then I see Stone walking toward me, smiling. His white teeth bright against his dark skin.

My hand comes to my throat. "How did you do that?"

"I have access to the Progress simulation." Berk speaks so quietly I can barely hear him.

"Why?"

"I am a Scientist in training." Berk shrugs. "I have access to almost everything."

I can't speak. Berk turns off the screen and sits back on the edge of my sleeping platform. "But I didn't know Dr. Loudin was testing on you until you told me. I promise. After I watched Dr. Loudin that day, I tapped into the simulation program. To make sure there weren't any more he was planning to put you in."

I drop my arm. Slowly. "This isn't a simulation?"

"No."

"None of this has been a simulation?"

Berk holds my face in his hands. "We are not a simulation. What we feel is not a simulation."

I want to cry and jump and shout. But those thoughts are crowded out by another thought. "Rhen is alive?"

Berk holds my good hand with both of his. "She was taken a few days before Pod C was eliminated. She is sick."

I remember hearing the strange sound that came from her mouth. The same thing Asta had. I remember trying to hide that from the Monitors, trying to convince her not to tell anyone. With me gone, she must have decided to follow her logic and turn herself in. "What is going to happen to her?"

Berk won't look at me. I hear what he is saying without him having to say it. Rhen is going to be annihilated.

"No." I jump out of the sleeping platform, nearly tripping from the weight of my arm. "She can't have survived the pod's elimination to be sent here to die. We have to do something. We have to save her."

"I am trying." Berk sighs. "I've been trying."

"She's much smarter than I am." My voice is loud, but I can't quiet it. "Convince Dr. Loudin that she is necessary."

Berk walks to me, then places his hands on my shoulders. "I don't want to see her annihilated any more than you do."

"I need to see her." I pull away, walk toward the door. Berk grabs my dead arm and pulls me back.

"You can't go there right now." He rubs my arm. I feel nothing. He realizes that and transfers his hand to my good arm. "You don't remember her."

"But the cameras. You said the whole wing was having technical difficulties."

"Yes, but what if someone sees you walk over there? Or walk back? We can't take any more risks."

I know he is right. But I don't like it. "But it's Rhen." I fall into Berk's arms.

"I know," he whispers into my ear. "You and she made a great team in Pod C. I am going to advocate to Dr. Loudin that that team remain intact."

"But how did she survive this long?" Pod C's termination was over a week ago.

"Testing." Berk helps me walk to the couch. We both sit.

"The Scientists always test those with illnesses. They want to know what caused it and how to prevent that particular malformation in the next generation."

"Is hers serious?"

"Not at all." Berk turns to face me, hope lighting his face. "It is very minor. That is why I believe I can make a solid case for her being allowed to remain here and work with you. She was given an antiquated form of medication and is showing almost no signs of illness at all anymore."

I think of Asta, annihilated for the same "malformation." Could she have been cured with a medication? Allowed to return back to us? If the solution was that easy, why annihilate her in the first place?

"What are you thinking about?" Berk turns on the couch so he is facing me.

"Asta." I swallow. I can see her in the simulation. Her curly hair, her bright smile. "If the cure is so simple . . ."

"The Scientists fear illness." Berk shakes his head. "They can be contagious, wipe out whole pods. Or worse. That's why they have taken such care to design us without the propensity to get sick."

"Just like they have designed us without the propensity to feel or question?" I raise my eyebrows at Berk.

"I am not saying I agree." Berk shrugs.

"When you are one of the Scientists, you can change that." I hold Berk's hand. "Right?"

"I will be one of The Ten." Berk looks down at my fingers laced in his. "I don't know if I'll have that kind of power."

"You have to try." My voice is getting louder, but I can't help it. "That could be your purpose. Maybe the Designer has you in this position to save people like Asta."

I can tell Berk is thinking. And I can also tell that I need to speak of something else, give him time to process this. I release his hand and lean back. "Tell me about my surgery."

"What?" Berk was still thinking about his future, I am sure.

"My surgery. I want to know what to expect."

"Dr. Loudin will go back into your brain and remove the scar tissue." Berk says this in his Scientist voice.

"What are the risks?"

Berk laughs. "You ask a lot of questions."

"I thought that was a good thing."

"It is a good thing." He leans into me. "Everything about you is good."

"Stop trying to change the subject." I smile.

"He'll be in your brain." Berk leans forward, his hands on his knees. "It's delicate."

"What could happen?"

"I don't know." Berk stands. "Hopefully nothing other than removing the scar tissue and restoring the feeling in your arm."

"But?" I can tell there is more. I know when Berk is holding back information.

"You didn't respond the way he expected during the first surgery." Berk is staring at the floor. "But he doesn't know why."

"So I might be in danger?"

Berk runs his hands through his hair. "I don't know."

Panic rushes through me. "Give me the worst possible scenario."

Berk shakes his head. "No. I can't think like that."

"Do we tell him the first surgery didn't work?"

Berk looks at me. "If we do, then you won't be useful anymore.

He'll either annihilate you or use you for even more invasive experiments. We can't take that chance."

"Tell me the worst that could happen." I hold my dead arm against my stomach. "I need to know."

"You could get worse." Berk sits back down next to me. "You could lose your eyesight. You could lose feeling in another limb. You could lose memory or motor function."

I lean back into the couch. "Should I refuse the surgery?"

"You can't." Berk holds my hand.

"What can I do?"

"John would say to pray." Berk squeezes my hand. "That the Designer protected you from the last surgery."

"And he allowed this to happen." I look at my left arm. "How much power does he really have?"

"But that"—Berk touches my left arm—"brought you back here. It allowed you to see Rhen."

"But I can't talk to her. I can't help her. I'd rather be back in the pod. We were together every day. Just you and me."

"John told me that sometimes the Designer puts us in seemingly impossible situations to demonstrate his power."

"But I wasn't waiting for a surgery that might turn me into someone else."

"True," Berk says.

Do I really trust the Designer? Is John right?

"I'll be there during your surgery." Berk holds my right hand with both of his.

"And Rhen?"

The alarm on Berk's pad begins to scream. "The cameras are being repaired."

"I guess that means you have to go."

"I'll try to make it to Rhen's room before they finish," he says, a hand on the door.

"Good. Tell her everything, Berk."

He leaves and I lean against the door. Berk is real. Rhen is alive. And I am in a nearly impossible situation.

# CHAPTER FORTY-FOUR

Y ou need to stay awake throughout the procedure." Dr. Loudin is standing above me. I am strapped to a chair in the operating pod. "Berk here is going to be asking you questions. Answer to the best of your ability."

"All right."

Berk is standing behind Dr. Loudin, a Scientist's smile plastered on his face. "If at any point you feel discomfort, see, hear, or feel anything out of the ordinary, please let me know."

"Of course."

Dr. Loudin moves out of my line of sight and Berk moves in.

"I am beginning the procedure now." Dr. Loudin's voice

247

sounds strange. Then I realize he is wearing a mask. The clarinet is muffled.

The wall screen in front of me lights up and I see what Dr. Loudin sees: the inside of my brain. Berk is blocking the center. I want him to move so I can watch everything, but Berk purses his lips and I know I cannot ask that. I shouldn't be that curious.

"What is your name?" Berk asks.

"Thalli."

"Pod?"

"C." I am sure Dr. Loudin wrote these questions. Berk would never ask me something so painful.

"Your design?"

"Musician."

"Age?"

"Seventeen."

Berk looks above my head and pauses. He nods. Dr. Loudin is communicating something. I wish the screen were a mirror so I could see what it is.

The room goes black. I want to jump up, but I cannot. "I can't see." I can barely get the words out.

"What?" Dr. Loudin's muffled voice sounds amplified.

"I. Can't. See." I try to speak clearly, try to remain calm. I close my eyes and open them. Nothing.

I feel someone's breath on my face. Berk. "Her pupils aren't responding to stimulus, Dr. Loudin." He is trying to keep the panic out of his voice, but I hear it.

"Interesting."

I want to scream. I am blind and Dr. Loudin thinks it is interesting?

"She is certainly an anomaly."

"Can you repair it?" Berk asks.

"Let me see." I hear Dr. Loudin's fingers tapping against his pad. What is he doing? What is happening?

"Her heart rate is accelerating." I feel Berk's knee touching mine. It is slight but reassuring.

"Thalli." Dr. Loudin's voice is clearer now. The mask must be off. "You need to calm down. Your blood flow must be normal for me to do my best work. If you get excited, I will have a hard time completing this repair. Do you understand me?"

"Yes." I try to will my heart to slow down, my lungs to take in enough air.

"Do you have any other unusual sensations?" Dr. Loudin asks. "Assess your body from your feet to your head. Dr. Berk, help her with that."

"Of course." I feel Berk move. His hands are on my feet. He is rubbing them with his fingers, squeezing hope and love into them. "Do you feel this?"

"Yes." I try to sound clinical and not grateful.

His hands move up to my ankles. "This?"

He continues. Each touch calms me, reassures me.

"This?" His hand is on my arm. My left arm.

"Yes."

"The scar tissue extraction was successful," Berk says, his hand still on my arm.

"Excellent," Dr. Loudin responds, still tapping.

If I could choose, would I rather lose feeling in the one arm than sight in both eyes? But, of course, I don't get to choose. My status as a project has never been so horrific.

"I think I have found the problem."

He *thinks?*

"Continue asking her questions, Dr. Berk. Ask the second set of questions."

I feel Berk move away. He is tapping on his screen. "The square root of 225."

Math? I am blind and in brain surgery, and he is asking me to do math? I calculate in my mind. "Fifteen."

"Single unit of a quanta?"

Science? Is he trying to punish me for rushing through my lessons as a child? "Quantum?"

"Correct."

"A few more and I should have the exact location," Dr. Loudin says. I remember the image of my brain, with all the colors. He must be using that again.

Berk drills me on calculus next, then history. Finally, I get a music question. I can answer that easily. He gives me a few more of those. I relax and shoot off the answers without thinking. I wonder if the image of my brain is projecting the treble clef.

And then I see it. My brain, lit up with reds and blues and yellows. "I can see."

"Excellent," Dr. Loudin says, the mask off once again. "And the arm?"

Berk touches it and I feel his fingers. "Yes."

"A complete success then." He walks around the chair and looks at me. "You are truly unique, Thalli."

I don't know what he means, but he is smiling, so I reciprocate.

"I will send some Assistants in to help return her to the recovery cube," Dr. Loudin tells Berk. "We need to observe her for at least twenty-four hours before we can release her back to her own room."

"Yes, sir."

Dr. Loudin turns his face toward me. "Rest today, and tomorrow you should be feeling well. Maybe even well enough to take a return trip to the performance pod. I would very much like another recording."

"Of course." The thought thrills me. I lift my arms—both arms—from the chair and sigh.

I am whole. I am safe. I am an anomaly.

# CHAPTER FORTY-FIVE

I have been back in my room for a full day and the only one to come in is the Assistant with my food. I haven't heard from Berk, haven't dared to walk down to see Rhen or John. I have played my violin, composed some new songs, slept, and worried.

Where is Berk? Dr. Loudin? I feel abandoned. And confined. I want to get out. I have asked the Assistant if I can go to a recreation field and walk, but he says I cannot. Not without Dr. Loudin's permission. And Dr. Loudin is busy right now and cannot be disturbed.

Is Berk busy too?

The door opens. I jump up from the couch, but it is only the Assistant with my dinner. "Any word from Dr. Loudin yet?"

"No." He places the tray beside me.

"What about the other Scientist with him?" I take a deep breath. "Dr. Berk?"

"All the Scientists are engaged right now. They have requested that they not be disturbed."

The door shuts and I groan. Why do they not want to be disturbed? What is going on? Something doesn't feel right.

I want to know what is happening with Rhen. There has to be a way to talk to her without being seen. Berk was able to create a technical difficulty in this wing. Could I?

I pick up my pad. It is locked on the learning mode. I can't get past it.

I remember the stairwell, where Berk and I went so many weeks ago. If I could get Rhen there, we could talk without anyone hearing us. But how do I get her there? Is she locked in? Am I locked in?

I look at my tray. Soup, bread, and grapes. A plan forms.

I take the bread and grapes and stuff them into my pockets. I crack open the door and peer out into the hallway. No one is there. I walk toward Rhen's room, trying to look confused, like the last time.

I open the door to the room before Rhen's. No one is there. I rub my head and crane my neck, hoping that if anyone is monitoring the cameras, all they will see is a disoriented patient out for a much-needed walk in the hall.

I open Rhen's door. She is sitting on her sleeping platform. Her eyes widen and I shake my head. Then I drop a grape on her floor and walk away.

When we were kids, we would play this game. I would hide and leave clues for her by dropping bits of my lunch on the floor.

I keep walking, dropping a piece of bread or a grape every few feet. I try to place them as close to the wall as I can so they will be inconspicuous to Assistants who might happen along. The Sanitation Specialists only work at night, so the mess should not be in danger for several more hours.

I try to recall the way to the stairwell, stopping along the way to stretch my arms and roll my neck.

I find the door to the stairwell. A final grape and I am in. I sit against the wall and wait.

In a few minutes, I hear footsteps approaching. I stand and begin running up and down the stairs. If it is a Monitor, I need to look like I am here to exercise, not to meet a doomed friend whom I am not supposed to remember.

But it isn't a Monitor who opens the door. It is Rhen, her hands full of bread and grapes, her eyes wide.

"Thalli?"

I jump down the stairs and almost knock Rhen over. "Are you all right?"

"My sickness was discovered so I am waiting to be annihilated," Rhen says, pulling away from me, as logical as ever. "But how are you still alive?"

"It is complicated. But Berk is helping me. And we're going to help you too."

"Help me?" Rhen's blond ponytail shakes. "I cannot be helped. I am malformed. There is no room for me in the State."

I want to shake her, to tell her everything. But I don't have time for that. "We can't stay here long. I just wanted to see you, and to tell you to have hope."

"Hope?"

The idea is foreign to her. It makes me sad. I forgot that the lack of emotions in her makeup was not malformed. That part works perfectly.

"You are going to live."

I see the familiar look in Rhen's eyes, the look she would always give me when I spoke from emotion and she didn't understand. "I am surprised I have been allowed to live this long, but I suppose the study of my malformation will aid the Scientists in the design of the next generation."

"You are so much more than a science project, Rhen." I say this, even though I know she won't comprehend it. Yet. But I am sure someday she will. The Designer did not spare her so she could be annihilated. I am sure of that.

"We shouldn't be here." Rhen looks around. I can only imagine what she thinks of this old stairwell.

"You're right." I sigh. "I just wanted to see you. But we should go back before anyone notices us."

"We are too old for children's games." Rhen folds her arms, but I am sure I see a slight smile on her face. She is happy to see me too.

"You should go back first." I peek out the door. We are still alone. I turn back to Rhen. "If you see me anywhere else, I have to pretend that I don't know you."

"Pretend?"

"Please, Rhen." Frustration battles with relief. "I am not supposed to know you."

Her brow furrows. "Why?"

"I can't tell you everything right now."

Rhen shrugs. "Okay."

"I'll try to meet you again and tell you everything." I look at my friend, memorizing her face, so glad to see her alive.

"When I figure out a good time, I'll knock on your door twice. Come here ten minutes after I knock."

"This doesn't sound like a very good idea."

"It is all I have."

"It is good to see you again." Rhen's face softens. "The cube was very quiet without you. And very clean."

I know she isn't trying to make a joke, but the statement is funny.

"I believe my time for annihilation is coming soon, though," Rhen continues. "So I might not get to see you again."

"Don't say that." I do not like how calmly she says this. Like annihilation is a field trip to the water tanks or a lesson to complete on the learning pad.

"Everyone is eventually annihilated." Rhen raises her eyebrows.

I think of John. He is allowed to visit those scheduled for annihilation. "Has anyone come to your room?"

"Of course. Assistants and Monitors. Every day."

"How about an old man?"

"An old man?"

Why hasn't John come? She has to have been here for several days. Surely he knows she is here.

I hear a sound outside, a door slamming. "Go. I'll see you soon."

"The probability of that is quite remote." Rhen looks at me, waves, and is gone.

The door to the stairwell shuts loudly and I lean against the wall. I need to find a way to save Rhen. I need to talk to Berk and find out what is going on with the Scientists. I need to find out why John hasn't visited.

And I need to do all of that without being caught.

# CHAPTER FORTY-SIX

I cannot stay in this room any longer. Three full days have passed with no word from anyone. I haven't visited Rhen again. I don't have anything to tell her, no hope to give. But I listen at the door every time I hear footsteps in the hall, making sure they aren't taking her. I don't know what I would do if they did, but I know I would do something.

Where is Berk? Why hasn't he come? What if something happened to him? What if Dr. Loudin found out about us, about me?

I begin pacing the room and am interrupted by talking. Someone is talking. Here in my room. I look at the wall screen.

There are no images. I listen more. No, the sound can't be coming from the wall screen. It's too small to come from there. I hear the wall screen from all sides. I just hear this from one place. From my couch. From my learning pad.

I peer into it and see Dr. Loudin in a lab I have never seen. He is speaking to another of the Scientists. I look closer. It is Dr. Williams. She looks older than the pictures I have seen in my lessons, but I recognize her face. She is responsible for the solar panels and for much of the electrical engineering in the State.

Berk must have placed a camera on his lapel and found a way to link the transmission to my learning pad. I don't have time to think about the genius—and the danger—of this plan because Dr. Williams is speaking.

"As I said, the oxygen we are producing is no longer sufficient." She is looking at a complicated machine.

"We will simply have to do away with a few more people." Dr. Loudin says this without any emotion. "We can function with as little as 50 percent of the current population. We will just have to train the remaining population in more than one specialty."

"That isn't the solution." Dr. Williams shows Dr. Loudin something on the machine. "The annihilation of Pod C has not improved conditions at all. The problem is not those who are breathing the oxygen. The problem is in the oxygen itself."

I feel sick. All my friends, gone. And for nothing. I want to curl up and cry, but I need to listen. Berk wants me to hear what they are saying, what is happening.

"Then what is the solution?" Dr. Loudin folds his arms.

Dr. Williams looks at the camera, at Berk. "This is why I have asked Dr. Berk to join us. I have had him working on a possibility."

"Dr. Berk?" Dr. Loudin turns. I feel like he is staring right at me. "I have had him working on something for me as well."

"As you said." Dr. Williams smiles. "We can teach more than one specialty."

"Go on."

Both Scientists are looking at Berk. "I believe we can treat the air from above the way we treat the water."

"We dismissed that possibility years before the war occurred." Dr. Loudin rubs his temples.

"I know." Dr. Williams places a hand on Dr. Loudin's arm. "But that was over forty years ago. We have developed newer technology. We have created Scientists even more evolved than we are." She points to Berk.

"If we allow air in from above, we could all be poisoned." Dr. Loudin is shaking his head.

"Not if it's treated."

"And how do you plan to treat the air, Dr. Berk?"

Berk takes a deep breath. "I don't know exactly."

"You don't know?" Dr. Loudin looks at Dr. Williams as he says this.

Berk's hand goes up. "*I* don't know. But I believe we can discover the solution by modifying one of your cerebral studies."

Dr. Loudin's brow wrinkles.

"As you know, I have been working to analyze the connection between the musical and the linguistic centers of the brain."

"Yes."

"There is a link between the two, but not in the conscious mind," Berk says. "I believe if we can find a way to make that connection, to break the barrier between the conscious and unconscious, we can discover solutions to this and many other problems."

"If?" Dr. Loudin's face is red. "You are coming to me with a hypothesis? I thought you said he had a solution, Dr. Williams."

"I do," Berk says. "I mean, I believe I do. But I can't go any further without your help."

"I do not have time to help you with your projects," Dr. Loudin says. "I have far more important things to do."

"Listen to him," Dr. Williams shouts. Dr. Loudin folds his arms and glares at Berk.

"If I can use your simulation program, I believe I can place someone inside a piece of music."

Dr. Loudin expels a heavy breath. "That is ridiculous."

"You created an entire village aboveground," Berk says. "The subject says it was so real, all five senses were engaged."

"Yes, and the results of that project helped me better understand the mind." Dr. Loudin is speaking to Berk like he is a child, not a Scientist. "I can pass that understanding on to the Geneticists as they develop the next generations."

"And I can use it to help ours," Berk insists.

"By taking someone inside a piece of music?"

"Not just anyone." Berk's hands emphasize each word. "It has to be someone gifted in linguistics. In logic."

"Why not use one of us?"

"As you know"—now it is Berk's turn to speak to Dr. Loudin like a child—"we were designed to have several areas of specialty. Those designed to be the logical members of their pods had that segment of their brain amplified."

"Of course I know that."

"They are designed to be logical, to decode messages, to

ANOMALY

make sense of difficult problems," Berk continues. "And they are designed to do that without being distracted by anything else."

Dr. Loudin opens his mouth and closes it again. "If they could break the barrier in the simulation—"

"Then we could use that to tap into the subconscious brain. And who knows how many solutions we can discover then." I can hear the smile in Berk's voice.

Dr. Loudin walks up to Berk. He stands so close I can only see his neck, the Adam's apple bobbing up and down. "You believe the solution to our problem lies in music?"

"I cannot answer that with a definitive yes, but I do believe exploring that possibility is worth our efforts."

"What materials do you need?" Dr. Loudin steps back, and Dr. Williams is smiling behind him.

"I will need access to your lab and your program," Berk says. "I will also need two subjects. One gifted in music, one in logic."

"Do you have a pair in mind?"

"Yes, sir. I certainly do."

# CHAPTER FORTY-SEVEN

P lay it again."
I am in the performance pod. Berk brought his own recording equipment and attached it directly to the piano. I have been playing the same piece for four hours, stopping to explain everything about it—the chords, the key, the values of the notes and the rests. I haven't thought about music theory in so long that I have to pull up old lessons on my learning pad to find the answers to some of the questions Berk is asking.

I know this frustrates him. He wants to get this part of the program set so he can move on to the next part. I want to ask him when we will begin, how Rhen is doing, if John is all right.

But Assistants are at every corner so I can't. I can only play and answer his questions. I am getting frustrated as well.

But I play and try not to think about my fingers aching, my back aching, my legs aching. Berk stays hunched over his equipment, tapping and adjusting and stopping me so he can play back what I wrote.

"Are you sure you played exactly what was written?" he asks. Again.

"Yes, I am sure." The new Thalli is not supposed to have any emotion, so I work to keep my voice level as I answer.

"But you didn't look at the music."

"I don't need to look at the music."

Berk looks at me. I raise my eyebrows. Slightly. But enough for him to know that I do not need him questioning my musical ability.

He sighs and leans back. "You know, I think we may need to stop for the day."

The Assistants suddenly stand straighter.

"You all may leave." Berk stands and motions to the door. "We will begin again tomorrow morning."

"Would you like me to return the patient to her room?" one of the Assistants asks.

"No, thank you." Berk rolls his neck from one side to the other. "I might need her help."

The Assistants file out the door and I storm into the practice room, needing to be away from cameras—and from Berk—for a few minutes.

I shut the door, making sure the soundproofing seal is in place, and I scream. Long and loud. It feels wonderful. A violin sits in the corner, but for the first time in my life, I can't stand the thought of playing any music. I jump up and down, my muscles begging to be exercised after being forced in one spot for so long. I place my right leg on the wall and stretch my fingers to my toes. I do the same with the other leg and then I raise my arms above my head, leaning right and left, bending down.

I feel much better. The screaming and stretching technique is quite effective. The door opens and Berk walks in.

"Is it safe for you to be in here?"

"I think I'm in more danger from you than I am from the cameras." His grin melts away any remaining frustrations I might have been harboring.

"You were very demanding." I lean against the padded wall.

"I am trying to save your and Rhen's lives." Berk sounds like he might need a little scream and stretch.

"I know." I walk to Berk and hold him close. "Thank you."

Berk relaxes. I lay my head on his shoulder and rub his back with my hands. His muscles are so tense. I forget that he has also been working all these hours.

"Turn around." I pull away and point him toward the door.

"What?"

I rub his knotted muscles. "How is that?"

"Worth working all day for."

I keep rubbing, neck, shoulders, spine. "Brilliant trick with the learning pad, by the way."

"It took some work." Berk turns his head to look at me. "But I knew you'd have a million questions if I just grabbed you and brought you here."

"I still have a million questions."

Berk laughs. "So I did all that for nothing?"

"No. I would have had two million otherwise."

"All right. Go ahead."

"How dangerous is the situation?" I ask. "How much time until the oxygen supply is gone?"

"We're not sure." Berk turns me around and begins rubbing my shoulders. "No one has been able to determine an exact formula to measure the deterioration. Some days are better than others, but we don't know why that is either."

"That's why you're working so hard to get this completed."

"Yes. So that's one question down. Only 999,999 to go. What's next?"

"Let's sit." I pull away and ease down on the carpeted floor. Berk sits beside me. "How is John?"

"He was sick," Berk says. "I wanted to tell you."

"What's wrong?"

"He is old, Thalli." Berk's eyes are sad. "It is amazing that he has lived this long."

"You didn't answer my question."

"He just got sick." Berk shrugs. "I don't know what was wrong. I just know he was in the medical pod for a while, but now he is back."

"Have you seen him?"

"No, I can't."

"Has he seen Rhen?"

"No," Berk says. "She isn't scheduled for annihilation anymore, so he isn't allowed."

"Can I see him?"

"You aren't supposed to remember him."

"Can't you turn the cameras off in our wing again?"

"I'm a little busy right now." Berk bumps my shoulder with his.

I lean my head back against the wall. "What happens when this is over?"

"Don't worry about that right now." Berk takes my hand, lacing his fingers through mine.

I think again about the Designer. Is this really all part of his plan? If it is, it seems awfully risky, awfully complicated. I wish he would make things simpler. Show himself to the Scientists, convince Berk he is real.

But maybe making things easy isn't part of his plan.

# CHAPTER FORTY-EIGHT

W e're ready." Berk is standing at my door.

We have spent the last four days in the performance pod. I have written a five-page piece of music that includes everything I know about music. It had to be complicated, with a variety of keys and rhythms. I had to use every note on the piano at least once. And when I was finally done and had rehearsed enough so I could play it flawlessly, I had to perform with a dozen probes stuck to my skull and another dozen attached to the piano.

"You will come along with us." Dr. Berk is speaking now. The Assistants around him surround me as we walk down the hall. "You will not be part of the simulation. We may need you, however, if there are any difficulties with the program."

"Of course." I get to see inside my music. This makes all the hours of work worth it. To see my music. What will it look like, inside a brain, in three dimensions? Berk has had little time to tell me the details of the simulation. I try not to reveal my excitement.

We walk down the hallway that leads past John's door. I want to look into his small door panel without drawing attention. I slow slightly. Berk knows what I am doing and he slows as well.

"Just a moment," he says to the Assistants. "I think I am receiving a communication." He stops and pulls out his pad, just ahead of John's door, forcing me to stop right at the window.

John is sitting on his chair. He looks pale, but he smiles when he sees me. He nods and points up. I turn my head so the Assistants cannot see me and I smile back.

"I was mistaken." Berk replaces his pad and we walk on.

We take an elevator I have never been in to a part of the facility I have never seen. Except on my learning pad when I first listened to Berk's plan.

Dr. Loudin's private lab looks different in person. Berk's camera only showed a small portion. But this is huge. The room is deep and pristine. Dr. Loudin is sitting at a desk near the center. It is surrounded by machines that look vaguely familiar. I am sure I learned about them at some point in my childhood, but I do not recall what they all are. Each has lights and knobs covering its surface. Some are taller than I am and some reach only to my waist. Dr. Loudin touches one with expert hands, reading something on its small screen that makes him grunt.

Berk clears his throat. "Dr. Loudin?"

"Yes?" He is still reading the screen. When he looks up and sees me, he stands and adjusts his rumpled jacket. "Ah yes. Of course. You have retrieved our Musician."

"Yes, sir."

"Our patient is prepared." Dr. Loudin walks to a door at the side of the room. The interior is quite similar to the room where I had my surgery. But this one has a panel on the wall opposite the surgical chair.

I see the back of Rhen's head, the probes already in place inside her brain. Dr. Williams stands in front of her, asking her questions and adjusting the screen behind her. Berk leads me into the room on the other side of the window. There are chairs so we can sit and observe the procedure without being in the room itself.

Rhen doesn't appear frightened. Her voice, coming through a sound portal in the observation room, is calm, normal. She has no problem answering each question. I look above her at the screen. Her brain is lit up, a different color for every question that is asked.

Finally, Dr. Williams nods to Dr. Loudin. They each place a thick mask over their mouth and nose, the Assistants leave the room, and within minutes Rhen is asleep.

I don't see any medicine being administered. "How did they put her to sleep?"

"It is a gas that is released into the room," Berk says, still in doctor mode. "She has a screen above her that looks like a garden. The gas smells like flowers. It is designed to calm people before anni—"

He doesn't finish. But I know. This is how people are

annihilated. A garden scene, a sweet smell, then sleep and death. It is beautifully cruel.

"This gas will only put Rhen into a sleep deep enough to allow her to be placed in the simulation."

The wall screen behind Rhen changes. In the top corner, I see her brain, but a new color is lighting up, a purplish-pink. The rest of the screen shows my music, but in a way I never could have imagined. It is a place. A three-dimensional location, with each note residing in a specific position. The treble clef is the ceiling, the bass clef is the ground. It is like a maze. I can't see a beginning or an end. But then I see Rhen. She is there. In my music.

She looks at the music. I see the image of her brain in the corner. It is filled with so many colors, all moving and growing. Blues inside reds, yellows inside purples.

Dr. Loudin looks up from a machine to stare at the screen. He is amazed too. He walks to the image of the brain and moves it around, examining it. He is smiling the entire time. I have never seen him smile so much.

I look back at Rhen. She is moving the notes. They are light, so light that all she has to do is touch them and they float to a new position. In minutes, she has created a straight line. Berk leans forward. Dr. Loudin sits in his chair, ignoring even the lighting of the brain as he watches this.

Whole notes, half rests, flats, and sharps are all lined up. Rhen makes rows upon rows out of the music. What was once a maze is now an organized passageway. Rhen even adjusts the notes themselves so they are all the same height, blending into one another. She walks down one row and up the next, touching notes that are not lined up exactly right.

The notes aren't in the order I wrote them, but as I read the measures she has lined up, row by row, it makes sense. She is creating a new song. She is lining up all the parts by the key in which they were written. She has started with the up-tempo parts, those notes are closer together. Where I have written a slower tempo, the notes have spaces between them. They are in their own row. They stand taller than the faster notes. It is beautiful. What I wrote as a compilation of my musical knowledge, Rhen—logical Rhen—is adjusting to create beauty.

And she doesn't even realize what she is doing. She is simply following the logical progression, being given clues to the meaning of the notes, the tempo, the keys, through the probes in her brain. Information I gave to Berk that he programmed into the simulation, that guides Rhen to make choices I never would have considered.

Then the music begins to play. My music. Rhen's music. I recognize it and I don't recognize it. The room vibrates as it plays, a synthesized sound. I think it would sound better with a piano or violin. With a wood and string or even brass instrument. It is too beautiful for the computerized notes. They can't express the complexity of each line the way an instrument could. The way I could. I want to ask the Scientists to pause the simulation, to allow me to return to my room, to get my violin, to show them what this music is truly capable of. But they are far less concerned with the beauty of the music than with the message that music conveys.

Then the music stops. It is so sudden, I am sure its echoes are still bouncing around the observation chamber. I look through the panel at Rhen. The screen in front of her is black. The music has disappeared. But Rhen is still there. In the simulation.

The image of her brain is still lit up. She is confused. She cannot see. I know that feeling. I want to help her but I can't. Dr. Loudin looks to Dr. Williams. She is adjusting the knobs on the machine by Rhen's chair. She shakes her head and looks back at Dr. Loudin.

"What's happening?" I ask. No one answers.

Then Dr. Loudin's voice comes through the room, barely above a whisper. "She cannot get out."

# CHAPTER FORTY-NINE

jump up. "She can't get out?"

Berk puts a hand on my shoulder and I sit back down. Dr. Loudin is still staring at the image of Rhen's brain. Dr. Williams is tapping into the computer.

"I didn't prepare an exit for her," Dr. Loudin says. "When we programmed the simulation for Thalli, we programmed her return. She began and ended in the same room."

I remember the pink room. It is strange to miss something that doesn't exist, but I do.

"Why didn't you prepare an exit for Rhen?" Dr. Williams asks the question that I want to ask.

"I assumed she would do that herself."

"Why would you assume that?"

"This is a different simulation." Dr. Loudin turns from the screen and looks at Dr. Williams. "It was important for Thalli to believe she was in actual reality. This was obviously not a reality-based location. Rhen should have been able to decode that and remove herself."

I want to burst into the room and hurt that man. How can he blame Rhen for being trapped in *his* project?

"What will we do?"

Dr. Loudin looks at Rhen, still sitting in the chair, electrodes attached to her. "Annihilation is the most humane solution."

I jump up again, but Berk pulls me down before I can speak.

"But all this work would be lost." Dr. Williams looks back at the screen. "We don't know what she had decoded. It would take months to understand what she did in there. We need her to tell us."

Dr. Loudin sighs. "We would need to create a simulated reality then. That would take just as long as decoding would."

"Couldn't you create a reality using the music?" Dr. Williams asks.

"What do you mean?"

"Before her surgery, Thalli experienced excessive emotions, correct?" Dr. Williams says.

"That is why she was brought to us." Dr. Loudin nods gravely. "She fell to the ground crying after playing a piece of music."

"Could we connect her emotions to the music?" Dr. Williams looks at Rhen again. "If Thalli's emotions are connected to her music, couldn't she also connect memories and locations?"

They want to see what I feel when I play? The thought

frightens me. But then I look at Rhen. Without my help, she is trapped. Forever. She will be stuck in the darkness of the music until she is annihilated.

Dr. Loudin blinks several times. "I suppose that is possible. But her memories have been erased and the emotional excesses have been removed."

"Could you reverse that surgery?"

"I suppose." Dr. Loudin says the words slowly. "But I have never attempted a reversal."

My stomach tenses. I have to tell them the surgery wasn't a success. Berk looks at me, his eyes wide. He knows what I am thinking, but he doesn't want me to say anything. His life will be in jeopardy if I divulge this—Dr. Loudin will know that Berk and I have conspired to keep this secret from him. But Rhen's life is in jeopardy if I remain silent.

I close my eyes. I want to pray, but the Designer feels distant. Has he abandoned me? Why is this happening?

When I open my eyes, I see both Scientists coming into the observation chamber. I see Rhen lying in the chair. I feel Berk, tense, sitting beside me.

I know what I must do. I cannot allow Rhen to be annihilated so I can keep my secret. I could not live with myself if I did that. I pray Berk will understand. And surely he is too valuable to be punished as severely as I will be punished. They need him too much.

"I do not need the reversal surgery." I speak before I have a chance to change my mind.

Dr. Loudin looks at me, his brows raised. "Excuse me?"

"I have a hypothesis." Berk's hand is on my arm. "I believe she can record the music she composed before the surgery. The memories she had while she was writing should still be in there, deep in her subconscious. She will not know consciously what she is playing, but it will translate in the simulation."

What is he doing? My mind races through this scenario. If they choose music written since I arrived here, they will see me and Berk. Together. They will know. And Berk will be punished. But I will not be, because they will still believe my memories have been erased.

"That is an interesting hypothesis." Dr. Williams nods.

"But it is just that," Dr. Loudin says. "A hypothesis. We have no way to know if it will be successful until we test it."

"Which is what Scientists do," Dr. Williams argues.

"When we have the luxury of time, yes." Dr. Loudin shakes his head. "But we do not have that. We need to assume this entire experiment has been a failure and start over somewhere else."

"No!" I don't mean to shout, but I can't help it. "Let me play. Please."

"Two more days, Dr. Loudin." Berk is trying to remain calm. His tone of voice reminds me that I must do the same. "We can surely spare that. If it works, we are on the way to finding a solution to the problem with the oxygen. If it doesn't, all we have lost is two days."

"If I perform the reversal, the music will be both in Thalli's subconscious *and* in her conscious memory. We can be certain the memory is intact, and we do not lose any more time."

"What if something goes wrong with the surgery?" Berk is trying to keep himself controlled. But the muscles in his jaw are twitching. "We risk losing the patient altogether. We do not have another like her—both musical *and* emotional."

"We do have others like her because she is no longer

emotional." Dr. Loudin's face is red. "Which is why we must reverse the surgery."

Dr. Williams steps forward. "Dr. Berk makes an excellent argument, Dr. Loudin. This mind is our best hope right now. Let us not do anything that could potentially damage it unless we have no other options."

"Very well," Dr. Loudin says after a long pause. "But I want the music recorded today. And I want to use her most recent composition."

My heart plummets. I know exactly what I was thinking and feeling when I wrote that. I played about the Designer and love and Berk and freedom. Any one of those thoughts can result in annihilation. All of them combined guarantee it. And not just mine. Berk's. Possibly even John's.

Rhen's life may be saved. But I have just sacrificed the lives of everyone else I love in order to save her.

I pray I have not made the wrong choice.

# CHAPTER FIFTY

I cannot make my fingers play the notes. I have been sitting at the piano for half an hour. I can't play scales, can't play chords, can't play anything. Berk is silent. Assistants are everywhere, so I know we cannot talk about this, we cannot go into the practice room. His eyes are willing me to play. He is resigned. He is at peace.

I am not.

Berk walks over to me and leans down, his mouth inches from my ear. "John once told me that the Designer said, 'The truth will set you free.'" He pulls away and arranges the music in front of me. If the Assistants noticed the exchange, they do not say anything.

*"The truth will set you free."* In choosing not to tell the truth, I have certainly experienced the opposite of freedom. But wasn't it right to conceal the truth of my relationship with Berk? Of the surgery's failure? So much damage would have occurred if I had revealed those truths.

Damage that will occur anyway now, with consequences that could be even worse than what they might have been had I been honest from the start.

"Are you ready to begin the recording?" Berk looks at me and nods.

I close my eyes. I have not felt the Designer's presence the last few times I have tried to pray. Is it because I have wanted him to help make my deception a success? Would he answer that prayer? I try again, this time asking him to give me the strength to be free, to be truthful. No matter the cost.

And I feel him. He is here. He is with me, helping me. Despite my lies, despite my trying to manipulate circumstances and come up with my own solutions, he is here.

I nod to Berk, and he attaches the probes to me and to the piano. With each touch, he communicates love and hope and faith. I am not alone. I was designed for a purpose. The Designer works in impossible situations. He has done it before. I choose to believe he will do it again. I ask him to play through my fingers, to bring life and freedom to my friend, to me. To use my gifts to help the State.

And I play. If this is my last time to touch a piano on this earth, I vow to make it my best. I will not hold back. I play a way for Rhen to get out of her simulation. I play my love for the Designer, my love for Berk and for John. I play faith and truth, and I pray that the Scientists will see that and know that in their desire to maintain peace at all costs, they have removed from the world what the Designer never intended to be removed.

I am crying as I play, but I don't bother to try to hide the tears. The Scientists will know soon enough that I am not playing from repressed memory. I want them to know. I want them to see how beautiful feeling and loving is.

I know I have never played so well. I have never felt so connected to an instrument. I am not just doing what the Scientists designed me to do. I am doing what the Designer designed me to do. This may very well be the purpose John told me I was made for. And so I play.

And the truth sets me free.

# CHAPTER FIFTY-ONE

An Assistant comes for me. He doesn't speak as we take the long walk from my room to Dr. Loudin's laboratory. I recorded my music yesterday. When I finished, as I wiped the tears from my eyes, an Assistant began tapping on his pad. I am sure he was alerting Dr. Loudin and Dr. Williams of my status, my deceit. I am also sure those two Scientists were watching the cameras in the performance pod, seeing my reaction, my emotion. They knew. Their response was immediate. The Assistant looked from his pad to me and frowned.

"Dr. Loudin requests you return the patient to her room," he said to Berk.

"I have not finished compressing the file."

The Assistant's blank stare revealed nothing. "Dr. Loudin says that will not be necessary. This test has been deemed a failure."

I looked at Berk. The freedom I felt in listening to the Designer, in trusting him, was so much greater than anything I had felt before. I no longer feared the Scientists' power.

Berk walked me back to my room and held me before I went back inside. We didn't care that cameras were watching us, that Assistants might come by and see. We didn't bother going to the stairwell. We held each other in the open, defying the Scientists' rules. There was no purpose in continuing the pretense.

"I love you, Thalli." Berk whispered the words in my ear, and I repeated them to him.

I visited John last night before I went to the sleeping platform. I told him everything, and he hugged me and assured me I made the right choice. He shared more of the Designer's words with me, words about heaven. It is a wonderful place. And there will be no tears there, he said, because there is nothing to cause tears. There is only joy and peace and worship. I found myself longing for this place. Ready to go.

"I have to admit, though," John said, smiling, "I'll be disappointed if you get there first."

I slept better than I have slept in weeks. Even knowing this might be my last day on earth, knowing I have sentenced myself—and possibly my friends—to death. The truth has set me free. I know that whatever will happen is part of the Designer's plan, and I can trust him to make far better decisions than I ever could.

The Assistant is walking quickly, and we are in Dr. Loudin's laboratory before I realize we have even reached his floor. The door opens and I see Rhen, still attached to the probes. Berk is in the observation chamber. Dr. Loudin doesn't look at me. His mouth is set in a tight line. Dr. Williams is working, her head down, fingers flying.

I enter the observation chamber and Berk motions me to him, his hand holding mine even before I am seated. He squeezes my hand and we look ahead.

"Why are we here?"

"Dr. Loudin changed his mind." Berk speaks quietly. "He realized we were too close to a solution to give up."

"Even though he knows about me?"

"About *us*." Berk squeezes my hand again. "He called me back to the performance pod late last night and had me complete the file compression so we could attempt the simulation with the new music."

I look at Berk closer. There are bags under his eyes.

"And if it works?"

Berk shakes his head. "I don't think there is any hope that we will be allowed to live. But he will keep us alive until this test is over."

Berk will be annihilated? My heart constricts. Surely not. Surely they wouldn't sacrifice him because of me. I refuse to believe that.

"And Rhen?"

"I don't know." Berk sighs. "She has done nothing wrong, and she is no longer sick. Hopefully they will find that her logic is too useful to destroy."

The screen in front of Rhen is still black. Her brain is no

longer lit up. Just a few spots of color. She is sleeping, mercifully unaware that she is stuck inside a dark simulation.

And then the screen lights up. The music from yesterday plays again. Rhen wakes and is caught again in the structure she assembled. It is vibrating, the synthesized notes humming, and then the music changes. It is the music I recorded yesterday in the performance pod. A light comes from the corner of the simulation, brighter than the notes Rhen assembled from the first simulation. The light changes into a door.

Rhen opens the door and the music is only sound. The notes aren't in this room. I am there. With Berk. We are in Pod C. He is holding my face, looking into my eyes. The scene is so intimate, I am upset that others are watching. These moments are ours. But this is the only way Rhen can return.

The music plays louder and Rhen looks around, assessing the situation. She knows where she is, but she doesn't know why Berk and I are there, doesn't understand what we are doing, why we won't speak to her. She walks from cube to cube and all are empty, except for the one that has been set up for my surgery.

She bends down and touches the bare floor in the living area. When she stands, the couch is there.

Dr. Loudin steps forward. Rhen is adjusting the reality in there, the same way she adjusted the reality in the music. She moves around the living area, tables and chairs coming up from the floor. The image of her brain is once again lit up, all colors, all over. Dr. Williams is frozen, her eyes watching Rhen.

Rhen is calm. Logical. I can see she is trying to understand where she is and what is happening. She looks back toward the music room. She retraces her steps until she is there again. She knows she must find a way from there, through the pod, back to the laboratory. She understands that she is trapped in this simulation.

She reaches up to grasp the treble clef in both hands. It is light but it is huge. She lifts it above her head, pulls back, and hurls it with all her might toward Pod C. The entire side of the pod crashes in. But we don't hear the crash. We only hear the music. Notes from the music room drift into Pod C. Yesterday's music combines with today's. It should sound horrible. But it doesn't. Rhen knows something I do not. The music fits. Yesterday's music is played an octave lower. It is the accompaniment to today's melody.

Of course. How did I not know that?

My melody plays of love and faith, what I was thinking of when I composed it. But the other piece, even though written to be technically superior, filled with as many differing notes and keys and rhythms as possible, still tells a story.

The music drifts out of the pod toward the Scientists' pod. Rhen reaches for a half note, stretches its stem, and sits on it like a floating chair. It takes her directly to the pod, the other notes following. She floats up, outside the pod, until she is outside this room. She points the stem of the half note toward the wall, pushes it forward. She breaks the wall from the outside. She is here, in her chair, probes attached to her head.

And then she wakes up.

# CHAPTER FIFTY-TWO

Rhen is gasping for air, trying to stand, brushing invisible debris from her shirt.

Dr. Williams rushes to remove the probes before Rhen is injured. Dr. Loudin is tapping intently into his pad, trying, no doubt, to make sense of what just happened, to find the code that allowed Rhen to move from subconscious to conscious thought.

Rhen stands and turns around to see Berk and me. She is confused. I want to go out, but Berk holds me tightly to his side. "Wait."

"All of you may leave." Dr. Loudin dismisses the Assistants

with a wave. He walks to the observation chamber and opens the door, motioning us out.

Berk never lets go of my hand. We stand and walk into the laboratory.

"Sit there." Dr. Loudin points to a couch in the corner of the room. Dr. Williams calls to him, pad in hand, and the pair exit. The door slams behind them, the metal echoing in the large room.

"What happened?" Rhen rubs her head, smoothing back her hair from where the probes had been.

"What do you remember?" Berk turns so he can see Rhen, who is seated on my right.

"A room with music." Rhen's eyes are far away. "Darkness. Then Pod C. But it was empty. Until I . . ."

Rhen shakes her head. What happened is so illogical, she cannot even bring herself to speak of it.

"You made the furniture appear," I finish for her.

"But that is impossible."

"It was a simulation," Berk says.

"What?"

Berk explains the simulation and the test, the experiment to find a connection between logic and music.

"But how did my being in the simulation help determine that connection?" Rhen asks.

"Dr. Loudin has been studying the brain for years. He applied one of his programs to your simulation."

"And what did he find?"

"I am sure he is discussing that with Dr. Williams right now." Berk looks at the closed door.

"And I am sure he won't bother sharing those results with us." I lean back.

"We will be annihilated," Rhen says. She isn't upset or angry. Just stating facts.

"Unless they need your assistance in the decoding." Berk rubs my hand with his thumb.

"What are you doing?" Rhen leans over and sees my hand in Berk's.

I want to explain that we are in love. I want her to know what love is and where it comes from, to break through her logic and help her find emotions. I am sure they are somewhere in her, suppressed, yes, but not gone. Her loyalty is proof enough that she has some feelings. She has just never allowed herself to connect with them.

But I don't have time to tell her anything because the door is opening and the two Scientists are returning, huge smiles on both their faces.

"While we commend you both on a job well done"—Dr. Loudin replaces his pad on the desk—"we regret to inform you that your assistance is no longer needed."

"Of course," Rhen says. "I am pleased to have been of service."

"You were of great service," Dr. Williams says, still smiling. "With this data, we are well on our way to being able to access the subconscious brain. There are so many possibilities from there. I am certain we will be able to use this to discover a solution to the oxygen problem."

Berk steps forward. "Then why not keep them here? Continue to use them?"

"Why not keep them here?" Dr. Loudin glares at Berk. "Rhen is physically unstable and Thalli is emotionally unstable. Both conditions are contagious. As we have seen." Dr. Loudin looks from Berk to me and back again. "Which is why your services will no longer be needed as well, Dr. Berk. You have been infected by Thalli. Your reasoning has been compromised."

"No, please—" I step forward, but Dr. Williams silences me with her eyes.

"We allow free thinking in our Scientists in order that they may have complete cognitive function." Dr. Loudin's voice gets louder with each phrase. "You took that freedom and applied it not to your position, but to *her*."

I feel sick. I knew this would happen. What other possible outcome could there be? But the reality of it is too horrible to comprehend. Talking about heaven with John last night is not the same as facing it with Berk and Rhen today. Where is the peace I had? I only feel fear. Numbing, crippling fear.

Dr. Loudin doesn't stop. He walks closer to Berk. "You had such potential. Your annihilation will set us back. But what choice do we have? You lied to us, you manipulated us for her. You placed this one life above the laws of this State. We can never trust you again."

"Erase his memory," I shout. "Make him forget me. Make him forget all this."

"And how will I know if the surgery is successful?" Dr. Loudin raises his eyebrows at me, anger radiating from his hazel eyes. "You have demonstrated exactly how to circumnavigate the system. We believed *your* memory was erased until last night."

Tears form in my eyes. I wipe them away, needing to be as logical as possible so Dr. Loudin will be convinced that he should not annihilate Berk. "You can review that surgery and determine what went wrong. Then you can try again with Berk."

"Interesting idea." Dr. Loudin presses his lips together.

"This is a procedure I would like to repeat. And Dr. Berk is a worthy candidate, despite this unfortunate occurrence."

"No. I don't want to be tested on."

Berk is looking at me, but I refuse to look back. He must live. I won't allow him to pay for his feelings for me with his life.

Dr. Loudin looks from Berk to me, ignoring Berk's outburst. "I believe I discovered what went wrong with your surgery. Your brain doesn't work the way most people's brains work. Your memory lives somewhere else, somewhere different. As does your eyesight. You are an anomaly. If we weren't so focused on finding a solution to our oxygen problem, I would have liked very much to have continued testing on you."

"Then why don't you?" Berk says.

"No." This time I do look at Berk. "I don't want to be tested on any more than you do."

"And you see why emotions are so dangerous." Dr. Williams spreads her arms out. "No, Dr. Loudin. We must stick to the plan. These three must be annihilated. It is the most humane and the most logical solution."

"Not Rhen. Please. She has done nothing wrong. And she is healthy now. The medication worked. Rhen has never deceived anyone, never pretended. She doesn't deserve to be annihilated. Her logic is superior. You saw that in the simulation. Imagine what she could do—"

"Enough." Dr. Loudin slams a hand down on the desk. "I will not have you dictating to me who should live. Dr. Williams is right. The decision has already been made."

Berk squeezes my hand.

"But I will allow you some comfort." Dr. Loudin says this softly. I hold my breath. "You will go first."

# CHAPTER FIFTY-THREE

I am clinging to Berk, our cheeks pressed together. I can't tell which are his tears and which are mine. My head drops to his shoulder and I hold him tighter. I know I will see him again. I know this. But saying good-bye is terrible, even with that knowledge.

Dr. Loudin allowed Berk to walk me to my room. He did not tell me where Rhen was being taken or what would happen to her. He feels that he is being kind in leaving me unaware of their futures. It does not feel kind.

"When?" I finally ask.

Berk pulls away, places his hands on my face. His green eyes are bright from crying. "Soon."

"Today?"

Berk closes his eyes.

"Don't answer that." My hands are on his shoulders, his chest. "It doesn't matter."

"Of course it matters." Berk leans his forehead against mine. "I need time to make a plan."

I shake my head. "No more plans, Berk."

"Thalli." Berk cannot speak. My heart is breaking for him. I know the pain of being left behind.

"Death is only the beginning, remember?"

Berk steps back and swallows. "Is this really our purpose, though, Thalli? Did the Designer bring us to know him, to love each other, only to be removed now, before we could accomplish anything?"

I think about all that has happened. "Maybe knowing him and loving each other *was* our purpose. We have accomplished it, so he is letting us go to him. Where we will truly be free." That thought frees me, brings me hope. Other than Berk, John, and Rhen, this world has not been a place that has brought me much joy. The thought of never knowing pain or sorrow again is exciting.

"Amen."

I didn't hear John enter the room. I have forgotten how white his hair is, his beard. How old he is. I rush to him and take his hands.

"I might get there before you." I think of our conversation the night before.

John shakes his head. "Then you tell our Maker I am ready. Take old John home."

"How can you laugh about this?" Berk's voice fills the room. "She is being killed because I love her."

John walks to Berk and taps a wrinkled hand to his chest. "Do not be afraid. Perfect love casts out fear."

"I'm not afraid." Berk bites the words out. "I am angry."

"Anger is all right." John nods. "You have reason to be angry when sin reigns. But I don't see anger, Berk. I see fear. And I see guilt."

Berk deflates. His eyes drop to a spot on the ground. "It's my fault."

"No. This is not your fault." John forces Berk to look him in the eyes. "Remember when I told you about Job?"

Berk nods.

"He was innocent. Completely innocent, yet the enemy sought him out and destroyed everything he held dear."

Tears roll down Berk's cheeks. I want to comfort him, but I need to let John finish.

"And do you remember what he said?" John asks. "'Though he slay me, yet . . .'?"

Berk wipes a tear from his cheek. "'Will I hope in him.'"

"Trust him, Berk." John pats Berk's chest again. "'Trust in the Lord with all your heart and lean not on your own understanding; in all your ways acknowledge him, and he will make your paths straight.'"

John turns from Berk and walks to me. "And you, my dear. How blessed you are to get to say good-bye to the ones you love."

John's eyes are moist, and I know he is remembering that day so many years ago when he thought he was just going on a quick trip to see his son. He didn't know that was the last time he would see the ones he loved.

"I love you, John." I hug the older man. "Thank you."

"Thank *you*." He pats my back and steps away. "You have

given this old man hope and joy. I am like Abraham. Except God has given me *two* children in my old age."

I watch John leave. I am no longer crying, no longer grieving. John's presence has reminded me that this day would have come eventually. If it were not now, it would be when I was older. But it would come. Death is inevitable. But I do not fear it.

I am ready.

# CHAPTER FIFTY-FOUR

Fifteen minutes and twenty-three seconds.

That's how long I have to live.

The wall screen that displayed the numbers in blood-red letters now projects the image of a garden. The trees are full of pink and white blossoms, the green grass swaying a little in the wind. I hear the birds as they call to each other. I smell the moist soil.

But the countdown still plays in my mind.

Fourteen minutes and fifty-two seconds.

It isn't really soil I smell. It isn't really the garden breeze I feel on my face. That is simply the Scientists' "humane" means of filling my bloodstream with poison, of annihilating a member of the State who has proven to be "detrimental to harmonious living."

The wall screen is beginning to fade. The colors aren't as bright. The blossoms are beginning to merge together. They look more like clouds now. I don't know if the image is changing or if it is the effect of the poison. I could try to hold my breath, to deny the entrance of this toxic gas into my body. But I would only pass out, and my lungs would suck in the poison-laced oxygen as I lie here unconscious.

No. I will die the way I finally learned to live. Fully aware. At peace. With a heart so full of love that even as it slows, it is still full.

Because I know something the Scientists refuse to acknowledge.

Death is only the beginning.

# CHAPTER FIFTY-FIVE

feel myself being lifted, but I cannot open my eyes. Is this the Designer? Is he carrying me to heaven?

But it cannot be the Designer. My head aches and my body feels heavy. I try to open my eyes, but it is impossible. I hear a voice. It seems far away. "Stay with me, Thalli. Stay with me."

Berk. Berk is here. I try to stay awake. I fight against the fatigue.

And I remember. The annihilation chamber. Assistants came for me right after John left. Berk was crying, but I was not. I walked to the room, refusing to be assisted. I was going to go on my own. I wanted to show the Scientists I was not afraid.

And I wasn't.

I sat in the chair, watched the wall screen change from clock to garden. I must have drifted off. And then . . . this.

I am disappointed. I expected to wake up in heaven. I was prepared to wake up in heaven. But I am not in heaven. And though I love the feel of Berk's arms around me, I would rather be in the presence of the Designer.

"Hang on, Thalli." Berk sets me down. He begins placing something on my legs. Pants? I try to open my eyes. The light hurts them, but I keep trying. Berk is wearing a thick white uniform of some kind. There is a kind of helmet beside him.

"Help me with this." Berk is speaking to . . . Rhen?

"I still think this is unwise." She says this, but she bends down and forces my arms into the heavy sleeves.

"We need your logic up there." Berk zips up the uniform. It feels twenty degrees hotter in this.

"But my sickness."

"Doesn't matter," Berk says. "You are well now."

"Are we ready?" John. John is here. And Rhen. And Berk. Maybe this *is* heaven.

I feel myself being lifted again, feel the ache in my head intensify, feel the weight of the uniform pressing down on me. No, this is not heaven. But it is an escape.

"Where are we going?" My voice sounds strange, but everyone stops as soon as I speak.

"Thalli." Berk's face is by mine. His eyes are on me, assessing me. I am sure he is wondering how badly I was damaged by the gas.

"Where?" I need to know the plan.

"We're going outside."

"Outside?" My mind is still fuzzy. He pulled me from the annihilation chamber to take me, Rhen, and John outside?

Berk sets my feet down and puts his arm beneath my arms to support me. With his other arm, he points toward a large metal door. "Outside."

Rhen and John put on their helmets. Berk follows, then helps me put mine on. It is heavy, but with a flip of a switch, it pumps in oxygen. I cough as my lungs adjust to the concentrated air in the helmet.

"They won't bother us up there." Berk's voice is beside me, coming from a speaker attached to the side of the helmet.

"But we cannot live up there." I begin to panic. Death by garden sounds much better. "We won't make it more than a week."

"Have faith, Thalli." John's voice fills my helmet. "As we have seen, the Scientists don't know everything."

I look out of the helmet, the clear front allowing me to see only what is ahead of me, nothing to the side. John is opening the door. I imagine our uniforms being melted off, eaten away by the poison in the air.

Berk steps forward, pulling me with him. "We walk by faith, right, John?"

"We certainly do."

"But there's no food." I lean back, trying to delay our steps. "No water. No air. The earth isn't habitable."

"Berk's logic is difficult to refute." Rhen is speaking, her voice calm and measured. "We can either die up there or die down here."

Yes, irrefutable logic. So I allow myself to be propelled forward, outside. Walking by faith.

# EPILOGUE

Do you see them?" Dr. Loudin speaks into his communications pad.

"See for yourself." The wall screen in front of the Scientist comes to life. He sees an image taken from a recently recovered satellite. Four dots of orange move across the surface of what was once Colorado.

"They are alive."

Dr. Grenz enters from the side room. "It all worked brilliantly, Dr. Loudin. I must congratulate you."

The remaining Scientists enter and seat themselves at the round table, all looking expectantly at the wall screen.

"Was all this really necessary?" Dr. Turner says. "My father would have gone gladly. As would the young woman."

"But we needed Berk and Rhen to go as well. I have been talking to Berk about the possibility of living above for a few weeks, showing him some of the technologies we have been preparing for that," Dr. Loudin replies.

"Which is how he knew about the suits," Dr. Grenz says.

"Exactly." Dr. Loudin's eyes never leave the screen. "And the food and the transport and the map."

"They have everything they need?" Dr. Grenz asks.

"Of course. I made sure of it. It was quite a brilliant plan, if I do say so myself. I have watched these two since they were young. I knew there were feelings even then. I had gotten several calls from the Monitors about Thalli, but I kept waiting for the right moment. The Bach piece confirmed my suspicions in a way even I had not expected."

"And the surgery?" Dr. Grenz asks. "Was it really unsuccessful?"

"Of course not." Dr. Loudin laughs. "But I needed to see where, exactly, their loyalties lie. I was fairly confident in the young woman's rebelliousness. But I still wasn't sure about the young man."

"Ah." Dr. Grenz smiles. "So you observed their interactions while she was in Pod C."

"I observed everything."

"And the other young woman?"

"Rhen?" Dr. Loudin folds his hands, finally looking away from the screen. "I knew of her illness and I waited with her as well. She is quite brilliant. If this group is to survive, I knew they would need her logic."

"Very true." Dr. Williams nods. "With any luck, at least one of this group will survive and find one of the pockets of survivors that remain in North America."

"I still doubt that the other Scientists made it that far." Dr. Grenz follows the orange dots with his eyes. "It was over thirty-five years ago, Loudin. They had a crude map and barely enough food. The nearest pocket of survivors is nine hundred miles away."

"And we don't know what shape those survivors are in," Dr. Williams says. "They could have been contaminated."

"We have discussed this already." Dr. Loudin slams his hands on the desk. "The State will not survive more than another five years if we do not solve these problems. With Dr. Spires gone, we are shorthanded. And five of our best Scientists are out there."

"Perhaps they are out there." Dr. Turner leans forward. "But they chose to leave. They objected to the decisions we were making. They were undermining our authority. Even if they are alive, do we really want them back here?"

"If they are alive"—Dr. Loudin faces Dr. Turner—"they will have been living away from technology and intelligence and innovation for over thirty-five years. They will welcome a return to civilization."

"So it all rests on these four." Dr. Williams points to the orange dots, moving farther away from the State. "Don't you think one of us should have gone?"

Dr. Loudin growls. "Of course not. You know we are all needed here. But I trained Berk personally. And I have been in Thalli's and Rhen's brains. If anyone can find our colleagues, it is these three."

"And if they do?" Dr. Turner asks.

"*When* they do." Dr. Loudin looks at Dr. Williams.

"Our transports will be ready."

"And so will we." Dr. Loudin leans back. "Our lost Scientists will help us get the State functioning at its peak."

"And the four?" Dr. Turner motions to the map.

"Will be annihilated."

# DISCUSSION QUESTIONS

1. Do you think a worldwide nuclear war is possible? If so, who do you think would survive and what do you think the world would look like afterward?
2. The Scientists argue that the ultimate result of excessive emotion and freedom is conflict. Do you agree?
3. With which character do you most identify? Why?
4. Thalli "hears" God in the music she plays. Do you think music has the ability to communicate truths?
5. John says that God will always leave a remnant, no matter what people on earth try to do. Do you agree?
6. What about the State did you most dislike? What did you like?
7. Imagine you are one of The Ten right after the war occurred. What suggestions would you have made for this "new world"?
8. What do you think happens next? Will Thalli, Berk, Rhen, and John survive? Will they find the other colonies?

# ACKNOWLEDGMENTS

am incredibly grateful for the team at Thomas Nelson Fiction. They believed I could write this even before I did. I am humbled by your faith in me.

My amazing agent, Jenni Burke, helped me create and tweak the proposal that would outline this trilogy. Throughout the process, Amanda Bostic and Becky Monds were part sounding board, part cheerleader, and all friend as the manuscript went through several changes before I started writing and even more once I was finished. Julee Schwarzburg, as always, saw through my messes into the possibilities and helped me see those possibilities as well. Kristen Vasgaard created the fabulous cover. And Katie Bond, Ruthie Dean, and the whole marketing and sales teams worked so hard to make sure this story got into the hands of readers all over the world. Thank you, thank you, thank you!

Special thanks go to the Citrus Park Christian School class of 2015. This is an extraordinarily creative group of young men and women. I brainstormed with them several times, asking their opinions about the direction of my plot, asking their advice for what else I should add. Their ideas are all throughout this book and the next (and the next!). And all they got for it were just a few days of "rabbit trails" in English class.

I am grateful to Kathy Johnson for talking me through what it's like to play the violin, to Leann Williams for making sure there wasn't too much fiction in my science, to Amy Busti for reading the manuscript with a musician's eye, and to Lauren Webb, proofreader extraordinaire.

My family, as always, is my greatest inspiration and they are my biggest fans. My husband, Dave, is one of the best men to ever walk the face of the earth. Our kids, Emma, Ellie, and Thomas, are the most wonderful gifts God has given us.

A huge thanks to you, my readers. Thank you for your e-mails of encouragement, for "liking" me and "following" me. I am so grateful for you.

But the reason that I write, that I live and breathe, is because of my wonderful Savior, Jesus Christ. He has made each one of us beautiful anomalies. I pray that every person reading this knows how very special you are to the Designer, how unique and precious and valuable you are to him.

*"First Date* is a great debut from an author who's sure to make a splash in the inspy YA market."

—USAToday.com

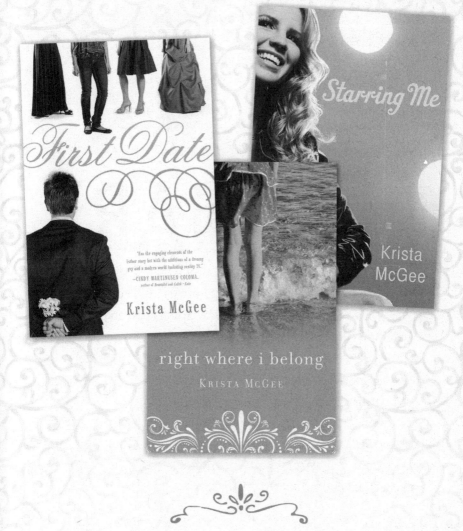

She was an anomaly.

Now she is free.

# LUMINARY

Available in print and e-book
July 2014

# ABOUT THE AUTHOR

Author photo by Ruth Kegel

When Krista McGee isn't living in fictional worlds of her own creation, she lives in Tampa and spends her days as a wife, mom, teacher, and coffee snob. She is also the author of *First Date*, *Starring Me*, and *Right Where I Belong*.